Scatteree,

A Novel

Roger Porter Denk

DEDICATION

To every character, real and imagined, in the small fishing village of Chatham with whom I have come in contact; I dedicate this book. I have changed most of their names to protect the guilty and at the same time to shield the innocent. While I have used actual locations in the little town, there is no implied or actual connection to the events described in this novel.

I also dedicate this book to my former colleagues at the Defense Intelligence Agency, the Pentagon in Washington DC, where I worked for two decades. By accident (and answering the phone at the right time I found myself on the road to being an ambassador for the United States, sent to Europe numerous times, to solve a Cold War Problem, or not to create one. I should mention the late Richard Higgins, Colonel, USMC, and the late Secretary of Defense, Caspar Weinberger, both of whom helped me grow. Last, for Sepp Von Radowitz, retired General Bundeswehr; a good friend and ever better equestrian.

Other books by Roger Porter Denk

Stepping Stones,

A Novel

(2007, revised 2013)

The Reunion,

A Tale of Vegas,

Reunions and Redemption (2012)

Anadyr,

The End of the Cuban Revolution

(2013)

Skunk's Neck,

A Novel

(2013)

ACKNOWLEDGMENTS

Mentioning the legions of people whom I need to thank would consti-tute a book in itself, but here are just a few. My wife, Adrienne, of course is first among the ones to be thanked since she lets me engage in these (not so profitable) literary pursuits. Our daughter, Kecia, reads these books with care and makes great suggestions. It is always nice to have a family of readers.

PROLOGUE: OVER THE ATLANTIC

The Horten jet bomber was fast. It was also extremely uncomfortable. It was very cold inside the cramped cockpit. The sleek design of the plane seemed to keep the cabin eerily quiet. It seemed to the three men inside that they were piloting a glider, though the Horten's jet engines were powerful and gave the plane plenty of power.

The pilot, a younger man than he appeared, was intent in flying into the mist over Newfoundland with only a vague idea of his heading and speed. Radio silence was mandatory, he was told.

"Can you see anything," one of the two passengers asked.

"*Nein*, I mean no, Doctor, but I am trying my best to acquire a landmark. This plane flies very fast, and it has almost none of the pedals and the controls that I am used to."

"Herr Göring would hate to hear that you are uncomfortable in his fantastic toy, young man. This weapon will change the course of the war. I suggest that you refrain from making derogatory comments about the design of the magnificent aircraft, if you please."

The pilot winced. "Of course sir, I am deeply sorry for my comments, and given the work to which I have been entrusted, it will be my honor to die if necessary for the Fatherland on this mission." He added the obligatory words 'Heil Hitler' as an afterthought.

The passenger turned to his companion, a man sitting in the back of the cramped cockpit. The man was looking at a glowing green screen. He looked up from the screen and arched his back.

"Werner, we are going to make history this day, I know it. We will overfly the enemy and he will not even know that we are up here. This is the genius of *Heimlichkeit* is that we are virtually invisible to their ancient so called Chain Home radars. If they were able to acquire us on radar they would have seen us by now and sent their fighters to meet us."

"We must stick to the plan," the front seat passenger said. "Only speak English, remember that we are merely lost seaman if we are forced to land, and always remember our first priority is not to show anyone what is on board this aircraft or what is does. Now we need to place the special markers down there, as a guide for the planes that will follow. This is our primary concern, and the aerial photography should be a secondary one."

"I studied English," the pilot interjected, "and I have to remember not to say 'also' at the end of a sentence."

Both passengers laughed and the man in the rear of the plane looked at his screen again, putting on headphones to screen out the noise of the powerful jet engines.

"Well, we certainly do look like seamen, after that rolling around on a merchant steamer that took us to the islands."

"Yes we do," the pilot said. "I only wish for a taste of my Schnapps, since that damned Rum they fed us daily was not the best for my digestion."

The mist and fog cleared. The Horten bomber was flying toward a landmass covered in green forests and white beaches. The pilot announced that they were now at the first part of their destination.

"Karl, we are here at last. I have not been here since my days with the Americans at M.I.T. Those were good years."

Werner stretched again. "I hope that we can reestablish ourselves with the university once the war is over and we have won. Victory will be sweet and we can finally work toward our scientific goals."

"Werner, I am in agreement. While there are some things that I would have wished we would have done differently, like finishing our work against the British, we cannot turn the clock back."

The passenger spoke to the pilot. "Have you been here before, North America I mean?"

"This is my first visit. I certainly hope it will not be my last," he said. "I have been told that if we get the information that is desired there will many more overflights. I would be pleased to again make those flights."

Werner scratched his ear. "You know gentlemen, these Americans are a very interesting bunch. They spend countless hours worrying about their families and their personal automobiles, and yet they do not see the fallacy of their democracy—that allowing divergent views to be expressed is dangerous to national identity. Unlike the Fatherland, they are a nation of racial impurity, one of their own making I should add. Yet there are Aryans like us, many working with us to achieve our goals, down there. For the most part the Americans are a group of sleeping fools. It would my honor and hope to make them more like us in the coming years."

Karl remained silent, lost in thought.

Werner turned to Karl. "Are you dreaming of something or just not interested in our grand plan?"

"I am very interested," Karl said. "But I see that we have some radar activity according to a sound that I just heard in my ear."

"Impossible," Werner said. "These Americans cannot see us in the air and cannot see us on their primitive radars either."

"Impossible perhaps but they have managed to acquire us, if I am correct. Pilot, where are we?"

"We have just flown over the city of Boston and we are headed for that arm shaped piece of land they call Cape Cod, sir."

Werner looked at his glowing green screen. "The problem may be that we have someone interfering with a signal coming from down there. We may have been targeted by some kind of countermeasure like the English used to confuse our bombers using our X-Great beams during the Great Britain air campaign."

"Perhaps Werner," Karl said, "but as we told Reichsmarshall Göring the British were using our very own technology to defeat us. I recommended that we find out how they acquired it, whether by espionage or even a disgruntled man within our government telling them, and root out the traitor."

"Did Hermann actually agree with you?"

"Werner, he is an enigma, and he merely smiled and then he told me to get back to work. I took that to mean that he either had no interest in discovering the truth. But more likely he already hatched a plan to tell Hitler. Like his other entreaties to Hitler, making it seem as if he'd been able to root out someone and have them executed, guilty or not."

The pilot interrupted. "Doctor, I have to report that the skies are clearing, and we might have a reflection from the sun on our fuselage. Do you want me to fly higher?"

Werner consulted a small notebook. "What is the maximum altitude at which you have flown in the past?"

The pilot looked at the altimeter. "This time is my first above ten thousand meters."

"Then take us to fifteen thousand meters young man, and be quick about it."

The pilot pulled his stick back toward him and then nosed the jet upward to level off.

"I hope," Werner said in a low voice to Karl, "that our cabin pressurization works in reality as well as it did in the lab."

"I do as well, but if it does not we can always get our medals presented posthumously."

"That is not at all funny my friend. I intend to live long after the current war and to become the man who reconstructs the new world into the new world order."

The pilot smiled. *"These scientists are only as clever as they think they are, and they need constant reassuring to keep their spirits up,"* he thought.

The Horten's left jet engine whined, and sputtered. The pilot needed to hold the stick hard right to compensate for a lack of power. The jet was without a tail so he could not compensate with rear flaps. He struggled with the controls and eventually maintained a level course. The engine returned to normal.

"Problems, Lieutenant?" Karl asked.

"None that I cannot handle sir. We had a momentary fuel line issue that seems now to have corrected itself. I have cut back from full cruising power to conserve fuel and also to give the left engine some rest. We should be able to finish our mission and return to our recovery base as scheduled."

"Please deploy the camera then, and we shall start the run over the targets," Werner said.

The pilot pulled a lever on the floor and heard a soft mechanical squeak as the bomb bay doors opened slowly, revealing a stereoscopic camera that began to take photos every few seconds. The film moved smoothly along its track from one side, the unexposed one, to the exposed film side, one side balancing the weight of the other.

"We have used all the film," the pilot reported. "Should we turn back now?"

"No, let us enjoy the blue ocean below for a few moments, if we can," Werner said.

There was a loud cracking sound and the plane lurched upward.

"What was that?" Karl asked.

The pilot frantically checked his instruments and meekly turned back to Werner. "Sir the film canister and the camera have become dislodged and I am afraid that we've lost them both."

"Them," Werner screamed. "You mean we've lost the entire roll of film and the camera?"

"Yes sir, I am afraid that is so. I am sure that…"

"We'll all be shot, that is what I think. Taking aerial photos is espionage and we have just been committing it."

Karl put a hand on Werner's shoulder. "I should hope not. After all we had our art department mark everything with that American Kodak label, so if it is found it will be presumed to be American cameras and film.

"Now please let us review what just happened. We've learned that the gravitational forces at this altitude and speed are sufficient to make our normal anchoring bolts ineffective, so I suggest we get back in the lab and make stronger ones."

"Fine, spoken like a good engineering designer. We've just overflown much of the enemy territory and we have nothing to show them when we get back."

Karl turned to the pilot. "Where exactly where we when the event happened. Do you have the coordinates?"

The pilot checked his leather map pouch and pulled out a wax-covered card to determine what they had just flown over, and said, "Seems sir that we have reached the elbow of this Cape Cod place, and according to my map we have lost the camera over the town called Chatham."

"I thought we had also bombed another location called Chatham, the one in England during the attacks, the ones they called the blitz," Werner said.

"Werner," Karl answered, "We took out a major shipyard in that place some time ago, but some of our bombs did not detonate, as I recall. The problem has been rectified, so when we come here again we will not have that problem."

"Yes we can only hope, but that still leaves us without film and without a camera form which the pictures we taken," Karl said.

"I have an idea my friends, but it will be how-do-you-say-it, a 'long shot' for it to work."

"I am listening," said Werner.

"We have many duplicate cameras at the base, do we not?"

"Yes we do?"

"And we have rolls of film as yet undeveloped that could easily be sent as being from this mission. Am I correct?"

"Yes, that is true."

"We have one problem, however, our young friend the pilot must be willing to engage in our subterfuge, and never tell."

The pilot blanched. "I am certainly willing to remain silent, sir. You can trust me."

"I would hope so. That is because not telling anything is in your best interests. Lest you forget let me remind you that we can have anyone, I mean anyone, and taken to the camps for just making an anti-Nazi remark, and I am sure you would never want to be in that situation, would you?"

"No sir," the pilot said. "You can be assured of my silence."

At that moment both of the plane's engines stalled and the Horten dropped like a stone. Werner pulled his ejection seat lever and he was thrown out of the jet knocked unconscious. The Horton jet spiraled down and crashed into the ocean near George's Bank, some 100 miles from the New England coastline.

Werner was floating in the ocean for only a few moments. Bobbing in the blue ocean he was spotted by a German U-Boat.

Dragging him to safety the sailors never knew that this man, Werner Rasmussen, would fight another day. He looked at them and said "*Jedem das Seine.*"

CHAPTER 1

Andy Reid sat in a trance. The security briefing was an exercise in patience for him. The poorly dressed briefer was inexpert in making slides and he was also a poor briefer. If Andy was going to be read onto yet another special program, he had to check off this hour of painful sitting and listening. Hemorrhoids for the mind, he imagined.

The briefer was slowly extolling the virtues of the program, most of which were in the eyes of the beholder. Andy had a thought that many mystery writers could have guessed what the whole thing's purpose was.

Andy began to drift off. His eyes began to close. Maybe it was the dark room, the voice of the briefer. Andy thought about why each of these special programs, these intelligence compartments, was so enamored not with what they did, but who was included and who was not? Andy waited for the last slide, the one which suggested that the free world depended on keeping the program's details out of enemy hands. It was there in red letters on the last slide.

The briefer approached Andy with a folder full of papers, most of which Andy would skim, and one page he would sign as he left.

"Mr. Reid, I wanted to ask if you have any questions." Tapping his pencil on the desk, the briefer seemed to want Andy to answer. One way or the other, it never makes a difference, he thought.

Andy paused. "Well, as you may have heard this was the only program that I was never read on to. I am leaving for Europe in a couple days and I need to have this access according to my orders."

"Where in Europe will you be going?"

"Mostly London, a little side trip to Paris, then NATO, then West Germany. Why do you ask?"

"I did not cover this in the briefing. I should have. This program requires approval for any travel outside the continental US. I am afraid to tell you that you might have to cancel your trip."

"I know you're going to think I am just another smart ass, but I was going about my business when I got the call to come in, to listen to this spiel of yours, and then sign the papers and leave. No one mentioned travel restrictions. For all I care I hope they cancel the trip. Seems like a colossal waste of time and money to send me there anyway. I have been on inactive status for a while in case you did not know."

"How long were you inactive?" the briefer asked.

"Years actually. I thought I was not longer cleared. I was sitting at home in Maryland with my wife and young daughter enjoying a respite, a long one. The phone rang, I threw on a suit and tie, and here I am."

"Mr. Reid, someone much more powerful than me sent word that you needed to be briefed into this program. It is a very small group of folks who have access to this program, and now you will be one of them. If that person who calls can attest that your trip to Europe does not conflict with your access to this program then you can sign the agreement."

"If you need to call him or her then go ahead. I have nowhere else to go today, and I have another hour in visitor parking before I get a ticket."

"Cute. We have marked your car and you will not get a ticket. In fact, the police force will be extra vigilant about your vehicles once you're in the program."

"Amazing, this is the first time I've actually gotten special treatment instead of harassed by one of these special access programs," Andy said with a grin.

"I take it you are not a fan of secrecy for secrecy's sake?"

"Look, I have been privy to lots of secrets over the years since I entered the service. I have seen some things that make me cringe. I have stumbled on things that were hidden, some in plain sight, and they needed to be stopped. Twice I nearly died while trying to uncover the truth. My wife was a victim the first time as well She's better now.

"Frankly, I am wary of all special programs. I find that each one of them seems to be fulfilling a need for someone to spend lots of cash and not be accountable. Just my personal observation."

The briefer raised a hand. "We cost the taxpayers nothing Mr. Reid. Our funds come from…"

"Yes, I know, I was paying attention. You are siphoning foreign funds from international banks. Salami slicing I think you called it. And no one is the wiser, at least not yet."

"That is correct. Is there an issue in your mind about that practice?"

"If you think it works then it works. I guess that morals are what you make of them. I have found that people in a special program write their own rules. They make decisions based on what I'd call a warped sense of right and wrong. Just my opinion, but one based on firsthand experience."

"Mr. Reid, I get what you are saying. Your comments will be passed up the chain. Of course given the nature of this program I cannot guarantee that you will hear from anyone else that the comments have been accepted or rejected. Now I have to make a quick call to verify that you can be in the program and travel too."

The briefer left the darkened room for five minutes. When he returned he looked perturbed.

"Just got my ass chewed out for asking that question, Mr. Reid. Whoever wants you to be in the program carved out an exemption for you. Essentially, they tell me you are free to do whatever you want, even while being read into our program. Please sign this acknowledgement."

Andy signed the three pages of paper. He stood to leave.

"Nice to meet you," he said shaking the man's hand.

The briefer shuffled his papers and said nothing. He pressed a small button to let Andy out the door. As the door closed Andy saw that the lights in the room were being turned off.

As the briefer promised Andy's car was alone in an otherwise full parking lot for visitors. A uniformed policeman approached and tipped his hat to Andy. It was a day to remember.

Brass bells larger than house cats hung from the necks of sleepy, determined cows weaving their way home after a long day of cud chewing. Each was ready to move anyone out of the way. The cows were heading to their night jobs—the heating of many homes in the village.

Andy Reid walked slowly through dimly lit streets of Garmisch-Partenkirchen, avoiding the slow-moving cows as best he could. He needed to find his hotel, the Garmischer Hof, before dark. The owner, Frau somebody unpronounceable, was not a tolerate person. She insisted that her guests adhere to her rules, no questions asked.

It was a long day, and it was part of a long trip. Andy was hassled by the French *Gendarmes*, the police because of heightened security on the Auto Routes leading into Paris. The police officer mumbled something about being on the lookout for Direct Action Terrorists, but laughed when Andy produced his Black Diplomatic Passport. Andy was quickly waved through the roadblock.

The side trip to Belgium was relatively uneventful, except for a flap at NATO Headquarters in Mons, a Brussels suburb. An unauthorized vehicle tried to ram the front gates. Andy was a material witness to the incident. He had pulled in directly after the car.

The driver, later found to be intoxicated, was not seriously hurt, and allowed to spend a night in the drunk tank before being questioned again. NATO, as always, was a genteel place to visit, with the occasional official meeting sandwiched in between trips to the excellent in-house cafeteria for mussels, pommes frites, and mayonnaise. Beer flowed, cares were forgotten, and from time to time information was shared and then quickly forgotten.

West Germany, Andy's last stop for the trip, was calm except for some raucous parties held at the United States Embassy in Bonn. The building complex was huge. It was among the largest embassies anywhere. Andy was on a mission to convince the Germans to work with the United States on a sensitive intelligence program, and they had agreed quickly to everyone's surprise.

There was one night spent drinking excellent German wines at Roland's Bogen; a restaurant just across the Rhine from Bonn in Petersburg. Andy told his hosts he was cured of drinking German wine, at least for a few days. His head pounded as he fell asleep at the Embassy Guest House, only to be awoken by sirens from a neighboring street.

Last stop was the southern part of the country. It was a chance to see Bavaria again, Andy thought. This was where his great grandfather was born, or so the legend went. Seems that the little town where he was born, Lam, had been part of several states depending on the war.

But Andy loved the feel of Bavaria, the mountains, the beer, and sometimes the people there. His business in Bonn done as fast as ever, Andy made for Garmisch for a weekend of rest and relaxation. First, he'd called in to tell his contact in Bonn where he'd be. The hotel Garmischer Hof was strongly suggested. Most official visitors stayed there and the rooms were swept weekly to remove Soviet and even German listening devices or secretly installed cameras.

The dimly-lit sign for the Hof was a block ahead. Andy sped up, looking left and right for last minute Bovine jaywalkers. Twilight was a dangerous time he remembered, cows or no cows.

He walked into the front door of the Hof and was greeted by the Frau, who announced loudly that he had had a call from the United States. "You know Herr Reid, we take pride in keeping our guests aware of their communications," she said with a forced smile.

"I thank you and will gladly use your phone if that is acceptable, to return the call." Andy bowed slightly. "Where shall I take it?"

"We have here a system that accounts for the time you spend on calls, and there is a counter here at my desk. Please feel free to use the phone as long as you please, but I will need to provide you with a bill for the amount of marks that you spend."

"Understood and I shall be brief, very brief. Can you tell me who called?"

The Frau consulted a small pad of paper. "It was a woman named Nancy and she was calling from Massachusetts, she told me."

Andy rubbed the stubble on his face. "Thanks for that I assume it was my wife, she's a stay-at-home mom, you know, and…"

"We shall connect you to the international operator, so please you wait for that time."

Andy stood by the phone, and waited for the sign from the Frau that he was going to be connected. She gave him a sign and a nod. He picked up the phone.

"You OK there Andy?" Nancy asked.

"Sure Babe, why do you ask, everything OK back home?"

"Just that we got a really strange call a few hours ago, a person who knew my name and well, he was kind of rude."

"Nanc, that describes most of the people I have worked with over the years. Did he leave a name, or tell you a number to call back?"

"He asked where you were, and I remembered not to tell him specific details, but he guessed or maybe he knew that you were in Europe and he said, in a weird way, that he could find you. Then he hung up."

"He gave you no name I take it. Not even a hint about what he was calling about?"

"Andy, it was all very creepy. This guy seemed to be watching me as I spoke, you know. He sounded as if he was looking at my reactions. I know that's not possible but I felt that way. Isn't that odd?"

"Very odd and very unlike the strange people that I hung out with in the past couple years. Do you think he was calling from DC or maybe from Chatham?"

"If he was, he did not have a Cape accent, you know all those 'ers' and 'aaas.'" Nancy laughed, her voice wavering as the connection moved across the ocean.

"Nanc, I need to call back to my DC contacts to track this down, but first let me tell you how much I miss you. I never thought my so-called career would bring me here, and definitely not so much."

"Hey, we're fine here. We write pretend letters to you every night. Alicia dictates and I scribble it down. We make it a day's work to lick the envelope, and then walk to the post office to mail them.

"Grace next door gives me a break, in fact lots of breaks with the baby. All's well but I guess being a single parent is harder than I thought. I know that they have you on a leash, and I've gotten used to it."

Andy winced. "Well, the government, no never mind. They rule all things, even my life. They gave you and me a short period of doing nothing, but…"

"But you almost died again, don't forget that. Anyhow, I know that it's almost feeding time and I gotta go, so love you, and goodbye. Call again when you can. Love you."

Andy replaced the phone, and the Frau motioned for him to come over to her desk. He reached for his wallet.

"It was, Herr Reid, a longer call, and I think my machine it tells me that your time on the phone cost 50 marks. I must tell you that a kind person has offered to pick up the costs, in fact he has paid for your room rent. So, you owe me nothing."

Andy thanked her and walked into the parlor of the Garmischer Hof. If there was really someone picking up his tab he wanted to meet that person and thank him. He looked at the people gathering for their evening meal, many red-faced from a day in the sun, or Volks Marching, or too much beer, or perhaps all three.

Someone tapped Andy on the shoulder and he turned slowly.

"Reid, you stupid shit, how have you been?"

The man was carrying a large satchel and had his Bavarian hat pulled low to cover most of his hair and forehead. He was about six feet tall, very fit and thin, and had a handlebar moustache.

"Well, I guess that must mean we know each other, and maybe it's the piss poor lighting here, but I have no idea who you are."

"Andy, Andy Reid, you disappoint me. I am one of your oldest and dearest friends. In fact when you were in the Pentagon; I was the doctor who fixed you up when you got mauled by that stupid cart. Tell me you at least remember that?"

Andy scratched his head. "Yep clear as a bell, were we introduced? I mean formally, of course."

"Doubt it, since you were actually knocked out cold. I gave you some pain killer. You most likely spent a time in another parallel universe somewhere." He stuck out a delicate, long-fingered hand. "Bud Steinmiller's the name, Andy. I'm pleased to finally meet you now that you're in a more conversational state."

"Well Bud, or should I say Doctor Bud, how are you? Thanks for making me well after that fall. What was it, twenty years ago?"

"Bud's fine, and yes I'm out of the Army now, did my time. After the Pentagon tour I went to Nam, that kind of thing. While there I met some other govies, and they kinda hired me on." Bud winked. "In fact I am here with 'them' right now, taking a sojourn through scenic southern Germany. Work is a bitch you know."

"I get it, Agency business, and I have no need to know. But why pay my way here, including my phone calls back home? That's very nice and totally unnecessary. You may have heard that I have a stipend from the government and only occasionally have to work for a living."

"Andy, we should all be so lucky. I am here…"

Someone ran into the room yelling *"Gibt es einen Arzt im Haus."*

Bud approached the man and spoke loudly, *"Ich bin ein Arzt,"* and asked the man what he needed.

Switching to English the man told Bud that his father had fallen in the room they rented in the Hof.

"Andy, why don't you come along, we might need another set of eyes and hands here. I've got my bag with me. You might just be watching."

Andy, Bud and the German raced up to the third floor of the Hof and then sprinted down a long hallway to room 210. Unlocking the door, the man pointed to his father, a man of eighty or so, lying prone on the bed.

Bud asked, *"Enlgisher Sprechen?"* The man nodded and held up two fingers close together, signaling a little.

"Where is the pain? It is here?" Bud felt the man's stomach. No response. Bud probed his kidneys, "Here?" Again, there was no response.

The son, who had introduced himself to them as Hans, told Bud and Andy that his father suffered from heart disease and high blood pressure, and that he sometimes forgot to take his medicine. "Father is a proud man," he said, "but stubborn like many of his generation."

Andy asked Hans, "What does or did your father do?"

"Father was a man who defied the Nazis. It was ironic since he also worked on several projects for them and was given awards for his work."

Bud was busy, so Andy asked, "How is that possible, to be against and work for someone at the same time?"

Hans looked at the window, not at Andy. "Father was preeminent in his field, the area of theoretical physics, and his work was far ahead of other practitioners. He knew that Hitler and the group that surrounded him had no knowledge of elementary science so he was able to concoct experiments that seemed to be very ground-breaking but in fact were nothing more than parlor tricks, designed to fool the gullible."

Bud looked at Andy and Hans. He was hard at work on his new patient. "Look, let's get your dad stabilized first and maybe we can talk later."

Hans drew back. "I am afraid that I might have said too much already. You see my father is a secretive man, and if he saw that I was discussing his past he might be angry."

Bud looked up. "Reid, make yourself useful and call the *Haus Frau* to call someone to get this gentleman to a hospital really *snell*, OK?"

"Will do. Hans do you want to stay here with your father or come with me to speak with her, my German is poor, and..."

"I can leave father. You should know that his name is Werner, here with the capable doctor. Certainly, we can go. Father, be calm, I will return."

Bud watched them leave and bent over the patient, switching to German in a low voice. "Look I am your friend, and in fact I can save your life on one condition."

The older man opened his eyes and murmured something, mostly inaudible.

"See, I am a friend, and I have many friends, even in your community. My country and your country share many secrets. I know that you know what I mean. Now, have we a contract? Will that allow me to let you live?"

The older man closed his eyes, and then shook his head back and forth. Again he murmured something, but Bud could not hear what he was saying.

"Suit yourself, I will make sure that your death is seen as nothing more than routine. An autopsy will show only advanced stage cardiovascular disease resulting in your death."

"Wait," the older man said gasping for air. "Who are you, are you one of them, the people who escaped capture, and who hope to bring the Reich back?"

"No my friend, I have no ideology, just my own preference for international intrigue and justice, no more than that. My goal, as a medical professional is to do no harm, except in exceptional circumstances like this one.

"How fortunate that we met this way, but I can assure you that it was not an accident. You see I have been looking for you for several years. Your son was kind enough to make your presence known to my people, not by his own choosing, and that led me here to you."

Werner coughed. "You are a clever man. You will not make me tell what I know. I have faced many strong men in my eighty years. You may do what you want with me, go ahead, I am ready to keep my secrets to myself."

Bud leaned closer. "What about your son, your grandchildren, and your other family members? Are you willing to sacrifice them as well in the name of some long-forgotten thing you worked on?"

"You would not…"

"Trust me, I would and I shall."

Andy and Hans walked back into the room interrupting the conversation. "Bud, the ambulance on the way, thanks to Hans's authoritative voice."

Hans was embarrassed. "It was my duty to help, and my father is very precious to me, as you can see."

"Bud, how is he doing?" Andy asked.

"Seems to be stable, but I am ready to give him an Epi Pen if things get worse. He should be able to get some rest at the hospital and then maybe we'll see about an EKG. His heart is beating normally now. All is good." Bud gently squeezed the older man's shoulder.

Hans smiled for the first time. "Good news Doctor and thank you. Papa, can you tell me how you are feeling? Are you in pain?"

The older man stared straight ahead and said nothing.

"Hans, it would be better if we did not excite your father too much. I will see to his personal care, here and at the facility. I can have him transferred to the US Military Hospital in Kaiserslautern if you'd like. I have connections there from my military service."

"Doctor, that is very generous, and I thank you." Hans waited for the ambulance gently stroking his father's hand. "Werner, if I can call you that, you will be fine."

Andy and Bud waited just outside the room. Bud was fidgeting with a stethoscope and said little. Andy paced from one window to the other looking for the medics.

"You smoke Andy?" Bud asked as he pulled out a pack of cigarettes.

"Nope, too much bad news about that addiction, that habit. My folks never did, and I guess I never had the desire."

"Glad to hear that, but I picked up the habit in Nam. And then I graduated to stronger stuff, if you catch my meaning. Damn Germans are more anti-Marijuana than Reagan is these days, so I have to be content inhaling these smelly German cigs." He lit an unfiltered dark cigarette and inhaled deeply.

"Bud, I have to tell you straight up that smells like horse shit."

"Hmm," Bud said with a smile, "no label ingredients so you may be correct."

"Also I thought doctors were supposed to engage in model behavior, like being thin and not smoking."

"Who said that? Was that our fictional friend, Marcus Welby? I ain't buying it whoever it was." Bud looked in at his patient for a minute and then turned back to Andy. "Sorry, everyone in the office gives me the same crap about smoking but I remind them that they are all boozers."

"That must be helpful," Andy said with a laugh. "But seriously, how is that old guy in that room? He gonna make it or not?"

"This time he has a good chance. I suppose given his age and overall state of health there's not much time left or even things we can do to prolong the inevitable."

"Bud, what did you make of Hans's comments about his father, Werner I think he called him, and what he did in the war? Think that's embellishment or just misremembered stuff?"

"Who can say? I've met many men his age who are absolutely sure they were Medal of Honor winners, or that they came close. All they did was man a desk stateside before, during and after D Day.

"Our current president, the former actor, seems to have a vivid memory of visiting the death camps but he never left Hollywood, as I recall. LBJ, bless his conniving soul, was fond of detailing his experiences in the war, though he refrained when Jack Kennedy was around."

Andy looked down at his shoes and shook a small piece of lint from his trouser leg. "Bud, I've met some characters since I saw you last. Many of them were real heroes, a lot were not. My own take is that the real achievers, the ones who did great things, are reluctant to talk about it."

"Werner is the right age to have been involved with the Nazi regime, but without proof we may never know if he's telling the truth. If we saw him mentioned in the Party's newspaper, *Völkischer Beobachter*, I still might not be convinced."

"You seem to be a real student of the Third Reich, Bud. What's that about, are you a secret Nazi hunter or something?"

"I leave that work to the good man, Simon Wiesenthal. As for me I am sworn to secrecy my friend, I'll never tell, and you can take that to the bank." Bud slapped Andy on the back and laughed. "But yes our mutual friends in the Agency are certainly interested in the whereabouts of the *leavers*, as they call them, the Nazis who escaped Nuremburg and are living large somewhere in South America. As a group they are of interest to the Agency not so much for where they are now but what they know or knew."

"What they knew, what does that mean?"

"Andy, the Germans had a slew of advanced technology projects on the drawing board before and during the war. As I recall reading in the classified reports even you had a hand in foiling a couple of them."

Andy nodded that he had been involved.

"We, I mean all of us, are drilling down, looking for additional details that we can use for our own defense and offense."

"It's been forty years since the war, Bud. How do we know that we haven't gone beyond where they were in their efforts in the last forty years?"

"Good question. Do you remember the UFO sightings, the rash of them, especially over downtown Washington?"

"Yep, sure do."

"Just think for a minute about who might have been flying these UFO things if not some extraterrestrial. Could have been us flying one of the many German designs. That's all I can say."

Andy said, "Well Bud, I gotta admit that nothing surprises me anymore, and I guess there is a lot I do not know. But back to Werner, did you have a chance to ask him anything other than how he was feeling?"

"Not really, he seemed uncommunicative."

Werner and Hans waited in the Garmischer Hof room. Werner's breathing was erratic. He seemed to be calm. Hans leaned close to his father and asked, "Was I wrong to mention your time in the war?"

"I wish you had not, but as you know, they will find out about my past eventually. Perhaps it is for the best. Recall that I fooled them once before. Now I can do the same."

"Clever father. Like always. But recall that these people are smart too, and they can see when you are lying."

"I can and have beaten their detectors, the ones that tell if you are not being honest. It is quite easy and I have done it with the Russians and Americans too."

"Rest now father. We will be hearing the ambulance arrival soon."

"Hans, there is something I need to tell you. That medical man, he is not who he seems, he threatened me when you and the other man were gone, and threatened our family also."

"How…"

"He wants information, and he has me at a disadvantage now that I am weaker. Please watch him for me."

Hans smiled. "Father I will be your guardian as I have been for many years. Rest now, I think I hear a siren." Hans opened a small cigarette case and withdrew a small syringe.

Hans stuck the needle into his father's neck and watched as Werner's breathing slowed then stopped.

CHAPTER 2

The flight back from Frankfurt to Dulles was going to be uncrowded. Andy was upgraded to First Class when the Pan Am customer service agent saw Andy was flying on a government fare. Sheepishly he walked to the separate gangway leading to the B-747's luxurious cabin normally reserved for full-fare paying VIPs.

As he sat down he was offered a glass of Champagne in a crystal goblet. Looking around he saw the cabin was virtually empty, and those who were there were immersed in their newspapers or magazines. *The First Class syndrome*, Andy mused, *apparently comes with the supposed prestige and the seats, the larger than normal seats.*

No one sat next to Andy and he was getting ready to nap before takeoff and the next round of food and drink. It would be a long haul back to Washington with headwinds. The steward announced that the door was closing after one more passenger arrived. Rushing in was Bud Steinmiller, the doctor who tried to save the older man in Garmisch.

"Andy. Great to see you again, where've you been? I missed seeing you after I took Werner to the morgue. Did you check out?"

"Yes, I did and I wanted to thank you for taking care of my bill at the Hof, it was really not necessary but appreciated."

Bud smiled. "What are friends for? Hey, I am bound for Dulles and have a car there, can I drop you somewhere?"

"Nancy, my wife is coming to see me and pick me up, so thanks but maybe next time. Have you got a business card?"

"Seriously, me, *moi*, have a card? What would it say? Physician and active duty spook of something like that?"

"Ha, that's good Bud. But seriously, what and where are you located in case I want to look you up."

"Well here's the scoop: just call the number that I'm going to give you and they'll find me so I can call back." Bud recited a seven digit number and Andy memorized it.

"Andy, did you think that Werner died a little too conveniently the other week while we were waiting for the medics?" Bud looked serious for the first time.

"Conveniently?"

"Yes I mean, one moment he's stable and the next bingo, he's dead."

"You're the professional; you tell me what I should think."

The steward walked toward them and collected Andy's glass. He motioned to Bud to buckle up, and promised to return with more bubbly in a few minutes after takeoff.

"Well Andy it seems that Werner died of something other than a heart attack. Our friends at the hospital let me watch their autopsy, and it was clear that something was introduced into his bloodstream that caused him to die."

"What and who did it?"

"My money is on the son, Hans. He was the last person alone with his father."

"Son kills father, got it. But why, I mean for what possible reason?"

"Who knows, there could be many reasons. I assume that the information I sent to Langley is being analyzed right now and they'll come up with something."

"Bud, I have had some dealings with your employer over the years, and I know that there are many experts there, people who specialize in analyzing other people, sometimes from afar. Is that what you mean?"

Bud scratched his head. "Andy, one of the things that make the Agency so much fun is that you are led to believe that you know everything when in fact you know part, a very small part of the entire story. In this case I really doubt that I'll know the entire story of young Hans and old Werner."

"We're alone here," Andy said as he pointed to the large cabin almost totally devoid of passengers. "Fess up, what do you know?"

"You got me at a weak moment, Andy. No Champagne yet and I am very thirsty, so this is the worst kind of torture. What I know is that Werner; actually Werner Rasmussen, Ph.D., in Physics was a legendary man in the 20's and 30's. Got his doctorate at age 17, and then went to work immediately on atom splitting, worked with Heisenberg on the German bomb."

"My dad…"

"Yes I know, your dad was a great man and his work with ALSOS is still part of the entry-level agent curriculum we all took down at the farm."

The pilot came on the intercom and announced a small delay without giving a reason. Andy settled back and put up his footrest. "Go on, please Bud," he said.

"Werner's son was telling a half-truth about his father's time under the Nazi's. He may not have been an ardent Nazi but like many others he was required to join the party in order to advance. Seems there is some anecdotal evidence that Werner met with Hitler and others on numerous occasions, subjects discussed unknown He was promoted through the ranks to Chief Scientist of the Third Reich in 1943."

"No Nuremberg time in the dock or what was it called "Operation Paperclip," the bringing back of all those rocket scientists?"

Bud yawned. "Not sure since most of those files are still under wraps, even nearly forty years later. Someone must be covering their ass somewhere, and that's why the information is still classified."

"Good old classification. Protect the guilty, torture the honest and the innocent. Must be someone or something embarrassing in those files? Maybe some other UFO stuff?"

"Andy, like I said before the whole ET thing is one that I wouldn't touch with a twenty foot pole, to coin a new phrase. But I agree with you that after all these years we've gotta see what Truman was thinking when he approved the immigration of these Nazis en masse. More to the point, we need to see where Herr Doctor Rasmussen fits in this scheme."

The Pan Am pilot left the cockpit and walked quickly down the stairs to the First Class cabin. He was searching for someone. As he approached Andy, he leaned down and asked him to follow him to the jet way.

Andy followed, telling Bud he might be back or might not, and to stay there.

"Captain what's wrong?" Andy asked.

"Mr. Reid, I have to tell you something, and this is confidential. Someone took a shot at the president today during a meeting he was attending in Washington DC, just outside the Washington Hilton.

"At this point we assume he was not hit but he's being rushed to a hospital just in case. The reason that I am telling you this is that Pan Am Operations in New York is holding all flights bound for Washington until we know exactly what's going on."

"Thank you but how do I fit in this? I mean I am concerned that the president is in danger, don't get me wrong, but I'm a small cog in a much larger wheel."

"Not according to the call Pan Am got from the National Security Council. They want you off my plane and are sending an Air Force contingent for you. You're welcome to go back to the Clipper Club for the time being until we've cleared it out. You'll be comfortable there.

"Your bags will be out of the plane in a little bit in case you need anything from them. It's been my pleasure to have you on board sir." He stiffened and saluted.

"Captain I am honored to be given such special treatment. But can I at least say goodbye to my seatmate? He and I are..."

"Let's leave the good doctor alone shall we? My information from New York is that you and you alone are to wait in the Clipper Club."

"You must know him," Andy said.

"We need to act quickly. We know him, yes, he's a frequent passenger. HE cannot go with you in the interest of time. I insist you follow our steward to the Club on the second level. You'll need to show your passport to gain entrance."

Andy walked from the jet way up to the second floor of the terminal. He stopped at the door to the Clipper Club and rang the buzzer. A serious-looking man holding an Uzi submachine gun stood there. He was not smiling.

"Can I help you?"

"Yes, my name is Andy Reid, I was told to come here and..."

"Passport, and please turn over any weapons you might have on your person."

Andy grimaced. "No weapons, I can assure you and here is my passport." He handed over his black passport.

"What about the red one? Gotta be sure of that name on that one too."

Andy reached in his jacket pocket and fished out the official government passport he rarely showed. The man nodded and ushered him into the nearly empty Clipper Club.

A man approached and asked Andy to follow him to the conference room. Closing the door he told him to wait for the arrival of a special phone.

"Got you a sat phone to use, it's secure they say, just hang on." The man reached into a cabinet and pulled out a large black phone with a three inch antenna. "Gotta wait for the satellite signal, ah there it is, here you go."

Andy stared blankly at the phone, wondering why he was there and what would happen next. Suddenly the phone chirped.

"Andy Reid," he said hesitatingly.

"This is a secure line. One moment please," the anonymous voice on the other end of the line said. "Reid, we pulled you off that plane because we have reliable intelligence that it was going to be bombed over the Atlantic."

"What? What about the passengers there on board, shouldn't they be warned? And whom am I speaking to?"

"The Cold War is particularly hot right now. Who knows if this guy who shot our president was acting alone? We might be seeing a wet operation by the KGB, the kind they've used for years, against the man.

"We've just begun a major search of the plane, tip to tail, and we'll know soon enough if this is a hoax. Most on board think it's a mainte-nance issue, so they're stuck aboard. Pan Am carries a lot of government folks like you and your seatmate, and would be a great propaganda vic-tory for the terrorists if they could bring one down."

"Can I ask you again whom I am talking to?"

"Sure Andy. You're in touch with a senior member of the National Command Authority. Is that specific enough? Anyway, we've got you on our radar back here. It's my job to make sure you remain safe and sound. Can I ask you another question?"

"Sure, go ahead. I'm an open book."

"You met, supposedly by accident, another Agency employee, a medical doctor, and then also by happenstance, a German son and father, is that right?"

"Spot on, as they say. Now tell me why this is important and how I fit in?"

There was a long pause. "How can I say this without sounding overly dramatic? Well there is no way to do it easily, so here goes. You've been identified as lead on a special program, that's all I can say here, and it involves you going into deep cover, and well, the rest will be explained when you get back here."

"May I ask if this has anything to do with the German father and son, or from what I've just been told that shots were fired at the president in DC?"

"Both Andy, but that's all I can say. Your air force escorts will be there in a couple hours so rest up and have a drink on me, and Pan Am of course."

"Good idea, but how?"

"Bar looks empty to me so help yourself. Bye for now."

Andy looked around but saw no Pan Am personnel. He did just that.

CHAPTER 3

Air Force passenger planes were more comfortable than some commercial ones but not nearly as luxurious as Pan Am's Clippers, even in coach. Andy reclined in the cramped jet. He soon fell asleep. Landing at Andrews Air Force Base in Maryland just over six hours later he was whisked to a remote location. The reception was correct, the base seemed to be in lockdown, and Andy's plane was the only one visible on the tarmac.

The military staff car took a route that doubled back on itself, but he was tired and slept most of the way. He realized that he had not called Nancy to let her know that he was back in DC. No one offered a phone to call anyone.

"We're here, watch your step," the driver said.

Andy left the sedan and stood alone in a large cave entrance. The cave appeared to be made of solid granite. Water trickled from the ceiling on the highly polished cement floor. Fluorescent lights gave the cave a bluish tint. They were strong and nearly as bright as daylight.

Walking toward him was a senior Navy Chief, who extended his hand to shake. "Andy welcome to the new world, as we call it, glad you're here. C'mon let's get you settled."

Andy followed meekly. "Any chance I might get a shower in this place, maybe?" He asked.

"I can arrange that, but I gotta warn you the water's rock hard!" The Chief laughed. They walked through a set of massive doors and entered what appeared to be a hotel lobby.

"Reid needs a room and a shower, chop-chop," the Chief said to a young black female civilian.

"Can do, come with me Andy," she said with a seductive lilt to her voice.

Andy followed meekly. "Guess who all know a lot about me and I know virtually nothing about you all. That a fair enough assessment?"

"Bingo, right on target, my man. Here's your room. I am getting off from work at about ten so if there's anything you need between now and then or especially after that, they can find me." She brushed hard against Andy as she left the room and blew him a kiss as she walked down the hall to the lobby.

"*Must be my magnetic personality,*" Andy thought.

The room had a phone so Andy took the chance that he might get through to Nancy. He dialed zero and was connected to the same girl he just met at the front desk. "Miss me already?" she said.

"Of course, I just wondered if I could make a call to my wife. That's all."

"Where and how long? The call I mean."

"Maryland, and I'll be quick I promise."

She paused. "Let me check with the big guy. Normally there are no outgoing calls allowed. Some stupid rule about security they came up with, I guess. But you're a special guest and maybe I can get them to relent."

"Appreciate it, thanks. Call me back when you know one way or the other, please." Andy hung up and took a long steamy shower. He was toweling off when the phone rang. "What did you find out?" he asked.

"Actually this is not the person who you talked to before," a distant sounding female voice said. "I am calling about your request for a long distance call to your home."

"And, the verdict is?"

"I can't allow it, but be assured that your wife Nancy knows you are back in the States. She's been told to expect you back home in a few days. That's the best I can do under the circumstances. We're in an emergency mode most of the time around here, and we're not singling you out, believe me."

"You assure that she know. We have a young child, a little girl. She worries a lot about me being gone all the time."

"Honest I do understand. I spoke with the person who spoke with her and with Grace, your neighbor. We didn't even have to pull out the national security card, like we sometimes have to. This time she agreed that your life is convoluted and that she's used to it."

"Thanks I guess," Andy said feeling very tired.

"One more thing. Try to keep your hands off the help, can you? We know that some of our staff can be a little too forward at times, but it is in everyone's best interest to keep things on the up and up here. We don't have an OB on staff, so we try to keep things Platonic."

"Ma'am, whoever you are, I have no intention of attempting anything, and as you said she was the one making all the suggestions. So, thanks for the warning but be assured I won't be doing anything."

"Andy, we know that you have a history with women, and at least one was a hot chick up there in Chatham, but now we've got to toe the line, get it?:

Andy smiled and waited a few beats. "Understood. Hey, do I know you; you seem to know a lot about me?"

"We may have crossed paths somewhere in the past, but I'll leave it up to you to find out where."

"Let me think about it, bet I can discover where." Andy hung up.

Suddenly he was very tired. He dropped onto the bed and slept.

Hans Rasmussen walked slowly though the underground tunnel. It was beneath an abandoned Bavarian barn. Some of the incandescent lights installed during the Second World War were still operative, but many had blown out, leaving a rabbit's warren of shadow-filled corners and dimly lit corridors. He reached the room at the end of a hall, and pulled up his collar to ward off the dampness and cold.

Pushing open the heavy door he had a hard time adjusting to the bright lights in the room. "Anyone here?" he asked tentatively.

"Just us, the old people," someone said. Two men approached Hans and shook his hand warmly. "Condolences on the end of your father's life, Hans. Though he was one of us, we were never sure how much he believed in our cause."

"Father was a great scientist, and science for him was everything. There was no other thing in his life that mattered. Sadly it was this way for me and for my sister, who now resides in the United States.

"Father was an absent man for most of our lives, and when he became incapacitated he ordered me to take care of him. You know that I would have done that anyway."

"We know this is true, Hans. Werner was a great man, a single-minded one. If he had been successful the War would have ended much sooner, and…"

"Everyone would be speaking German; yes I recall that old line. But, he did what he could with what he had to work with during those times."

"*Ya*, he was a man of honor. We and many others will miss him."

Hans studied the older men's faces. "As you know both my sister and I are also in the trade, I mean the Physics one. We could possibly be of assistance in the work you are still pursuing."

"Alas, Hans, the Führer is long gone, and that leaves us with no one to sell our ideas to."

"This is a new world. There are nations interested in what you've done here. I have been exploring contacts to the east. I think I know of others who might be interested, and these persons are willing to pay and pay handsomely. I would like to make contact with my sister and set up a meeting here, or there with you both, and we can discuss the details."

"Seems reasonable, after all we are both approaching 80 years of age and have not that many years left. It would be nice to see your father's work come to fruition. After all, we are essentially non-ideological here, the best bidder is always the most generous one."

"Perhaps," Hans said pausing for emphasis. "We should plan for a meeting here in the old country rather than subjecting you to the grueling airplane ride to America?"

"Grueling perhaps, but nothing can compare with our missions over the Western Hemisphere in the War," the first man said. "Sadly we never got the chance to use the thing, the one your father developed."

"Maybe this time we will," Hans said and stood at attention. "Now I must call my sister and arrange a meeting.

The phone rang as Harriett was preparing to leave the office. She thought she might let the machine pick it up, but decided instead to answer. "Hello, this is Harriett, can I help you?"

"Bet you can, this is your friend from far way, Harold, and…"

"Hans, what's wrong? It is dad?"

"Please my dear, you are no longer Helga, and I am no longer Hans. More of that later. Can I interest you in a short all-expenses paid vacation to Europe?"

"Tell me more," Harriett said.

"Well, some of my friends are working hard on a project that may interest you and we need a third, no a fourth hand to get things under control."

"How long would I be gone?"

"A week or two should be enough. We have much of the early work to build on, and we'll just need to run some equations to verify the thing is possible."

"What am I going to tell my boss?" Harriett asked.

"My dear, your government agency seems to be very easily pleased and very gullible, after all they hired you!"

"Point taken Harold. I need to get the bus to Boston and then a flight from Logan, so can I call with those details?"

"Taken care of Harriett. A car will pick you up to go to Logan in about twenty minutes. Your seat has been booked on Pan Am. See you here soon."

Harriett looked around her Hyannis office. "Good thing I always have a bag packed," she said to the empty FBI spaces.

She called her supervisor and left a message that she was on special assignment and would call in when she was returning.

"Easy enough," she said.

CHAPTER 4

The scarred dull yellow Buffalo Springfield tracked bulldozer was pushing sand, plowing along a new road in the little town of Chatham
Massachusetts. The center of the village was nearby. This stretch of land,
the part north of route 28 in what they called North Chatham, was almost virgin land. Pine trees outnumbered people in this part of town,
even in the 1980s. Except for a few mega homes, the land was virgin,
probably the same as when the Monomoit Indians roamed, three hundred years ago.

The construction supervisor, Willie Billings, signaled to the earth
mover operator, Chester Billings, that it was lunchtime and to shut off
the noisy machine. The operator lowered his blade to the sandy soil and
was stopped the large diesel. As he dismounted, he saw something under
one of the tracks.

"Hey, boss. Come over here. Got us a thing, something looks like rusty
metal or something just under the tracks, stickin' outa the sand."

"So what," the supervisor said, "just pick the damn thing up and throw
it is the dumpster OK?"

The bulldozer operator reached down and brushed the sand away from the object. It was some kind of canister, very old from the looks of it, and had faint markings He tried to lift it but it was partially stuck under the large track of the dozer.

Lunch sounded much more interesting. The dozer operator decided to check it out in an hour or so. He had tucked a joint in his lunch box, so he might smoke a little weed. It would make the afternoon that much more bearable. If his lady ever stopped bugging him about his weight, he would be a lot happier too.

"Hey kid what the hell you doin' there?" the supervisor asked from across the job site. His hands were on his hips and he was not smiling.

"Boss, just jerkin' off if you need to know. I was getting' my lunch pail, that's all. Whatsamatter, we on some kinda time schedule?"

"Building inspector, that's what. Son of a bitch is on his way I just heard over the CB. So look lively and don't light up, whatever you do. Old Harold is one straight mother and he ain't in the mood to be smelling your homemade shit. So keep it down there OK, and by the way, try to look busy."

"I guess that means no eatin' lunch, right?"

Willie Billings grinned. "Even if'n you are my nephew you are one fat fuck, I'll say that."

"Gee uncle, comin' from you that sounds like a compliment."

"Get back on your machine Chester and look busy, even if you just push the damned sand back and forth."

"By the by I found somethin' else in the sand, what'ya want me to do about it," Chester asked.

"Damn it, just bury the thing deeper and keep rollin'. We don't want old Harold snoopin' around the lot. Ya know he's half in the bag most times, and pissed inspectors are the worst kind."

Chester hauled himself into the seat of the dozer and started the engine with a roar and lot of smoke. He backed past the object he'd seen, lifted it up with the shovel, and then dumped the object into a grove of scrub pines at the end of the lot.

A dirty Ford pickup truck pulled up. Harold Ryder walked out unsteadily to do his inspection. His voice was slurred. Just another day and an incompetent inspection.

Chatham was too quiet. It was the non-tourist season, one that lasted from Labor Day to early July most years. In this long period of colder, drearier weather and short spurts of daylight, Chatham natives found time to plan their annual Florida trips. Some even considered playing the new lottery game that the state had begun. Scratchers were a big hit, and every church-sponsored Bingo game sold them.

The Mayberry atmosphere was alive and well on Main Street, but as the fall wore on, many businesses closed for the cold and dark season, hoping to count their summer haul and make it through until the arrival of the tourists again in the spring.

At the town offices in the center of the village there was a definite lack of activity. Most employees had decided that it was time to pedal back and take a breather after the slew of new housing starts that had overwhelmed them.

"What say we take the rest of the day off," James Dunlap, lead permit officer said. He stretched his long frame and leaned back in his wooden office chair.

"Fat chance, but I like the sentiment. There is always the chance that a meteor will strike Chatham and we can all forget everything." Noreen Caruso, his secretary laughed. "We got to get these final figures ready for the selectmen; they meet in a couple days."

"Ah yes," Dunlap said as he stretched. "They who must be obeyed, our good and true leaders. What would we do without them?"

"Most likely we'd be clammin' full time, that's what. Fishing is way too hard and besides you need to get up early for a long ride out to George's Bank. Not my cup of tea."

"Could do worse. I know that I'd enjoy getting that rake out and diggin' for our suppa," he said broadening his New England vowel's accent.

"Aaayup, just like down East," Noreen said.

"What say we head over to the Dyke and get out pants wet? Get it?"

"What say we just tell your wife that you're hitting on me?" Nancy smiled and winked. "Remember dear comrade that we are here on another mission, and we need to focus."

"You know these wonderful folks we call our betters are often as stupid as the leaders back home." Dunlap said. "I for one would like to see the whole lot lined up before a firing squad, but that's not for me to say or do."

"Comrade, comrade, we have a problem here. Your enthusiasm for the state is lagging. You've been weakened by all this natural beauty and the friendliness of these capitalists, our enemies that surround us. I will need to report you unless you can be re-programmed."

"Point taken my dear. You know that I would never say this kind of counterrevolutionary thing outside the confines of this office. Alas dear comrade Nancy. I am, shall we say 'on top' of it. You know that I am just a horny guy. Must be my red Russian blood. I need to maintain my virility both here and at home."

"Four kids is certainly proof that that Jimmy boy, but speaking for myself I tend to like older men."

"Noreen, think of me as an older brother…"

"That's sick, but interesting," she said. She grabbed his belt and pulled him close. Her hand slipped over his zipper, slowly pulling it down.

A truck roared into the lot and backed into a space nearly ramming the railing leading to the town office front door. Harold Ryder stepped out and threw his lit cigarette away, then stomped on most of it. He walked slowly into the building fumbling with the door marked 'pull' while he tried to push it open.

Harold was a known heavy drinker, but the most part an honest guy when it came to building inspections. Chatham's building boom mirrored a drop in mortgage interest with the end of the Carter administration, a welcome change from the twenty percent rates.

"Hey, is there anybody here?"

"Just me and my girl," James Dunlap yelled. "Hey Harold, you been over to the monster house lot on Scatteree yet?"

"Just back, actually. Seems to be taking forever to get the lot cleared, if you ask me." Harold sniffed, reached in his shirt pocket, and took out a Lucky Strike. Tapping it on the desk, he lit it and coughed.

James Dunlap waited for Harold to speak, and to cough a few more times. "So Harold, what exactly did you find over there?"

"I guess you might say I found two of the laziest contractors in town over there, but that's not the main thing I found. I reckon that old Billings and his worthless nephew are the stupidest people in town, and they have a long ways to go to beat the others I deal with."

Nancy Caruso spoke up. "Harold, we know that the Ryder's and the Billings clan have been fighting for a long time, sorta Hatfield's and McCoy's, but…"

"They shot each other, those Hatfield folks, but the Billings crowd is inbred. If you want to know why just look. The real dumb ones are falling out of that family tree. Should be their coat of arms, that's for sure." Harold took another drag and waited for the cough he knew would be coming.

"Harold, we get it, but as the permitting officer I have to know about the progress over there, are they puttin' in the foundation yet?"

"Damn, they can't even level the lot. Chester is stoned most of the time and he can't follow a plumb line to save his soul, so Willie has to go over what he done and make it straight."

"So I guess I need to go over there, right now and see what's what." Dunlap said. "Noreen, let's go for a ride."

Ryder smiled. "Who's gonna be on top this time?"

Nancy turned red. "Harold, I guess that all that booze is making you more stupid than normal. Keep your comments to yourself, OK?"

Harold saluted and almost fell backward. "Yes, Ma'am," he said and turned to leave for his office down the hall.

James Dunlap whispered to Noreen, "I think we might have to deal with Harold one of these days. You and I both know that he's a liability around here. He's much too stupid to know who we really are. But if he makes a major fuss and gets the whole office involved, our covers might be in jeopardy. Besides, one of these days he'll hit someone when he's got a snootful and kill somebody, maybe even do himself in."

"That would be an unfortunate accident, darling, wouldn't it?" Nancy kissed James on the lips. "We've come all this way to do our jobs and yet we have this one pimple that we need to squeeze, just one little blemish on our perfect complexions. It seems to have the potential to ruin everything."

"Noreen, we can't all be prefect, and we need to focus on the job we are here to do. We've got these little people thinking we're just plain folks, and I'd like to keep it that way."

"I'll bet that woman, the one you call your wife, would be happy to know the truth."

"Noreen she is a fellow traveler. She knows the danger that giving away our little secret would cause. She is also a committed member of the party."

"Shall we adjourn to our secret hideaway and see if there are any new instructions from the home front?"

"As long as we can take our time. You know that I like to be slow and steady not rush in these things," Noreen said. "Do you need any more instructions my dear boy?"

"Not hardly," Dunlap said with a laugh.

Harold Ryder, who had overheard the conversation, closed his door and made some notes on a legal pad. He placed the pad in his briefcase, and headed to the local watering hole, the Chatham Squire, to meet his friend and pass on what he learned. Maybe the guy would even buy him a drink; after all it had been at least an hour or so since his last one.

He locked his office and turned off the lights. Walking out the front door, he set the alarm but did not lock the door. Someone will come along and then the cops will come, and what fun that would be, since Harold recalled James Dunlap was the first person they would call.

Ryder walked the three blocks to the Squire and was met there by a group of college kids. Each one was drunker than the other. They were trying to best each other in a game of vodka shooters.

As he pushed through the crowd one of the bigger kids reached over to grab him, and Harold was glad to deck him with a single punch. The others were suddenly more sober and headed for the door. One of them threw up on the sidewalk and then threw up again on someone's brand new car parked at the curb.

"Hey Ryder, over here," a voice called from the back bar. "Sit down and take a load off."

Harold hitched up his jeans and straightened his shirt collar, and walked slowly to the bar. The need for a drink was strong. The guy who poured at the Squire was a good friend. He'd often filled Harold's glass for no charge.

The back bar bartender, Alex Romanoff, looked at Harold, and said, "Got something for me, old boy? If you do and I like it then maybe we can see about getting you lit today. What the hell, you're lit most days, aren't you, so what's the difference."

Harold Ryder settled on the bar stool, and wondered what he'd would have and whether the bartender might go for something stronger, from the wall instead of the lower well area, the one beneath the bar. Harold pointed meekly at the upper shelves.

"Harold, don't tell me you're gazin' at our top shelf shit. You wanna get me fired. I tell you this is one dangerous time to be a barkeep what with the Cold War, those damn Russians, and all those loose nukes floating in those Soviet subs off Chatham."

"Alex, can I remind you that your parents came from that God-forsaken place, Russia, the one that you just told me you're worried over. What do you take me for a fool? Wait, never mind, that's been established already. I do have some good intelligence for you, and this might be a better than usual tidbit. You be the judge.

"Meantime can you spread a little cheer for me here, I just want to smell that Bourbon in that fancy bottle. How about putting it on the bar, just this once and lettin' me smell a bit?"

"Harold, you are a freakin' piece of work, know that? Of course, you can smell the bottle, but I ain't openin' it. If the boss sees me being overly generous then I am out of a job and that's not good for my little escapade here in Chatham. You must get that much in your booze-soaked brain."

"I have lucid moments Alex, in fact quite a few of them. It's part of my Dean Martin act, if you must know."

Alex laughed. "That's where the similarity ends my friend."

"Nonetheless, I have a great deal to tell you about my officemates, facts that I think you and your friends would be happy to know."

Alex uncorked the good Bourbon and poured a double for Harold. "Here's to the patriots and I don't just mean the football team!" Alex said clinking his glass and Harold's.

"Let me tell you what I heard over at the office just now. You're gonna like this one, I guarantee it."

CHAPTER 5

Andy Reid was tired of being debriefed, sometimes by the same irritating and anonymous bureaucrat. He told the last person he met that he thought the whole process was nothing but a sham, and got an earful back.

"Reid," the interviewer said, "you are in danger of being branded a non-cooperative subject and you don't want to do that, my friend."

"What else can I do, you've made me tired and confused with all these little intrigues and this bullshit about national security."

"Smart ass answers will get you in deeper shit, young man. It is not bull, Andy, and I assure you that the security of this nation rests with this program and others like it, and you'd better get that or else…"

"I am waiting for the 'or else'," Andy said.

"We've had people decide to go rogue in the past. Folks we thought we could trust. They met with a bad end. We could not trust them to be good soldiers on the outside so we had to silence them."

"As in cut their tongues out?" Andy smiled.

"No, much more severe penalties, the ultimate I might add. So if you're thinking that you can just walk, think again. Let's start over again, shall we, and try to be civil here. Is that OK?"

There was a long period of silence as both men decided whether to add anything, and then decided not to try.

Andy stood and stretched. "Fair enough. But can I at least go for a walk first, just to clear my head?"

"I guess that's OK. Want some coffee or something to eat? We can have it brought in."

"What I really want is to call home, to call my wife Nancy, and see how she's doing. Can that be so hard to do?" C'mon, are we going to let me call or what?"

"You have to understand that we're in a facility that theoretically does not exist, or not supposed to exist, and we're..."

"I know, we're invisible, I get it. How about we bend the rules just this one time?"

"We'll see if that is doable, but based on my experience..."

"It's not. I get that, but please."

"There is a pay phone in the little town less than a mile outside the cave, and I suppose I could drive you there to use it. Let me see, OK?'

"I appreciate it."

Andy paced the little room with the large camera in the corner, smiling from time to time to let the watchers know that he was watching them as well. In about five minutes the briefer returned with a smile on his face.

"You ever play golf," he asked.

"Nah, but maybe when I get older, then who can say?"

"Well, you just got a Mulligan, a do over. They allowed me to escort you outside the perimeter to make a call. Even gave me a roll of quarters for the Western Electric pay phone."

"That's great. How can I get some privacy when I'm making that call? You know my wife and me..."

"Mr. Reid, one thing you'll learn here is that you've already given up every shred of privacy when you came through that cavern entrance. Your life is now an open book. Everything you think about, say or even do, is goin' to be watched and reported to someone. It's the bane of the special people like us."

"I really don't feel that special, actually. I have been, as I am sure you know, a person who has been at the wrong place at the wrong time, and that's been my bad luck for over a decade. I'm sure you heard about that thing up on Cape Cod?"

"Who hasn't, after all we watched over you all those years…"

"What do you mean '*we* watched over me'?"

"Let's just say we knew what you were doing and when."

"Well, well. I am not that all surprised, but since you guys are all knowing why not step in? Just do something, like give me a hand? I could have used some help, especially when I was almost killed. And Nancy, my wife, she took the brunt of all this, she almost died."

The briefer stood for a moment, choosing his words carefully. "Andy, let's just say that our inaction was not aimed at you but in preserving the secrecy of what we do and how we do it."

"Which means? Give me a clue here, after all we've just had hours of this and that, and yet I don't have the full picture yet."

"Look, the Russians are a good deal more pissed at us than most people realize. We assume that the public face at the Kremlin is a front and that the real power brokers are ready to make us look bad, and do something somewhere in the world, we just don't know what. I know that you have seen some of what secrecy can do. That Stepping Stones place is a good example. What if the real intent of doing something there was part of a long buried Russian scheme? Would that make it any less terrible?

"Andy, one other thing. There is a lot that even I have no clue about. We compartmentalize here, and that's for the good of the group and individuals too."

Andy smiled. "What, are we expecting a major invasion and hordes of communists coming over the North Pole to tickle every last detail out of us?"

"Seriously Andy, I wish that was all we needed to sweat, but it's not." The briefer turned his back to the camera and spoke in a whisper. "Andy, there are moles in our organization and we're trying to find them right now, with little luck. It's a long slog, and you are part of the sloggers, as it were. I expect you to find out eventually that we'll be putting you in charge of a major effort to find the insider who's getting us more and more worried."

"Well, once again I find myself on the short end of the stick here. I am totally unqualified to do this. In case you care. Get that, I am not really a player in this game, whatever it is, and besides I thought I was relieved of any more responsibility after my little trip to Germany."

"Perhaps, but think back to the time you were in Garmisch for minute. Add to that the sheer coincidence of meeting Bud Steinmiller at the Garmischer Hof, and finally the very convenient medical emergency. All very nicely fits together don't you think?"

"I suppose it was," Andy replied. "But I have had weird things happen lots of times, starting with being run over at the Pentagon by an out of control cart years ago. That's where I met Bud."

"Well, that's his side of the story. Doctor Bud is an enigma to us, and someone we want to watch very closely. He is indeed an MD, but his career path with the Agency, the CIA, has been mostly out of medicine. Ever hear of something called the Pathfinders?"

"Seems familiar. Tell me more," Andy said.

"The Pathfinders were part of the '*we-were-not-there-but-we-were*' group that worked with the Hmong tribes in Laos. They based out of NKP, Nakhon Phanom, Thailand during the Vietnam War. Doctor Bud spent time there at a secret base the Agency had. I recall the folks referred to NKP as 'naked fanny,' and worse.

"We, as in the US, had Special Operations personnel at NKP starting in 1962. JFK had this fascination with unconventional warfare and this was his baby. Some idiot outed the whole operation to the press in 1968, but we kept it through the mid-1970s, when Vietnam fell to the Commies."

"What did Bud have to do with this, NKP Pathfinder thing I mean?"

"Amazingly Andy I have no goddamned idea. The cover story these folks had is so deep and so hard to crack that even I can't find out what he did."

"How do you know he was there then," Andy asked.

"We have contact with other members of the unit, folks we trust, we can verify that he was a part of their operation, but for how long, no one can say since these guys often went native, lived among the Hmong, spoke their version of Chinese, ate rice, ducked under triple canopy to avoid being tagged, that kind of thing."

"Bud is a big tall white guy so he must have been easy to spot, right? I mean he's definitely not Asian."

"You'd think, but he never got nailed buy us or them. His ability to avoid detection is the stuff of legend. But I digress; he is one mystery to us. He's got friends in high places, politically connected and protected, and he's very savvy."

Andy paused. "Well, you know I found it strange that he'd appear out of nowhere deep in Bavaria and be my long lost companion after these many years. Do you think he was looking for me, is that what you're saying?"

"Hard to say but I do not believe in chance, or fate for that matter."

"Well, now that we've got that straight, can I ask you a question?"

"Maybe. It depends on the question."

"For starters what is your name?"

"What 'sir' wasn't good enough?" The briefer smiled. "I am called by many names but my family calls me Bill, Bill Leonard. Is that common enough to be lost in the weeds?"

Andy reached out a hand. "Pleased to meet you Bill, and thanks. It gets somewhat impersonal here, wherever that is, at times. Other than the sweet looking black babe who made advances at the front desk when I checked in, it's been all business."

"And she may have meant that it was the paying kind of business, who knows. Actually I think she is just happy to see an unfamiliar face and a tad bit shy." Leonard laughed.

"I'd call her anything but shy. What's her story anyway? What brings her here?"

"Andy, I will tell you that this little corner of the world is a home for the homeless, the lost and the unhopeful. I am one of few still married in this group. My wife thinks I am an astronaut, somewhere in space."

"Space maybe not, but how does she, your wife, cope?"

Leonard was serious for a moment, and said, "She has another friend, one who satisfies her when she's lonely that's how. I know this because I also know the son of a bitch who's screwing her. Used to work for me, he did, back in the day. The little shit has used that connection to insert himself, if you get my meaning."

"I get it, and I'm sorry Bill, even though I have not been faithful myself over the years. Now that I am a dad I guess I have settled down and…"

"Never say never Reid, that's my motto."

"But you started on Doctor Bud, and his time in Southeast Asia and we got side-tracked. What's the deal with him?"

Leonard said, "Well he was essentially a non-person for years. He never checked in with the Agency's Chief of Station like he was supposed to. He apparently never got in trouble or needed an evacuation either. He just went underground, that's all. He finally reappeared after the truce, and he was repatriated on one of the last Air America flights from NKP to Saigon. After that he came home.

"We lost track of him after that. Someone told me he was involved in some serious doings down in Chile or somewhere else in South America. No one's talking about that now after the Church hearings and all that fallout.

"Bud became a mover and shaker when he got back to DC. Got a medal of some kind, which is a hell of a lot better than many other compatriots I know who got the shaft for doing their job. Good old Bud always lands on his feet. I will say that for him."

"Now the million dollar question: was he in fact the Doc who patched me up at the Pentagon a while back? Claims he was but I can't place him."

"Andy, he was there somewhere in the Pentagon during your time getting run over. He may have responded to the call for medical personnel when that happened. As for an assignment in that medical clinic, there's no record that he was ever part of the group, at least not on a permanent basis."

"Damn, Bud's little introduction might have been a setup. He sure knows plenty about me that's for sure." Andy frowned. "Maybe he was there, maybe not, but he sure knew a lot about me, what I had been through and where I had been."

"Your life is an open book within the intelligence community young man. Every student at the basic intelligence school studies your improbable journey through the two last decades."

"Well Bill, does that include the concept of dumb luck and incredible circumstances for which I had no desire to be part of?"

"Yeah, among other thing, that too. Your ability to survive in an extreme environment I guess the instructors are kinda comparing you to Luke Skywalker, the dude in the Star Wars movie who uses The Force to get through those tough times."

"Except that I am not a Hollywood actor and I had no special effects to make it look so real or even good. But back to Bud, what am I to do, no let me rephrase that, what are you going to do with him?"

"Let me and my good buddies handle that. Want to make the mad dash for the pay phone in town now?"

"Will I need a disguise?" Andy laughed.

Bill Leonard raised his index finger to his lips, and shook his head. "Not this time." They walked down a long tunnel and through a small door into bright sunlight.

Harriett Rasmussen was dead tired. Lufthansa managed to delay the flight from London for over six hours, making the long flight on Pan Am from Boston to Frankfurt even more odious. She had wandered through the shops at Heathrow for a time, tried to sleep on the hard plastic benches. She had been awakened by a curious German Shepard who was apparently looking for contraband or drugs. Finally listened as a two teens screamed to each other as they broke up then fell madly in love again.

"Miss, can I take this seat," a handsome man wearing a well-tailored business suit asked.

Harriett sat up straight, and involuntarily ran her fingers through her blonde hair. "Of course, thank you for asking."

"The man sat very straight, and held out his hand. "May I introduce myself? I am Percy Atwater, and I am traveling from here to Germany, West Germany that is. I hope that this delay in our flight will not be much longer, I have important business to attend to once there."

Harriett noticed that his sentence construction belied his perfect English accent, and that he had been a native German speaker as a child or perhaps later in his life. "I too am bound for Germany, family reunion, that kind of thing," she said.

Percy Atwater smiled showing large white teeth. "I am glad that we are both heading in the same direction. I find England to be a nice place but the food is terrible. They think that Sausage is something greasy and tasteless. I long for the Wurst of my youth."

"I am not much of an expert on food of Europe. I am an American with hot dog and hamburger tastes actually. Recently I've been working in the Commonwealth of Massachusetts, Cape Cod actually, and have been eating a heavy dose of seafood and shellfish. Lobster is actually quite good, if someone else does the hard work, the killing, the cooking and the cracking."

"I've often pondered the first time a human had the nerve to eat one of those marine dwelling beasts, and hope that he knew that the shell was not edible," Percy said.

"My exact sentiments, yes sir. I find the best delicacy is wrapped in the most perplexing package. Like clams and oysters."

"My excuses ma'am, I did not ask your name and that I must apologize."

Harriet smiled. "I am Harriett Rasmussen, and I should have made that clear when you introduced yourself."

"Not a problem. May I offer you a token of gratitude for speaking with me?"

Harriett was not smiling. "I find that the kindness of strangers sometimes comes with a hitch if you get my meaning. I want to assure you that while I am a nice person, I am trained in the martial arts. I also have extensive firearms training."

Percy held up a hand in surrender. "I give up Miss Harriett, and am glad that you warned me of your prowess. Let me assure you that I was being kind and not trying to make any advances, just conversation. If I can continue, I'd like to offer you a seat next to me in First Class on our outbound flight to Germany, no strings attached."

"Forgive me for being a little more cautionary and suspicious. But how might that happen?"

Percy smiled and stood at attention. "Ma'am, when you own an airline there is very little you cannot accomplish with a wave of your hand."

"I am impressed and skeptical at the same time. You own Lufthansa; I thought that was a state run airline?"

"Miss Rasmussen, I did not say that I owned that specific airline, just an airline. Let me tell you that you may not have ever heard of it, but it has a long lineage, stretching back to the era of biplanes. My grandfather was a pioneer in aviation. His designs are among the best ever, and his advancements in aviation are still being tested but not bested in air forces around the world."

"Was your lineage German? I mean was your family in the old country during the war? Many aircraft were developed during that time. As I recall the first operational jet fighter was built and deployed during the late stages of the conflict."

"Ah yes the ME 262, far ahead of its time, but alas the allies had bombed most of the sources of material by then. Only a few were actually flying but then grounded for lack of fuel. Grandfather was not a Messerschmitt man; he actually had a firm that carried his name."

Harriett was listening carefully. "I might be tempted to ask what that name was. Perhaps my dear Percy you'd rather keep that secret for another time?"

"If there is another chance to talk yes that would be a *bon mot* for us to share. But tell you what I am willing to speak freely now if you accept my offer of an upgraded seat."

"Yes why not?"

"My grandfather's name was Horten, perhaps you've heard of it since your father, Werner knew him very well."

Chapter 6

"Hey Babe, it's me, calling from, well never mind," Andy said softly. He cradled the phone against his chin, ready to drop in more quarters at the signal.

"Well I guess I can call the police back and tell that you're not missing after all. Last time I heard from you, you were en route back from Europe. You have a lot of nerve leaving me out in the cold, Andy. Couldn't you just have written a telegram or told someone with you to tell me you were OK?"

"The problem is that I was incognito…"

"And *alone* while you were I hope. You have a track record Andy so don't forget that."

"Yep, very true Babe. I need to keep reminding myself that I am married and faithfully married at that."

"Don't make fun Andy. We need to remind each other that this was for better or worse, and I have had a lot of the 'worse.'"

"I apologize Nancy, really if there was a spare moment. Well, that's a piss poor excuse; I just have been out of the loop and still am for that matter."

·"Can you tell me when you'll be back here and in the loop? I need to have some idea of what you are doing and when you'll be a good husband again."

Andy shifted from one foot to the other. "Babe, I am using a pay phone and yes I am back in the states, but I have no idea where I actually am. I was actually kidnapped and pulled off that Pan Am flight from Frankfurt the other day. The pilot took me off the plane, and…"

"I now, the aliens got you and have just let you off the spaceship. Spare me the details if you can. When are you coming home? I know it's too much to think about right now but when you do get home are you gonna stay for a while, I mean with us."

Andy looked at his handler, Bill Leonard. "Depends on what they say and what they do. Hey Bill, any idea when I can get back home?"

Leonard shrugged and said nothing.

"So, they have no idea. I will call you as soon as I know what's going on. I promise."

"I've heard those kinds of promises before Andy. I am very tired of it. Just get home as soon as you can. You are married and you have a family in case that little detail slipped your mind."

"Got it Babe, I will be there soon I hope, bye for now, love you."

The phone line went dead. Andy heard the dial tone and slowly replaced the phone in its cradle.

Bill Leonard was standing there, extra quarters in his hand. "Guess you won't need these?"

"Got that right Bill. I am in deep trouble with Nancy, not that that hasn't happened in the past. The poor girl does not have unlimited patience. Who would?"

"Andy, this is small consolation but most of us here are divorced or nearly so, and you are not alone in making a spouse give up waiting for you."

"Well, that is something. You know I love Nancy and I want to see her as soon as I can. Isn't there some way that we can speed up the process and get me back home?"

Leonard smiled. "If you are willing to submit to just one small experiment then maybe we can process you out fairly quickly."

"Experiment, what is this Frankenstein's lab or something?"

"Nah, Frankenstein was bringing folks back to life. We haven't got that far yet. But we're working on it," Leonard said. "Let's go back inside."

Andy and Bill Leonard walked back to the tunnel from the way they came. The door which they had left was held open by a small piece of wood. It was getting dark and looked like rain. The wind picked up and the air became colder.

"Bill, tell me something, if you can. What is so damned important that we need to play James Bond around here? What's with the tunnels, the briefings, and all that? What is this, another Fort Knox?"

"Fort Knox is an important place for sure, and I have actually been there. Let me tell you without divulging too much that what goes on here is as important as all that gold down in those vaults in Kentucky. The reason this place was built long ago was to survive a major thermonuclear bomb direct hit."

"OK, that much I get, but if this place is so secret how could the bad guys have it on their target list?"

"We assume that everything within a hundred miles of Washington DC is on the list that's why. Given the ability of the Russians to see everything we do and say we have to assume they know where we are and what we do. I know that sound cynical but it's a fact of life in the 1980's."

"Not at all reassuring Bill, and I agree that a good plan is assume that the evil doers, as we know call them, are evil and smart too."

Bill stopped and put his hand on Andy's shoulder. "Andy, we know that some of our people, some of them well-meaning or worse, naïve, are going to give away the farm every chance they get. Just a truism. My feeling is that we should consider everyone a security risk and then be surprised if they're not. Hey, maybe I have been insider the perimeter too long."

Andy smiled and said, "How long have you been here actually?"

"That's Top Secret Andy. Let's just say it's been over a decade. The place was built long ago, and some of the folks inside are plank holders, meaning that they were here during construction. They behave as if they're part of the woodwork, which for all intents on purposes they are. Hidebound, that's the term I use. They think rules are meant to be followed no matter how stupid or how outmoded they are."

"I know about the fallacy of rule following," Andy said. "I have often made my own rules, and suffered for making that decision. Overall I try to be a good soldier but I am not afraid to make waves, if I feel the time and circumstances are right. But I am still here and I guess that means it's OK to take some chances, if they fit the circumstances."

"Andy, I have only just met you. It was not under the best of circumstances, but I have to tell you that I find that attitude refreshing. Of course, if I am pressed in my next polygraph, I'll try to cover that fact of my feeling that way, since it usually means the rack." Bill Leonard smiled.

"One last question for you Bill. Where are you from, I can't detect any accent."

"True, that I am now unaccented. I have worked hard to get to the bland side of American English for a while, even when I was speaking Russian to shall we say, unfriendly folks. I am actually from Massachusetts, south-eastern as a matter of fact."

"Don't tell me that…"

"Aayupp, as we say, born and raised on Old Cape Cod."

"Where's Leonard, I need him right now," the colonel in charge of the facility screamed.

"Sir," a sergeant said meekly, "I have not seen him in a while. Last time I saw him he was with that Reid character, the civilian who's been here for a day or so. Do you want me to check and see if I can find him? He can't be very far away, can he?"

"Never mind, but when you find him tell him to see me immediately."

"Yes sir," the sergeant said snapping a hasty salute. He reached under his desk drawer and pushed a button, calling Leonard on his pager.

Bill Leonard got the distress call immediately and headed for the command center, walking briskly. Placing his palm on the reader he waited for the familiar whoosh as the door opened inward.

"Colonel, you wanted to see me?" He asked.

"I'm tempted to ask where you've been. I actually need to speak with you and not even bother with knowing that," the Colonel said.

Bill Leonard's patience with the arrogant officer was wearing thin. He decided to say nothing, and nodded.

"Well anyway give me a status report on this Reid character. I need to know what makes him tick and whether we can use him for the special project. Don't give me any of that mumbo jumbo that you guys are famous for. I don't understand it and never want to."

"Sir, there is a good possibility that Reid is the perfect match for our plan. I say that because I have had both on site and off site…"

"Off site, Jesus what the hell does that mean?"

"Sir, Reid wanted to call his wife and I escorted him into town. Not more than that. I heard everything that he said, even stood at the pay phone with him. He was a compliant fellow and never gave away our location."

"Thank God for that Leonard. We have enough to worry about the Commander in Chief in a hospital bed shot by a would-be assassin, for God's sake. I do not need a security breach to add to those troubles. Why was Reid so anxious to call his home?"

"Sir, he apparently has had a long history of being away from his wife and not telling her where he's been or why. I guess that coupled with a few times he's been in the sack with other women makes him doubly nervous about the future of his marriage. Now that they have a baby, well as you can guess, he needs to check in."

"Yes, we did snatch him off the Pan Am plane didn't we, and with only a bare minimum of explanations? I suppose that gives him the incentive to call. I would have appreciated advance warning that you'd be doing this."

"My apologies Colonel, I should have checked with you first. If I may sir, I think that Reid is the by far the best candidate we have for the project."

"And what does he know of the assignment?"

"Not a thing sir and that's the best course of action I think. If he's compromised we want to ensure that he can tell nothing of substance that would give away the plan."

"Agreed. But how can we send him on this adventure and not tell him the real reason for his mission?"

"Colonel, I have already started a cover story and am building a plausible scenario for that. Just one more thing, can we let Reid have a pass to visit his family?"

"Not now. Let's let the crisis down in DC die down a bit. Maybe then perhaps. Meantime, keep Reid here and keep him happy. If he has a wandering eye then fix him up with someone. I assume he's heterosexual so find some babe that he can work on."

Leonard smiled. "I think I have a couple of good candidates, yes sir, and I'll get right on that."

Andy Reid stretched out on his bed and put his arms over his head. He looked directly at the corner of his room. There was a small black spot there. Squinting to get a better view Andy thought he saw a small reflection on its surface. Thinking it was a camera installed since he had left, Andy wondered what other listening devices might have been planted in his room and when. He rolled over and was soon asleep.

Someone knocked quietly on at the door, waking Andy up. He heard the key turn in the lock, and then a click. Someone entered the room quietly. It was the girl from the front desk, and she was wearing a terry robe, and apparently nothing else. She took off the belt of the robe and let it slip to the floor. "Room service," she said and reached over to climb into the double bed. "Don't worry, I turned off the camera," she said.

CHAPTER 7

It was a media circus. In this case the clowns were wearing press credentials. Many of the men and a few scattered women had the chance to
cover the biggest story since Watergate, the shooting of an American
president. The perpetrator was in custody. His bizarre fixation with col-
lecting guns and a Hollywood actress had been replayed a number of
times, perhaps too many. Now the focus was on the president's health
and the succession, if there was to be one by the vice president.

Geoff Branstead, chief White House correspondent for Info News
Network, INN, one of the newest but least viewed cable news outlets
on TV, was hard at work. Using the phones in his tiny office just off
Pennsylvania Avenue, he called every person that he knew in the government and the military, scrounging for information. He was hung up
on five times, but he persevered.

At last he had someone, a man named Alex Cardozo, on the phone.
Cardozo was an important source for Branstead who was willing to talk
off the record. "I assume you know that I work for INN, and we're…"

"Yes you are pathetically off the charts in Neilson terms, with no viewers. Hell, how are you paid over there, do they hand out IOUs? But you called me. I am not that busy other than saving the world. Shoot."

"Yes there is a need for the public to know about the president's condition, health wise and more about this Hinckley character. Can you give me any tidbits that I might use later for our special report?"

"Shit, Geoff, can't you crib something from the big boys on the real network news? Reynolds and Cronkite are doing it live, wall-to-wall. Old Walter is retiring soon I hear and this is his final shot at greatness. So, back to my question: why can't you just plagiarize something?"

"Well, we pride ourselves in being on air with original stories and insights. So…"

"You want me to provide that? I can't remember who said it but I think it sums up the whole media bunch these days. Someone said that laziness had replaced incompetence as the hallmark of journalists."

"Hadn't heard that one before but it's cute," Branstead said with a laugh. "But really, what can you give me, off the record of course."

"Well, I can tell you that this was a one man shooting, and there was no grassy knoll to worry about or a second shooter. Seems the kid was delusional, obsessed too, and did this to make a statement. He succeeded in that, as you can tell."

"What about the government now that the president is in the hospital? Is there a contingency plan, some kind of marital law thing that was put into place?"

"I see you've been reading those black helicopter paperbacks that show up on my desk all the time. No, other than getting the big man well and guarding him at the medical facility, we have done nothing to change our everyday workload or security here.

"Let me ask you a question, and this is serious. What are you hearing about this kind of reaction, or overreaction to the shooting? Just curious that's all."

Branstead looked down at a paper he'd been given. "I have a source…"

"Whose name will not be given up to me?"

"I have a source who tells me that there's a real serious concern that this event, taking place less than seventy days after the man took office, was a shot across the bow by the bad guys to send a signal that we American need to be less bellicose."

"You're talking about the Russians, our once and former allies, I suppose. Fascinating and pure conjecture. You're way out in left field. We have no need to consider the bad guys, whoever they are these days, as anything other than disinterested in what happens on Washington streets in April 1981. Is that clear?"

"Well, my source tells me that there's a disinformation office buried somewhere in this city that takes the news of these events and then inserts false information for the media to chew on. What do you know about that?"

"Fantasy, Branstead, pure and simple. I've been in the government long enough to know that we're not that sophisticated. If we were, someone would leak that we were. Then we'd have to shut down the entire system to cover our asses."

"So, you're denying the whole thing, can I use that on air?" Branstead asked.

"If the ten people with cable television who get tired of those new kids down in Atlanta, what is it called, CNN or something like that, then sure go ahead. Just remember that I categorically deny any knowledge of any government plan to take over the world." He laughed and then coughed. "Damn, where are my cigarettes," he said.

"OK and thanks. We'll use this to fill in on what we have and launch it on the next newscast. Thanks for the help."

"Sure, call me any time, but as always no names please or you're cut off."

The call ended. Alex Cardozo pulled a heavy gray phone closer to his hand.

"This is Alex," he said into the mouthpiece. "We have a problem with one of the media goons. Since he is in a small time racket with a small time cable news outlet, there's most likely not much to sweat but I thought you'd like the head's up… Sure I can wait, or you can call me back."

Alex hung up the phone and was about to light his fifth cigarette of the day when the gray phone rang. "Yep, his name is Geoff Branstead and he's with something called Information News Network, INN. Based here in DC, Pennsylvania Avenue I think. Why do you ask?"

The other person on the line paused and then said, "Well Alex, we need to get into this fellow Branstead's house and office and see if he has any sensitive information. Maybe even get his phone records; you can do that can't you?"

"Sure, but I'll need a cutout since he knows who I am. After all he called me if you recall," Alex said. That's not that easy to do on short notice. I need some assurance that if this goes south I'll be able to escape with my reputation intact."

The person on the phone sighed. "You know my fiend we all signed up for this grand adventure knowing that it was a one way entrance into the program.

"Only way you get out is if you die, or if you get caught, then you can die with that pill we gave you. What is so hard to understand here? Just do it, no cutouts, nobody else involved. And if that reporter gets too close then make sure he disappears. Is that clear enough for you?"

"Very clear, and do you want me to call you back when the problem is solved."

"Of course, we cannot have any loose ends, you should know that. Didn't any of your Sicilian relatives ever teach you about loyalty, the *omerta*?"

Alex grimaced, but held his tongue for a moment. He was thinking that not responding to that comment was the best course of action. "Oh yes, one other thing, he seems to have a good source somewhere inside, someone who knows about our special access program, the one that no one is talking about. He mentioned having a source within the government who tells him that there's a disinformation office."

"He knew that much? Damn it! That is not a good thing. I appreciate you telling me about his information for this part of his story. Now it's our problem to find his source. Perhaps we can sweat the name out of him before he meets some unfortunate end. Let me think about that, but in the meantime, do a full scan on Mr. Branstead and call me back with updates. See you later. And we're going to have a random, but full polygraph scheduling for the staff."

"I get that sir, and will keep you in the loop as I uncover things."

Alex stared out his window, looking directly at the U.S. Capitol building, shrouded in clouds. *How apropos*, he thought.

He stood and walked out his door. A guard tipped his hat and asked, "Off to the subway?"

Alex nodded and smiled back. "I need to make a pit stop and my office bathroom is not working that well. Can you call our maintenance dudes and get them in here? My staff can show them the problem."

"Yes Senator I will, right away," the guard said.

Andy Reid was mad. He was yelling to the woman who had entered his room without his permission. "I could care less what you want, and get out now!"

"Calm down Andy, can't you see I am just here to make you more comfortable? I am not going to tell anyone what we're gonna do, just lay back and we'll let nature take its course," she said.

"Shit, lady, you aren't listening, are you. I said get out, what's so hard about understanding that?" Andy stood up. "And put your robe back on right now. I got the picture and I am not interested. I've had entrapment chances in the past and am not gonna make that mistake again,"

"No one will see or hear us," she said pulling her terry robe back over her shoulders. "Discreet, that's me. I can be very accommodating."

"Discretion is not my problem, it's you. Who told you to come here and when?"

"Andy, I am just an employee at this place. When they tell me to jump I jump. This is one of the parts of the job that I'm not fond of, but it's a paycheck. And if you fail to do something, then you pay for that. I'm here because they asked me…"

"Who is that that asked you?"

"Your constant companion, Bill Leonard actually gave me this task, but I know that Colonel Clink, I mean Colonel Jackson, is undoubtedly the man doing the ordering around here. He is a prototypical redneck!"

Andy paused. "Well that's one person I have yet to meet. What's he like?"

"Other than being a self-absorbed male chauvinist pig, he's not that bad. He once tried to get me in bed, sort of his reverse Mandingo fantasy I guess, but I've held him off."

"You know, I don't even know your name, so if you don't mind telling me"

She held out a manicured hand. "My name is Wanda Brixton, and pleased to meet you."

"Wanda, you seem like a very nice girl. How did you ever get here and what in the world is going on? I have only been outside once in the last couple of days. Seems we're in the middle of nowhere."

"Close to nowhere, but we're actually at one of the many locations the government has, and most likely forgot about. They were built in the last thirty or so years to survive the end of the world.

"Ironic isn't it, surviving the end of the world, no more Moon Pies or Twinkies but plenty of canned rations from the last great war to keep us alive."

"Yep, makes no sense, but then what does these days? How in the world did you get here?"

"It's a long story. I was a military brat, dad was an Army Ranger, met my mom at a PX overseas, had me, but they never got married. His parents did not approve of colored girls, as mom was called then, marrying white southern boys. They threatened to disown him if he married my mom. Dad was killed in the raid, the one that failed trying to get the Iran hostages, so it's just me and mom now."

Andy smiled. "Got that so far, but here, how and why?"

"Seems dad left me a trust fund, one that even mom did not know existed, and he tied it to some lawyer in DC. I went to see him after the funeral at Arlington. He tells me that I need to come here for further instructions on how to collect my inheritance. I wanted to give half maybe all the money to mom. She's had a tough time, no pension since they never got married. I fell for the lawyer's line. I was younger and stupid.

"That was bullshit, I know that now. If I ever get the money it will be a long time coming. I sit here day after day pretending to be busy, doing whatever they want me to do, including what we just did, and…"

"And you failed in that, so now what will they do to you," Andy asked.

"No whippings, at least not so far. I am gonna get a ration of shit over this I know."

Andy put his hands on her shoulders. "I have an idea. Why don't we give that camera a show to remember?"

"But you said that you weren't interested, remember. They told me the camera was disabled."

"You fell for that?" Andy asked.

"Dumb I know, but then what about you and me, are we gonna…"

"We're gonna go through the motions, and if I can stay focused, we'll give those watchers something to tell their good friends about over a beer. But we're gonna fake it, if you get my drift."

"Faking is good, but I am more than willing to go beyond faking."

"Wanda, believe me when I say this, but it will take all my self-control to just pretend."

"Ready if you are," Wanda said leaving her robe on and crawling into bed with Andy. He resisted all urges and soon they were facing each other, hands at their sides, making sexy noises.

In a control room several hallways distant a technician was sound asleep and never noticed that the two figures he was charged with watching were in bed together, apparently making serious love to each other.

His neck snapped forward and he heard a click as his outer door opened. Pulling himself upright he stared at the nearly visible couple in bed.

Bill Leonard entered the room and stared at the image. "Looks like Wanda is getting the young man saddled up, doesn't it?"

"Yeah, I mean yes, not much foreplay, just a lot of loud grunting. Whew, they're like rutting dogs down there."

"Well, our job is get them together, and they are doing just that. I wouldn't mind getting a little help from Wanda myself. She is one fine woman."

"Yeah, the colonel has been sniffing around her for a long time but as far as I can tell, it's been for nothin,' I mean he's struck out every time."

Yep, our good friend Colonel Jackson has got lots of problems, other than being a committed racist and an idiot."

"Hey Leonard, watch what you say I might have to report you to the proper authorities."

"Well then I might have to spill the beans about the little illicit drug trade that you've been working on here in the facility."

The man blanched. "How did you know, I mean what do you know?"

Leonard smiled. "What and how I know is not that important. What matters is that I know. Now that I do, I want to get something for keeping my silence. Is that too hard for a dealer to figure out?"

"I get it. But what is the price and how long do I need to pay for it?"

"Well, I need some personal stuff and that of course will be on the house, as part of our agreement. And I think you'll need to plant something on Reid and Brixton too."

"What for? They're not customers."

"Leverage, my man, that's what that's for. Now turn off that camera. I can tell Jackson that the Wanda Andy show was titillating. Now he and I can go back to whatever we're supposed to be doing here."

"Got it, yes sir I do. What about getting me a better job, something that I can use in my resume when I leave here?"

Leonard laughed. "No one cares what a drug dealer was my boy, only that he provides a good service to his customers and outlives his competition, that's all. You should know that."

"I have a degree in electrical engineering. I hope to go back to that someday. Drugs for me will always be a sideline, kind of an off the book income stream. That's why I asked for a better job."

Leonard sat down and faced the watcher. "My friend, here are some facts, and hopefully they can make your life better. Without giving away too much let me tell you of a program that we're starting. Maybe you can be of assistance, since you have the engineering background.

"We need to develop a machine that will allow us to find things that are buried, some of them decades ago, and then develop a means to get them without revealing that we've been there or that we've gotten something. Ideally, we'd like to find a way to snatch these things and replace them with non-working copies. Is that something you'd like to work on?"

"I am intrigued yes, but I can only contribute to the finding part. Can someone else be in charge of the snatching?"

"That depends on many factors," Leonard said. "You'd be in a team of folks, but given the sensitivity of what we're doing, you'd never know who the other people on the team are, just what they give you and take from you."

"Kinda like dealing drugs, keep the parties apart, and you'll live longer, that's rule number one."

"Exactly, and that's why I think you are suited for this job. By the way there's one other favor I need."

"Shoot, I can see that this is going to be a favorable arrangement."

"I need you to be my eyes and ears."

"Bill, are you forgetting that's my job here?"

"No I am not forgetting that. I just want to check with some other members of the group, and then let you know if we have a deal. In the meantime, to establish what we call your bona fides, I want you watch Colonel Jackson for me."

"Watch as in what kind of watch? I need more information."

"We, I mean you and I have to get the good colonel into a bind where we can manipulate him, in the future, for our own ends."

"I take it Jackson is not part of the little group that you mentioned earlier?"

"Hardly, since he's just an inconvenient part of this little gaggle of folks, that's all. Jackson was without a place to go in the army and someone with authority but no brains felt this was a good fit for a man like him. But he's expendable."

"As in really expendable, like 'removed from his position'?"

"Or *done in*, yes that is what I mean."

"Got it and thanks for that detail, nothing left to chance, that's my motto."

"Wanda," Colonel Jackson said over the intercom, "please get yourself in here, double time." She stood, stretched, and walked to his office. Wanda waited about a minute before knocking. She straightened her dress and roughed her cheeks.

"What is it, Massa? Been seein' problems down on the plantation?" Wanda curtsied and smiled coyly.

"That's enough young lady. As you know Miss Brixton, I am a southern gentleman, and a very liberal person as far a race relations are concerned." He smiled. "I've been to every one of those damned race relations seminars and have certifications in my record to prove what a wonderful fan of diversity I am."

I'll bet you've have plenty of race relations with other less fortunate young black girls, Wanda thought. "I know that colonel. Remember I was an army kid once."

"Yes you were, and your dad was a legend. I honor his service to our country. That's one reason you're here and in such a cushy job rather than something more suited to your talents. Never mind that. I asked you here for a reason. What' is new with that Reid kid?"

"Oh you mean was he good in bed? Fantastic, no, even better than that! All those urban legends about the shortcomings of white men, well I can tell you, in his case they are false. He is one hell of a lover, and I say that without hesitation." Wanda wiped an imaginary bead of sweat from her forehead.

"Miss Braxton, if you think that by making jokes you can escape answering my questions, then…"

"What colonel? You'll send me back to the smokehouse for being uppity, is that what you mean? I ain't finished pickin' out in the fields and I gots lotsa laundry washin' to hang up for the Missy too."

"No need to get your back up, young lady. I just meant have you and Reid had much interaction?"

"Wow, is that a softball question or what? We did not have any past balls, if I can use that baseball metaphor. Reid hit it out of the park several times. It was a complete rout, or rut maybe I should say. He had a grand slam, which means he scored four times."

For the first time Colonel Jackson turned away. "I suppose you can have your fun, Wanda. I would appreciate it if this question and your answer were just between us. No, I am telling you that what you've just said is not to be passed around this pathetic little community of ours. Is that clear?"

"Clear as clear can be colonel," Wanda said turning to leave. "But I do have one question for you. What exactly did your henchmen hope to achieve by sending me to mount his poor guy?

"He's married with a new baby, not that that prevents the horizontal mambo. But he is a married guy. You must take me for some kind of bimbo colonel. If you must know I am saving myself for my wedding night."

"How do you know that I sent the word for you to do this? Are you clairvoyant, prescient, or just guessing? I assume you did a little of all three and that's why you're asking."

"Colonel Jackson, you and I come from different times and different families. I was raised to speak the truth, even when that gets me in trouble and never to apologize for being direct and straightforward. In this case, and in all my dealings here in the bat cave, I tell the truth. I let the chips fall where they may."

Colonel Jackson walked toward Wanda. "You know you and I could easily be, let's say, more than just co-workers, we could…"

Wanda reached down and grabbed the colonel's scrotum, squeezing hard. The colonel gasped and doubled over, tears in his eyes.

"Maybe later colonel but not until after you're healed, if that ever happens. In the meantime don't get any ideas. I may work for you but that's all, no extracurricular stuff, now or ever." She turned and slammed the office door as she left.

Colonel Jackson sat down slowly and waited for the pain to subside. He was sweating profusely and short of breath for over ten minutes. He looked at the back of the name plate on his desk for a long time, waiting for his eyes to focus clearly.

Someone called on the intercom and he answered trying to conceal his breathlessness. "Jackson, what is it?"

"Colonel we've got a problem," the adjutant said.

"And that is what." Jackson said, his voice clearing.

"We've just gotten word that Reid is missing."

"Impossible," Jackson said. "There is no way that he could have gotten out. We have him on video surveillance and Bill Leonard is his body double."

"Yes sir, but that's another problem. Leonard has gone missing, and so has Wanda Brixton."

"Have you called the Secret Service? They are out backup outside the compound perimeter. Get them on the horn and when you do, I'll talk with them. Jackson, over and out." He hung up the phone and touched his aching crotch. It still was hot and painful.

"Bitch," Jackson said softly. "I will make sure that you get what's coming to you, and sooner than later."

"Where are we?" Andy asked Wanda. "I thought we were making a run for Washington, isn't that what you said?"

"Were you ever a boy scout?" Wanda asked, tickling Andy on the stomach.

"For just a little time, but what does that have to do with it? We're not on a camping experience weekend are we?"

"Not hardly, but we need to be sure that we've left a false trail for the government watchers to follow, just in case they get smarter than they've been in the past."

"Smarter, what is that all about?" Andy asked.

"See, I've been here long enough and had enough close encounters with the males here to hear most of the operational plans they have. Seems most of them are anxious to keep the curious people out, and there are only sketchy plans to deal with folks like us, folks who try to leave."

"I don't get it, but then…"

"What's to get, Andy? Most of the people who work here, not let me rephrase that, *all* of the people working here are here for the rest of their lives. They've all been erased from databases, taken out of their neighborhoods, lost to their families, for all intents and purposes. Kinda like the *Cosa Nostra*, you know, you get in but you never get out."

"That's not reassuring Wanda. Not at all. Now what is the plan, once we've spread the seeds of our disappearance? When can I get home, back to my family?"

"Well, Andy my boy, that is the question of the day. Actually it might be the question of the year? I will tell you that I have a friend coming to a location near here and he will certainly find a way to get us off this crummy reservation, I can guarantee that."

"Let's hope so, I am…"

At that moment a twin bladed helicopter flew overhead and circled near where they were hiding. There was a man hanging out of the left doorway with what appeared to be a long gun. The man was dressed in black, and he was looking down at them with a high powered scope.

Wanda walked into the shadow of a large oak tree and whispered for Andy to join her. "We need to stay perfectly still Andy, if we're gonna survive this game they're playing."

Andy crept up next to her, feeling the softness of her skin and the wonderful smell of her perfume. She turned to him and took his face in her hands. "You know, we should be as close as we can if we're gonna make it outa here, Andy. We need to be invisible, to blend in so we can fight another day."

Andy blushed. "You know that the last thing I am thinking about right now is fighting."

The man in the helicopter fired a burst of automatic weapons fire about five feet from where they were standing.

"Wanda that was really close, what now?" Andy hugged her harder.

"Andy, keep on talking like that and maybe we'll have to see a preacher. Oh I forgot, you're already spoken for, right? But to answer your question, watch this."

Wanda reached in her pocket and pulled out a metal object. She pushed a button and the device emitted a bright green light, brighter than any flashlight. Wanda aimed it at the cockpit of the helicopter and watched at the pilot shielded his eyes for a moment. His distraction caused the helicopter to lurch left and then head down sharply. Wanda aimed the small light emitting device at the cockpit again. The pilot lifted his hand to his eyes, screaming in pain. The craft whirled in circles and then came down to earth with a loud crash. There was a burst of flames and then silence.

"I'd ask what that was, but then you might use it on me." Andy said relaxing his grasp on Wanda.

"I have other means of making men beg," she said with a smile.

"I am sure of that, Wanda, very sure. Now can we get out of here?"

CHAPTER 8

Chester Billings had a fight with his longtime girlfriend, Bonnie. It was not the first fight, there had been many. It was always a contest, a fight when he got home. He knew that he was overweight, that his clothes were always dirty, but after all, he had been digging dirt all day. She ragged him about being in a low paying job, kissing his uncle's ass to keep that low-paying job he had, and a bunch of other issues,

This time Chester lost it and he hit Bonnie hard in the face. She left the house with a bloody cheek. He knew he was in trouble since her brother was a state cop and a hard ass. Chester had been in trouble with the law before, local stuff, some drugs, only marijuana. He had pleaded out with the magistrate on the last charge, but he was officially on probation. Last thing he needed was a domestic battery charge.

Chester decided that the best course of action was to hit his favorite bar and get stinking drunk. After all, he deserved to be treated as a man, and in a place where you were not judged by your weight or what you wear. You just needed a stool and some cash.

The Squire in the middle of Chatham was that kind of place. Coaxing his ten year old Ford Falcon, he drove slowly into town he watched for cops checking on drivers with expired state inspection stickers – like his was more than a month out of date – and he kept well under the limit.

He stopped and waited for a young man on weaving bicycle to turn left on Main Street. Chester congratulated himself for being nice, something he never was before. He was, in his own mind, a new man. *Hell*, he mused, *maybe she'll leave me, and then I can be on the prowl again. I might even lose weight, who knows.*

Chester reached the Squire as the lunch crowd as getting their last drinks in, and the staff was setting up for dinner. He shook the dust and licked the dried blood from his fist, wiping them on his jeans, and walked into the knotty pine walled bar.

Alex Romanoff was bending down under the counter, checking the connections to the beer kegs. He hit his head as he stood up to see who had come in. "Damn," he said. "Oh, it's you Chester. Thought maybe you was a paying customer." He laughed and bent down again to purge a beer keg.

Chester put his arms on the polished bar. "Hey Alex, how's about me getting' a beer?"

"Got a foamy one here if you want it, end of the keg, on the house. Here you go." Alex filled a mug with more than half foam and slid it across the bar. "Careful, the bubbles can make you fart!"

"Least of my troubles, old buddy, since I am probably gonna be arrested soon."

"For what Chester? You musta got caught jackin' off outside the women's restroom peephole again. Thought you got over that now that you're hitched to what's-her-name, that Harwich girl."

"Bonnie, that's her name. Yeah I'm sorta married, but not in the real sense. See we're kinda goin' steady and all. Alex, I mighta smacked her around a little. She got all pissed off and left the house. I guess she had some blood on her, but I really didn't hit her that hard." Chester licked the edge of the foamy mug, waiting for the bubbles to drop off. It would take a few minutes, but he was not in a hurry. The Squire was his second home.

The bartender leaned over and spoke softly to Chester. "Don't tell me you didn't hit her that hard, you dumb shit. You hit her and no matter how hard or how accidental, you're gonna get arrested, and pretty soon. Your uncle Willie, he needs you for that excavation work he's doin' in North Chatham. You spending time up in the lockup in Hyannis ain't gonna help him get that done. You get my meaning?"

"Yeah, I get it, and I guess I gotta go find her and tell her that I forgive her that'll make it all better. We've had some fights, most of them about money, but this time it was…"

"Chester, you're not gettin' what I'm tellin' you. You need to apologize and get her to come back home. She's most likely talkin' to a girlfriend of somebody else in her family. I'll bet they're tellin' her to go to the cops, maybe her brother, the Statie, to report what you done. Either way your goose is cooked." Alex stood up and wiped the bar.

"Maybe you're right Alex. Maybe I should find her. Maybe I should apologize and get her not to report me. I am sure not gonna go to jail over this. Maybe if she won't forgive me, I'll just pick up and leave town. There must be plenty of jobs for a skilled laborer like me out there, even off Cape."

"Skilled laborer, my ass. You pull some levers on a big yellow digger, that's all. Hell, even one of them Portagees could do it. Listen Chester, just find Miss Bonnie and ask her for forgiveness, that's my advice. Like the beer you just drank, it's free. Now get outa here and find her. Got that?"

Chester wiped his mouth and burped loudly. "Yep, loud and clear buddy, got it loud and clear. I'm headin' over to Harwich now, gonna find her and make this right." He hitched up his dirty jeans and walked to the door of the bar.

He walked to his weathered Falcon and found a parking ticket waving back at him under the windshield wiper. The ticket was for having an expired sticker for the State Inspection. Crumpling the ticket into a ball, he threw it away on Main Street.

"Damn cops," he muttered.

He started his car with a blast of exhaust and smoke, and made an illegal U-turn at the corner of Seaview Street beyond the Squire. As he left Chatham and headed into Harwich on Route 28 an unmarked black sedan with flashing lights in the windshield and grill pulled up behind him.

"What now?" he said under his breath. He pulled over and the other car did too, barely off the busy road. A large man wearing black pants and a long sleeve black shirt got out and approached his car.

"Officer," Chester said meekly, "I know that my sticker is, well a few days old, but…"

"Mister Billings, the last thing I care about is your ancient car or when it was registered," the man in black said.

"Well, if this is about my girlfriend Bonnie. Maybe I should explain what happened and how she cut her cheek."

"Listen I could care less about that. I just want to have you come with me over to Scatteree Road, the place you've been working, and show me that thing you found."

"Thing, what thing you talkin' about?"

"Don't be coy Billings. We noticed that you tried to hide it once you dug it up, and we know that you then put it somewhere in the woods. We just want to check out what you found."

"I didn't find nothin' there. I just was movin' the sand around so they could start the foundation for that big house there in North Chatham, that's all."

"Chester, you are a liar, and I know it. My associates and I are not known for our patience. Our game plan is to be direct, not to dick around with fat guys like you with half a brain. We hope that you understand this is not a favor we asking, it's an order."

"Yeah, yeah, yeah, order, I get it. At the moment though I need to get to find Bonnie and be sure she's not gonna turn me into the cops. We…"

"You hit her, I got that. Look stupid, we've got your back. We got her patched up, took her home, and we gave her a sleeping pill and maybe she'll forget the whole thing. You can screw her again next time she's in town."

"What kinda cops are you anyway?"

"Shit Chester, we're not cops, we're just interested parties that's all."

Chester and the man in black drove in his police car to the Scatteree job site. Each waited a moment before existing the car. The site was as he'd left it a few days ago with lots of construction debris and some new material that had been dropped off from the lumber yard. Chester walked over to the digger and remembered that he'd left the keys on the table in the hall of his cottage.

"Sure hope you don't want me to fire this up, because I left the keys…"

"Chester let me tell you something. We know that you are stupid, that's beyond dispute, and forgetful. We also know that. We just want to improve your memory about what exactly you found the other day. I'll start real nice and if that doesn't work, we move on to a better kind of persuasion."

Chester gulped, and started to speak. The man held up his hand. "Just keep quiet for a minute, OK. Now show me where you were when you found something, can you? I need to have you pretend that you're driving this rig when you see something, or feel something. Do a little play acting for me?"

Chester walked over to the Buffalo Springfield rig and hauled his large body onto the seat, touching the levels and pedals as if he were operating it. "I was about there," he said pointing to a patch of sand about three yards ahead of the front shovel. "I heard somethin' when I had the front end loader at about a six foot depth. First I figured it was a rock, or maybe somebody's old air conditioner, but it was a piece of metal, kinda shaped like a rocket, but no fins.

So's then I got off the rig," he said as he dismounted. "And then I looked closer at the thing. There was no rust on it, so it musta been made recent, and then I lifted it up, it was kinda heavy. And then…"

"You decided to keep it, that right?"

"Actually, I decided that maybe it might be worth somethin' so I chucked it over there." Chester pointed to a stand of scrub pines bordering the site.

"Let's take a look," the man in black said. "Hope for your sake it is still there."

"Who else woulda known except you and me, and I can't figure how you knew all this anyway."

"Chester, old buddy, I know everything about you, your family, your drinking, I even know about your fights at home. Trust me, checking on you at the helm of this yellow monster is no big deal."

"Who made you the damn king, whatever-your-name-is?" For the first time Chester summoned the courage to talk back. He needed another drink.

The man in black faced Chester, their faces a few inches apart. "Listen stupid, I am here to find something not to kill you. That might be a side benefit, so don't push me," the man said.

"If you kill me then you'll never find where I hid that thing that you're lookin' for, stupid!"

"Chester, it will be my pleasure to have you begging for mercy in a little while. I can make it easy for you to let me have the thing, or hard. I'd recommend easy."

"Look, I was on the high school football team and I can handle myself." Chester tried to pull up his dirt stained jeans.

"OK Chester, but you aren't scaring me at all. You are just making it harder for me to control my temper. People who know me tell me that I have a short fuse, and maybe I do. But I always get what I am after, even with a little bloodshed along the way."

Chester took a swing at the man and missed, falling into the sandy soil. He tried to get up but the ground was slippery and he stayed there on all fours trying to get his breath.

"You are pathetic, you know that." The man in black laughed. "You could be the lamest person that I've ever met, and the dumbest. I want to give you one more chance to tell me where the thing you dug up is, one more that's all."

Chester lunged at the man's legs and both men fell into the sandy dirt. The man hit his head on the track of the dozer and was stunned. Chester slowly clamored to his feet and found a nearby shovel. Raising it he hit the man's head until he was satisfied that he was dead.

"Dumb ass," Chester said. "That'll teach you to mess with a Billings."

Suddenly it dawned on him that he had to dispose of the body. "Shit," he said loudly. "Now I am screwed."

Chester looked around and found that the man had left the keys to his police car in the ignition. Dragging the body to the back of the car, he struggled to get the man's lifeless body into the trunk. Closing it, he took a rag from his dozer and poured gasoline on it, and then stuffed it in the gas tank opening He used his lighter to ignite the rag and it burned slowly. As Chester was about to give up he was blown back by a large explosion as the car burst into flames.

Alarm bells rang at the Chatham Fire Department on Depot Street. Most of the firefighters were washing their personal trucks, and had just a few seconds to get into the ladder truck and head off to the reported fire in North Chatham. Sirens blasting, they arrived at the Scatteree Road site and watched a sedan fully engulfed in flames burn itself out.

The chief arrived a few minutes later. He stepped out of his Ford Bronco and looked at the scene. "Anybody in that thing," he asked.

"Nah, seems to be an engine fire, heard that these kinda cars have fuel line problems. We've hosed down what's left."

"Well young man," the chief said to the young firefighter, "you may have noticed that the front of the car is less damaged than the rear, which tells me that it started near the trunk, maybe the gas line to the tank or the tank itself. The state cops need to get over here and see if there's any remains in the car. Looks like we might have an official vehicle here, based on the model. Have the cops run that number plate to be sure. We are gonna be done but I want to be sure there's nothing here but a car fire."

The young firefighter nodded. "I'll get on the radio and tell dispatch to call the state guys, chief."

"While you're at it, ask the owner of this rig, the dozer, to get over here. Might be Willie Billings' bunch doing this site, since he's got a lock on this neighborhood. Make sure he's sober and then tell him to get over here as soon as he can."

"Got it, chief. By the way when we got here we saw his nephew Chester, the fat kid headin' down 28 from this location. Maybe just a coincidence, I don't know."

"Well maybe so," the Chief said. "I just need Willie over here, that's all."

Chester Billings walked into the Squire again. He was strangely quiet. He kept his head down, but the majority of the drinkers hardly noticed. Chester was a true townie, a group of people that off-Cape folks ignored or even ridiculed. Come wintertime, Chester and those like him would sustain the few places like the Squire, those that were open all year.

"Well, well the king of dirt returns," bartender Alex Romanoff said. "Come back for a refill, did ya? I got plenty of foam if you're ready."

Chester said nothing at first, then waved his hand to signal that he did not want a beer. He finally looked up and mumbled something that Alex could not hear.

"I ain't a mind reader Chester, what the hell did you say?"

Chester was still quiet, and put his hands over his face.

"Well, if you get to the point where you can communicate, then give me a holler and we can chat. That's what I'm here for."

Alex walked down the bar to check the I.D. of a pretty fresh faced girl and to memorize her vital information.

"See, told you I was legal," the girl said.

"Well, well young lady. I gotta hand it to you, you've got one hell of a fake one here. Who's your printer, the US Mint?"

The girl blushed. "Honest, I really am of age, just ask my friends…"

Alex looked felt and right. "I must be blind because I am not seein' any other of your so-called friends nearby. Maybe they had even shittier I.D.s and decided not to chance losin' them."

The girl looked anxious. "They were here a minute ago, and must have left when I went to the Ladies. I guess you're gonna take my I.D. right."

Alex leaned closer, and whispered softly to the girl, "Nah, we got us a special dispensation for young ladies with great bodies like yours. We got us an exchange: you get a free drink or two. Then you give old Alex something in return." Alex smiled lustily.

"Well, it is just a free drink right, that I'd be getting. Maybe…"

There was a commotion at the other end of the long wooden bar. Someone was pushing Chester Billings to the floor, and had his armed held tightly behind his back.

"Don't go," Alex said as he ran around to the front of the bar and stopped a few feet away. "I'll be right back."

"What the hell…"

"Federal agent, stay away. This man is wanted for questioning." The man holding Chester down was having trouble getting him to cooperate.

"About what? Chester here is a good old boy, and he'd never…"

The man spoke louder, he never looked up. "Chester you better stop fighting me or I might have to knock you out. Got that?"

Chester tried one last time then stopped resisting. "I give up man, so just let me stand up."

Alex moved a step closer. "Is this about his girlfriend? I thought you feds were only interested in mail box theft and bank heists."

"Smart ass. Buddy, whoever you are, shut the hell up! Mr. Billings is being charged with interfering with a federal investigation, that's why I'm taking him in."

"Pardon me old buddy, I just work here, that's all. No offense."

The man handcuffed Chester and held his arms stiffly. "Stand up Billings, it's time to go."

Chester had a bloody nose and meekly asked, "where we goin'?"

"Hyannis, the local FBI office wants to ask you a few questions that's where and why?"

Alex looked at them and said, "No Miranda stuff, no rights?"

"Again, buddy, don't make me take you in as well. Just shut up and then help me get this guy out the door."

Alex raised both hands in surrender. "Got it. Hey Chester, take care of yourself and let me know if you need something OK?"

Chester didn't say anything. Alex helped him to the door holding it open so they could walk down the steps to the street. A black sedan pulled up and Chester was put in the back. The car sped away.

Alex came back in the bar, and saw that the girl with the fake I.D, was still there, looking his way. Something was actually going his way for a change.

CHAPTER 9

The moon was full but in this corner of Western Europe, it was seldom seen from the ground. Clouds and rain were daily occurrences, a thing that was never talked about, but frequently lamented. Most Germans had decided that other destinations fulfilled their desires for sun and sunburns, just not their homeland.

Helga, now called Harriett Rasmussen, FBI agent in charge, Hyannis Massachusetts was there, taking the airs at night along the Rhine, waiting for a ride to another destination. At nearly six feet tall, blonde and blue eyes with a stunning figure, she attracted her share of stares and at times, propositions. Her smile was her best feature, friends and enemies told her, but today she was not in a good mood.

Harriett turned her collar up again and pulled her wool scarf tighter to ward off the wind. Most nights it was better to stay inside, light a fire, drink Schnapps, and contemplate the music of Wagner or even discuss Liberation Theology. Not tonight, tonight was business, urgent business her father had started and her brother Hans, now called Harold, dragged her across the ocean to continue or complete.

Harold was not pleased when Harriet mentioned her not-so-accidental encounter with a grandson of an aviation pioneer, Herr Horton. He called himself Percy Atwater, but Harold did a background check and found that no one by that name existed in West Germany.

He cautioned Harriet to be very tight-lipped about everything, telling her that the slightest leak could damage their progress and perhaps even derail the entire project.

Harold pulled up in a new Mercedes and flashed his headlights. Harriett entered the car, sinking softly into the leather seats.

"So sister we meet again, how long has it been?"

"Well, if you count the time spent on the phone with you, not that long. In case you have forgotten my real day job is with the FBI. They appreciate me being at my desk or in the field and do not take kindly to prolonged and unexplained absences like this one."

"Well, I made sure that our other contacts in the FBI explained your trip as coming from higher authority and…"

Harriet held up a hand and laughed. "Harold, stop. You sound just like father when you say things like that, you know. I was never really part of his inner circle, though I suspect he treated us as if we were fellow scientists—low level of course—to be berated and then berated again for the greater good."

"Dear girl, how prescient of you to say that. Of course, father was a taskmaster, but he was also a good man. It is a shame his wartime work was not really appreciated, or fully implemented, but alas what can you do."

"We can thank those allied bombers for interrupting his real work, as I should not have to remind you. Father was a great man, yes that is true, but also a lucky one. Most of the time spent hunting men like him, they are found, and then they are jailed or hanged. Father was a fortunate one. I guess we should be grateful for that. But then I never heard about his last days, so please tell me what went on, how he died."

Harold was silent for a moment. Stroking his chin, he began slowly and deliberately as if every word needed to be weighed before he completed a sentence. "Darling sister, I wish I could give you a complete medical rundown, but as you know my field is physics, not the healing arts. Father had a weak heart and I knew that. I surmised that a trip to Garmisch, to smell the clean mountain air, might do him good, might revive him."

"Was he under the care of a cardiologist?"

"Well, he went to one but when he found out that the man was Jewish he suddenly felt no longer in need of his advice."

"Old habits die hard."

"Sadly they do. Father was not a racist by any means just a believer in certain tenets to which I do not subscribe, such as race purity and the like. But to go on, we were put up in the Garmischer Hof, a nice place we've visited many times. He was taken ill. I called for a doctor and an American came to his rescue."

"And the name of this American was, brother?"

"Bud, yes that was his name, a person called Bud Steinmiller. He was about 40 or maybe older and he had another American with him. The other man was Andy something, oh yes, Andy Reid.

"The Reid fellow was not a medical man but seemed willing to follow this doctor's orders without hesitating. I thought they must have known each other for a long time but overhearing some of what they said, it appears they had not spoken to each other for many years."

"Stop for one moment, will you. This fellow, are you sure his name was Reid, Andy Reid?"

"Yes why do you ask?" Harold stopped the car and drummed his fingers on the wheel.

"Andy Reid is a famous, some would say too famous person. He is on a watch list with us, the FBI. His…"

"Watch list, but why?"

"I always need and always have had friends in high places, my brother. When I arrived in the little town of Hyannis to run that office I was told in the change of command ceremony that Mr. Reid was not to be contacted, not to be arrested for any infraction, even for a capital crime."

"He seems to be leading a charmed life, does he not?"

"One could easily draw that conclusion, yes. Mr. Reid is a person of interest for the Bureau and also for me, personally. His file, the one that we maintain on troublesome individuals, leads me to believe that he is easily taken with beautiful women." Harriet smiled. "And he has proven that his marriage vows mean nothing. Recently we have tracked his little adventures, but he has thus far not given in to the attractive women he finds."

Harold Rasmussen interjected, "Sister, perhaps you could be that beautiful woman he desires and make, shall we say, contact with him."

"Not in the cards, as the Americans say. I find that he is much less interesting than others in my immediate circle are."

"But, Harriet dear, there is a higher calling. You are familiar with the cause. We are moving toward. Perhaps we can make a little compromise here. And then Mr. Reid can have a little taste, but a bitter one."

"Harold, your English, while without that tell-tale accent, is sadly full of German syntax. Might I suggest that you go back to the tutor and take a refresher course?"

"Helga I mean Harriet, sorry, you were always the teacher but if you insist I will submit to the language lab again. Now, let's get back to Herr, I mean Mister Steinmiller. Can you find out more about him?"

"Once back in the United States I can make inquiries. I would not trouble the FBI liaison here in the fatherland since that would raise too many questions, especially as to the nature of my visit here."

"Understood Harriet, and I leave it to your discretion as to the time and place of your inquiry."

"But, brother, you called me here, what is the problem?"

"We have been told that one of the items on which father worked and was thought to be lost is not lost after all. It is in danger of being found. Seems that another party or parties is also knowledgeable about the project on which father worked, and has been making inquiries around that location."

"Which location is that Harold?"

"About a half hour from your office, dear sister, in a hamlet called Chatham. It's not much of a place just a little place in the middle of nowhere."

Now, now, be careful, that German or should I say your Prussian side is showing."

"Suppose so, my dear, but then what can one do but give in to the darkest emotions?"

James Dunlap found the work at the Chatham Permits Office boring but useful. As part of his undercover work for the Soviets he had befriended most of the hangers-on and locals in town, the police officers and fire-fighters too. Taking a stroll one afternoon he overheard two police officers speaking of the job site on Scatteree Road. Seems a car had exploded in flames over there, and the state police and the coroner arrived to examine the wreckage and examine the charred body found inside the vehicle.

"Hey guys," Dunlap said, "what's goin' on over there at the site? We gotta a permit for those turkeys, the Billings boys, to excavate that sand-pit, and it expires next week."

"Permit issues, Mr. D., are far above my pay grade," one of the officers said with a laugh.

"Well, I just need a little more information on the events over there. Is it still considered a crime scene, or can we civilians go have a look some-time soon?"

"Gee, I can't tell you that. Police procedure is such a hassle, I mean such rigorous work that I can't even divulge that anything may or may not have happened over there. It's classified."

Dunlap frowned. "OK, I got it, but really guys can't you give me a hint or something on the situation there?"

"Well, if I was to tell you that we found a burned car with a body inside; would you promise not to tell anyone else?" The officer put his finger to his lips.

"Of course I would keep that secret away from everyone. But in Chatham there is a rumor mill that works hard to find things out as soon as they happen. Take it from me, over at the town offices there is no privacy at all. I found someone, not another employee, rifling through my filing cabinet a while ago, and…"

"Well, this sounds like a case for us," the officer said. "We might have to rubber hose the perpetrator, the *perp* as we say in police lingo, and make him talk." The other officer laughed.

"Him or her, actually, it was a woman." Dunlap smiled.

"Well, in that case the hose won't be rubber, if you get my meaning. But do you want to press charges in this case?"

"Nah," Dunlap said with a wink, "I got the information I wanted from the perp, as you called her, by taking her to a fine dining establishment for dinner."

"Wow, you musta been eating down main street to Friendly's I'd wager, for a real, good meal and a strawberry frappe. I took the missus there for a meal, she goes and orders a Lobster roll, can you imagine? She don't know that I am a lowly law enforcement professional on a small income. Hell, we're all in the same boat, right Dunlap? So I will do you a favor and fill you in on what we know, which ain't much, about that crime over there."

Dunlap put a hand on the officer's shoulder. "I'm all ears."

"Well the state boys, the forensic ones, they came down from Boston and went over the burnt car with a fine tooth comb. Seems that the VIN numbers on the car got filed off, which says organized crime to all of us professionals.

In addition, the body, the one that they found in the trunk, was burned so badly that nobody could get an ID. I overheard one of them saying that they got some new shit, some gizmo called DNA, and if they can get a clean swab, they can run the guy through evidence down at the FBI or somethin'."

"Fascinating," Dunlap said. "Are they sure the body is a man?"

"Suppose so, but I never asked. That's not my business anyway, you know."

"For sure, officer, that's a fact. Say, next time you're down at the town offices how about swingin' by and filling me in on this case?"

"Well, sure but let me ask why you're so interested in the Scatteree site. It's just another sandpit far as I'm concerned and not much more than that."

"Well," Dunlap said, lowering his voice and leaning closer to the police officer, "You see I am on special assignment for the CIA and they want to know everything about the place, maybe they might even pay for information."

"Gee, I can see that, I mean about you bein' a sneak and a spy, but what the hell. I'll keep my eyes peeled for stuff and let you know."

"What a gentleman you are. I will mention your fine work to the chief, when I see him."

"No need, he already knows that I'm the best on the force." The police officer laughed heartily and slapped Dunlap on the back.

Back at the Permit Office Noreen Caruso was filing some old papers. She waited for James Dunlap to return. He walked in and barely had time to sit in his chair when she approached and touched him softly on the hand.

"We should go to the coffee shop for a little break," Noreen whispered.

"And the rush is for what Noreen?"

"Follow me," Noreen said as she walked to the front door of the office. "We need to be quick about this and private too."

"My goodness girl, what do have in mind? Something naughty I hope."

"Later perhaps, but now it's just business I'm afraid."

They walked down the street to the local diner and sat in a corner booth. Dunlap slid into his seat and admired Noreen, as if the fluorescent lights made her look even more beautiful.

"Want to have me take my clothes off here or can you wait? After all we're not at the Arctic Circle now are we?" Noreen asked.

"Right to the point, that's you, I must say. We should engage in a little more foreplay before that dear."

"Calm down sweetest, there is work to do. I got a signal from our esteemed leadership today. They are anxious for us to get to the location and find the item they seek."

"We all are Noreen, and that is the truth. I want to leave this little peninsula as much as you or anyone. Who knew when we joined the force we'd get these kinds of shitty assignments? So who sent the message and how was it delivered?"

"Came Western Union amazingly, and was in the simple five letter code, the ones they've used since the war."

"I recall that our code was broken, isn't that correct? Why would they attempt such a crass move, knowing that the chances of it being intercepted were so high?"

"Perhaps they are as stupid as we think they are. I know that the leadership spends plenty of vodka-filled nights worrying about this new president, Reagan. He's an actor with a Hollywood past but he seems to see our side as the real enemy."

"Quite a change from that Carter fellow, isn't he?"

"Well, you might way that," Noreen said. "They see Reagan as a dangerous man, just read what the press here is saying. He's also very persuasive, and his followers are a tight knit group."

"Noreen, the cold war, as they call it over here, is not going away anytime soon, so we might as well get used to the new reality. That makes my life a lot easier."

"James, spoken like a true member of the party. As always I am never afraid that your loyalty is with us, even in the face of these temptations the capitalists put before us, is ironclad."

"Dear girl, there is no end to my fervor for the Soviet state, of that you be assured. When I joined the service I pledged my faith and my loyalty to the regime and to the state. I must admit that the new bosses are less than my favorites. They are in charge and I am not, so what can I say but 'of course, yes comrade,' and words to that effect.

"Let's get back to the need to get to work," Noreen said.

Dunlap smiled and rubbed the back of her hand.

"We certainly will be the talk of the town if we keep meeting like this James."

"We certainly will. Now, you mentioned that the need was there to get to work. I have just met with one of the knuckle draggers on the force here in Chatham. He tells me that there was a car found with a body at the site…"

"Stop, darling. That was one of our men who met his end. He was over there at the Scatteree location. Seems our betters in Moscow have several teams working on the same problem here. The others either do not know about us or they do, and no one has told us. Typical layering, typical KGB operational protocol."

"So if one of our people was killed, who was the killer?"

"Amazingly, we do not know. Seems that we are more than in the dark than we normally are. Our control officer is not forthcoming on any more details. He's gone back to Washington and I doubt that we'll have another chance to speak with him anytime soon."

"OK, where was the telegram sent from? That would be a starter for us to work on."

"Boston, according to the header of the telegram. Strange isn't it, the sender is just a few hours away by car and he's sending us a telegram. He could have easily sent a letter, or made a call, but no, he has to resort to this insecure way to communicate."

"Well, Noreen, no one ever accused the leadership of being smart, just of being ruthless. Perhaps it was cheaper to send a wire than make a long distance call."

"Sadly true, my darling. Is there no end to our loyalty to the state, no end to our being aware of the excesses of the party, and yet no end to our being good soldiers."

"We could defect Noreen, but there is a good chance that they would find us and make an example of us."

"How could that be since we are essentially sleepers, the kind of people that the organization feels does not exist at all. Would they create an international incident by blowing our cover?"

I think," Dunlap said, "they never seem to grasp the nuances of the public relations game, since in mother Russia there are only private and no public relations to speak of."

"Perhaps you are right. Our handlers seem as dim now as they did in our previous assignments. Now we can engage in a little subterfuge with them."

"And how might we accomplish that feat since we have an assignment. It's very clear as to what we should be doing and when we should be doing it."

"But we are told we need to get over to that Scatteree location and snoop around. How hard can that be? And how can we collect data that is not there?"

"I have a plan, and one that might work. There is an element of danger in this, I will not dismiss that, but I know we are up to the task and we can certainly provide information that is almost true. In the past we've seen other agents get away with less, so I am confident we can do this."

"You never cease to amaze me lover. I'll give you that. If we succeed then we can disappear into the ether can't we?"

"Of course we can, now let's drive over to the location."

His luck and timing was good. Chester was able to overcome the man who had arrested him in the Squire, choking him with his cuffed hands from the back seat where he was sitting. He waited until the man stopped moving then fished around for the keys to the cuffs. So easy, and the man was like the other guy, dressed in black. Two dead guys.

Now Chester Billings was having trouble getting his things together. He still had to dodge Bonnie's family. Though the man told him he had fixed whatever was wrong, Chester never believed it, especially after he was nearly killed. Whoever was after him might be more than two guys. He had eliminated two of them but there could be more, he thought.

Things were happening too fast. At first he'd thought about making a run for Maine, where his folks used to own a cabin. But then he remembered that the place was now condemned and might even be used by the local fire department for training. In any case he knew that he would not get the chance to be there without someone coming to find him.

"Maybe I'll just call my uncle, he'll know what to do," Chester said to no one in particular. Sitting in a beat up truck he could think, maybe come up with a plan, he thought. That was what he would do.

Willie, his uncle was smarter and more advanced in his ways, and he'd know. Chester drove to the Harwich line and found a pay phone. He dialed slowly and let it ring four times, and then hung up.

After he'd smoked a joint he got up his nerve and called again. Willie Billings was agitated and his voice filled with anger. "Who the hell is this and what do you want?"

"Hey this is Chester. Keep your voice down, OK?"

"Damn it you fool, what the hell you been doin'? I had the cops here most of the day grillin' me about you and the beatin' you gave Bonnie. They was here and then they left. I'm supposed to call them if I hear from you. Are you so stupid you think you can whoop someone and not get in trouble for it? Shit, what a dumbass you are."

Chester mumbled something and said, "I was a little hot about somethin' and she pissed me off, so…"

"Chester, you are one piece of work. You oughta not smack your live in girlfriend, ever. Damn it, you're a real fool, and I'm sorry to say that I am related to you. Where are you right now? Cops were lookin' for your truck."

Chester glanced back at his vehicle parked about ten feet from the phone booth. "I guess I oughta ditch it, maybe get somethin' else. So they can't find me?"

"Great thinking kid, but you ain't got cash and them car lots have been told to look out for you. What's plan B?"

"I got me a good sharp screwdriver in the truck, and think I can remember how to jimmy ignitions, just push it in and turn, ain't that right."

"Jesus, Chester, make sure that you turn it up not down, else you'll never get the damn car started."

"Right, I mean up, yep I got that. Guess I'll find me a new rig, yes I will."

"Look Chester, whatever you do, pick somethin' that ain't too fancy, and ain't too new, just in case the cops figure you for the guy what stole the car. That all sink in to your thick head?"

"Year I got it. Somethin' plain. Hey, I'll call when I can and let you know…

"I already figured that you're not gonna be at work tomorrow, and for a long time either. Now I gotta find another slave to run the rig and finish the job. You know that the cops have the place roped off as a crime scene?"

"What for, somebody find a that guy Squanto or some other dead Indian grave there or somethin'?"

"Hell no boy, you been under a rock? Actually found a burned out car and some body that was fried in the trunk of it. Cops have got the place secured for the next couple days, from what I hear."

"Any idea who the guy was?" Chester waited for his uncle to speak.

"Nobody said it was a guy, but I'm bettin' that it is. Weird thing is that the car, what's left of it, looked like an unmarked cop car, pretty standard sedan. Maybe it was some kinda cop, ain't sure. Sure are takin' their sweet time to get the place gone over, and that's no lie."

"Maybe they're lookin' for somethin' else?"

"Like what Chester? Hell, all I seen over there was sand and dirt, mostly sand."

"Sand, oh yeah, sand that's what's there. Hey you just reminded me of somethin' that I need to take care of."

"Look Chester make sure you ditch that crappy heap of yours first. Don't call me again unless they arrest you. Wait until you're somewhere safe, got that?"

"Got it, now I gotta get me into this blue Ford in the parkin' lot with the Maryland tags, some tourist I'll bet. He won't even blink when he comes out and sees his car's gone."

"Careful Chester. Remember they're lookin' for you."

"Yep, got that and will do."

Chester walked over to the blue Ford. It was unlocked. He pulled out his screwdriver but saw that the owner had forgotten to take his keys out of the ignition. Chester stared at the key hanging there. He decided to take this as a good omen. Maybe he was going to have good luck after all.

Getting in the car he turned the key and started the engine. The gas gauge showed that the car was full. He pulled out of the lot and watched in the rear view mirror as a family of four came out of the restaurant and starting looked around for their missing car.

CHAPTER 10

The hum from the large bank of mainframe computers was deafening. Harold and Harriett Rasmussen wore protective earphones to block out the noise. The computing machines generated heat, lots of it, and were cooled by several large air conditioners installed in the facility. Those cooling units generated their own hum, but at a different frequency, making conversation impossible. Hand signals were the norm inside the data center, at least for the time being. The trio walked outside and removed their headphones.

"Well, my young friends, your father would have been proud to see what his work has done, and how far we have come." Karl Schultz said.

"Doctor Schultz, I agree," Harriet said. "Father spoke many times about your work with him, he was pleased that you two had continued the work begun forty plus years ago. I know that he would be pleased to see this incredible science and experimentation."

"You flatter me, my dear, and I must admit that I am just a messenger here. I am following the lead of your glorious father and his incredible knowledge of physics. He was the groundbreaker, the man with the vision, the man who worked with the Reich. Yet never succumbed to their stupid changes of heart and direction.

"He was able to maintain his integrity in the darkest of hours and also avoid being sent to the camps. Many of our colleagues ended up in them when they made the mistake of telling the truth. Sadly I had many close friends who met that fate. To this day I find that they were right. Hitler was wrong."

"Yet, he, Hitler I mean, was able to permit development of advanced science projects such as this one," Harold said. "We should be glad that he allowed father and others to pursue their goals, even though at times the man was erratic."

"An understatement young man, very much so. Erratic is too kind a word for the short Austrian corporal who led us. I was there as a very young man in meetings with Hitler and Göring when the entire enterprise changed dramatically. Your father knew that the Nazis and these men had no training in the sciences. He was able to make them believe that he was following orders when in fact, he was not."

"But there was that disastrous incident in the jet, the Horton, over North America. How did father ever get through that without raising damaging questions?"

"My father, also named Karl, was with your father on that mission. There was a young Luftwaffe pilot, whose name I cannot recall. Much of what happened was never released by the Nazis, unless there was an oral briefing to Hitler that I never heard of."

"Who can say, father never mentioned it to my brother or to me, and he was not a man to hide his accomplishments from his family," Harriet said.

"Helga, I mean Harriet, you need not concern yourself with that mission. It was of little consequence."

"Your father perished in that mission Karl, as I recall as did the pilot, so that makes it consequential as far as we're concerned. Our father was picked up by a passing U-Boat and made it safely back to the fatherland for the remainder of the war."

"Actually," Karl said, "the pilot was killed. It was not by the crash. He died in service to the Reich, according to his citation. My father, Karl Schultz, was actually able to get out of the plane before it crashed. He was not carrying German identification, but rather papers that made him out to be a fisherman. Whatever the papers said he had carried they worked.

"I do know that he never spent a day in a prisoner of war camp in North America. Instead father, with the help of some sympathizers, went into the woods there and has been there, I assume ever since."

Harold was puzzled. "But if you can tell us all that, how can you not know where he is now. Can you be sure he is alive right now? He must be in his later years."

"My father was always secretive. In the absence of other information, I must assume he is awaiting further instructions from us."

"But it's been four decades since the crash; I wonder what he has been doing to keep himself going all these years."

"Harold, I assume that he has taken some position of power somewhere in New England. Our friends, the sympathizers, gave him a new identity. He has a new life. With his command of English, he would have the chance to blend in as an American, but of German descent."

"Fascinating Karl, all these years we assumed that our father was the only survivor that day. Now we know differently. I suppose you'll want my dear sister to check out this when she gets back to the United States."

"Actually, yes that would be fine. I would appreciate hearing any news that you might get about father. Just remember that he might not want to be found after all these years."

"Karl, are you saying he has lost the incentive to make the program work? I certainly hope not. It was his and our father's life work."

"Clearly," Harriet said. "We need to be sure

"And there is one more thing. Perhaps you do not know, but I will tell you now. The pilot, whatever his name was, was thought to be an American or British agent. He was sent on this mission with the intent to uncover our secrets.

"We have evidence that the pilot planned to eliminate both my father and your father to do this."

Harriet held up a hand. "Karl I would be surprised if this is true. My brother may have told you that I have combed the archives held in America for any trace of the Horten mission. I found nothing. Also, if this pilot was a double agent there would be some data on him. I have access to old OSS files. There is nothing there, and I have also checked thoroughly."

'Dear Harriett I am sure you have done that. But, as you know secrets can be kept if all the secret keepers are dead or afraid they will be."

"Which means?"

"It means that some projects were so closely held that the major leaders of the United States had no idea they existed. And given the rogue nature of many OSS operations, the leaders preferred not to know."

"Harriett smiled. "Go ahead then."

"I have always believed that the pilot sabotaged that flight, and that he manufactured the engine problems. He also probably engaged something to allow the dropping of the camera."

Harold said, "Are you sure? That would mean that the Allies had an agent in place for a long time. Only the best pilots were even considered for the Horten and the *Huckepack Projekt* flights."

"Ah yes the 'Piggy Back Project," the one way missions to the American mainland. What a pity it never got beyond the drawing board.

"Harold, please recall that the bombers from England had been quite active starting in the third year of the war. Both the Americans and the British were accurate in their targeting of our industries. They flew here in great numbers. They found our underground factories with almost no problems. Their fighters fired on our trains carrying raw materials to those factories.

"In other words, we were operating on the worst possible schedule with the least available resources. But back to the issue of which we are speaking. In this case I would presume that Herr Göring was taken with the man, the pilot. The pilot was a very handsome man, a poster boy for the Aryan man, as it were. Göring's tastes ran to partners of the same sex, as you may know. So, if this spy pilot was indeed a handsome specimen then the normal rules of qualification and pilot selection would be thrown out."

"Ah yes, the perversion that was always whispered about, was indeed rampant at the top. Sad that sex replaced common sense and common purpose in the fight back then."

Karl scratched his head. "Yes, that is true, and remains true today I fear."

"*Plus ça change, plus c'est la même chose*, I suppose," Harriet said.

"Actually yes, but it sound sounds better as *je mehr das sich verändert, desto mehr ist das dieselbe Sache*, for old time's sake." Karl said apparently thinking of times and things from the past.

"Karl, you've got the language thing down well, maybe you and Harriett could hang out on the Cape sometime."

Karl's face reddened. "I would not presume."

"No danger of me attacking you here or there, dear Karl, I am spoken for these days. And in what do the Americans call it, a committed relationship," Harriet said.

"Your dog may be your best friend, dear sister, but it's hardly a lasting romance, or at least I hope it's not even that."

"You are still a smart aleck Harold. You know very little of what I do and for that matter, whom I do it with. As long as I complete my FBI tasks, which are far from taxing, and I also complete the surveillance for out project, there is little for you to worry about."

"I surrender sister, I really do, now can we get back to our mission? I am sure Karl has some updates and we need to plan your next steps when you are back in the United States."

Senator Alex Cardozo was riding the members only subway from the Senate Office Building from the Capitol. He smiled as other members of the Senate climbed aboard at the first stop.

His time here in Washington came as a surprise to everyone. He had come from an obscure legal office in rural western Massachusetts. He had the Democratic Party's backing and easily defeated two tired and older opponents, first in the primary and the general election.

He was short, he had a heavy beard and thinning deep black hair, which he combed straight back to cover a bald patch that seemed to grow larger by the day.

His parents had come to the United States through Ellis Island. Through hard work his father built a successful business into a major real estate development empire. He managed to educate all five kids, sending Alex, the youngest, to law school.

When it came to Alex, his parents could not afford the tuition. They asked for help from a family friend who footed the bill. The gift was made with the proviso that Alex someday would need to be a good man, and become a 'made man' in the parlance of the mob.

Insider politics allowed him to advance as a junior senator to higher and higher positions within the august body. His alliance with several other high-ranking senators from the Northeast resulted in the formation of a Jacksonian group of conservatives, whose expertise on foreign policy was better than most and rivaled the long-in-the-tooth senior members of the State Department.

Alex stepped out of the car. "Hey Alex, can I have a word?" said a familiar voice.

"Why Angelo, what a pleasure to see you. How long has it been? How is your family?"

The other man, a tall, distinguished looking man in a very expensive suit and tie, walked up and placed his hand on the Senator's shoulder as he exited the subway car. "The family is fine, and nice of you to ask Alex. Can we go somewhere and talk?"

"Angelo, I always have time for my good friends. I count you among them."

"Senator, I have already voted for you several times. So you can't bullshit me, old friend. Listen, let's go somewhere private."

"Of course, we can go in my office, it's just upstairs."

"Alex, maybe but I was thinking of somewhere that you and I would not be seen talking, *capice*?"

"Si, let's take a walk outside, the weather seems to be OK for a DC day. Is that gonna work?"

"Sure, but let's get far away from this building if we can. I think the walls around here have too many eyes and ears, know what I mean."

They walked outside the building and crossed the street to a manse in front of the Capitol building. "OK Angelo, we're out of earshot now, and I was wondering what you needed and how I can help?"

"Well, Alex, you recall what we've done for your family and for you, I am sure. Now we need a small favor."

Alex winced, since this conversation was one he dreaded, but expected. "Shoot, I am all ears."

"Well, I know you are a Massachusetts man, a native in fact. Your glory is well established. Somebody told me you would make a good president. Given all that I need some information."

"Sure, what kind," Alex asked.

"See there is a colleague of mine, maybe we will call him my business partner. He is being hounded by those bastards at the FBI, the shits, about some damned dog track issue. He's clean, but you know, he's one of us, Italians I mean, and that makes him a suspect. I am sure that you as a member of the *familglia*, can see that prejudice every day."

"I understand, but isn't that a state issue, the dog track thing, gambling, gaming and all that, right?"

"Alex, see we, my partners and I, have an interest in the track, and we use it for various purposes, some of which the feds consider illegal, and we..."

"Let me interrupt for a minute Angelo. What is it that I can do for you? Anything is possible to a point."

"I'd like you to get some dirt on this FBI agent who has the lead in the case. The lady works out of the Hyannis office since the track is located near there. Her name is Harriet Rasmussen. Real looker. I wouldn't mind having a piece of that action, know what I mean?

"She's clean, I mean not willing to listen to reason from us or even take anything to make the track problem go away. She is from German stock and those people, don't get me started. They can't be bought, at least not by conventional means. We have tried and failed. Maybe you could speak with the regional director of that bunch and get him to get her to lay off, or something?"

"Angelo, the threatening might have raised a lot of red flags with the FBI, if she told them. This is a serious matter."

"That is why I am here, to fix this thing."

"I can try. We can always threaten the FBI with a hearing into violations of the statutes of whatever. With Hoover gone the goons over there play ball better than the used to."

Angelo shook Alex's shoulders. "I knew that you'd be willing to help Alex. Now what can I do for you? After all one favor deserves another as my sainted mother used to say."

Alex scratched his chin. "There is one thing. I need to get some dirt myself on a reporter named Geoff Branstead. He works at that new TV network, INN, over on Pennsylvania Avenue."

"Want him to disappear?"

"Actually Angelo, that's plan B, but thanks. I just want to get a little background on him, what he likes, who he screws, who he hangs out with, that kinda thing."

"A little of the best of the blackmail potential is my specialty and something that I can help with. I would be happy to make him very sorry that he ever spoke with you, if you get my meaning."

"Maybe we can do that down the road Angelo but for now the dirt will work for me."

"Got it Senator. It is my pleasure to have seen you this fine day here on Capitol Hill. Keep up the good work defending our freedoms and all that shit. I'll pass on the membership that you're a fine man and a good buddy to us all."

"Ciao Angelo. My best to the big guy. Please tell him hello for me will you?"

"Absolutely, hey there's my ride, *ciao*," Angelo said. He walked toward a black Lincoln with dark tinted windows.

Senator Cardozo walked back to his office. Entering the outer office, asked his secretary to call the director of the FBI. The call was completed but the director was in a meeting and the secretary told Cardozo told that he'd get back to him soon.

Cardozo made a list of topics to speak with the FBI. He put the issue of Harriett Rasmussen at the end of that list. As he finished his phone rang and he connected with the Assistant FBI Director, John Steadman.

"Senator, the director sends his apologies, he's got a real thorny issue going right now, and I suppose you'll have to put up with me in his stead."

"John always a pleasure. The Department of Justice is lucky to have folks like you, and that's not just a pat on the back for no reason. I've often said the same thing to your boss and the secretary."

There was no response to the comment so Cardozo continued. "Listen that appropriation bill in the house is not going anywhere but my sources tell me that if the director made a few phone calls, then the logjam might get cleared."

"Very good idea Senator, and I will pass that along. We feel that the money is needed for these new computer systems, the one that Mr. Hoover felt were not necessary, are vital to our mission."

"Good, tell your boss to work the phones. Now on another matter, I hear that there might be a movement on the hill to get your building torn down, did you know that?"

"I did not Senator. I am shocked. We're preparing a formal request to have some of the construction issues known since the building was completed addressed. We've only been here a decade and the place is crumbling around us. Thanks for that tip too. I'll pass that on, and we can always use this kind of actionable intelligence in our business."

"My pleasure," Cardozo said.

Steadman paused and said, "Senator, I appreciate all the help. I feel I am in your debt and if there's anything we or I can do, then let me know."

After a ten second pause, Senator Cardozo said, "Well, there is one thing and I really hesitate to ask, but what the hell, here goes. I hear via a constituent that there is an ongoing probe into a Massachusetts dog track and the notoriety is hurting his business. I have not spoken to my colleagues, the other Senator from the commonwealth. I assume that this would be considered a Massachusetts state gaming issue, but my constituent tells me that there is a wind blowing about a federal probe of their operation."

"I can check on this, and call the New England supervisor in Boston for you, and let you know what he says."

"John, why not do this? Would you call the Special Agent in Charge of the Cape Cod Office, the one in Hyannis? Can you let her know that there is a lot of interest in what she is doing?"

Cardozo could head the shuffling of pages on the other end of the line. He waited for whatever was being checked until Steadman came back on the line.

"The SAC is a woman named Rasmussen, Harriet is her first name, and she has been a fast riser in the Bureau. She got that job about a year ago."

"Good information John. I want this to be settled without interference on my end, so I'd rather you handle this internally."

"Sure, as best I can I'll find out what she's doing, and perhaps, no I will redirect her efforts to more significant law enforcement issues. The Cape is a big drop area for illegal drugs coming from fishing boats. I'll make sure she's concentrating on that issue. Will that work?"

Cardozo smiled and said," John, as always you've exceeded my wishes and done it quickly. I thank you for that. See you at the next hearing or at the next golf tournament, whichever comes first. Goodbye."

The Senator stood up and stretched, both arms raised to the ceiling. *Guess I'll wait until tomorrow to let them know up north that the problem is being handled*, he thought.

Geoff Branstead looked in the full-length mirror, noticing that he was getting a paunch. He pulled the sides of his shirt together hoping to make the fat less noticeable. It was not working. He needed to get more exercise, he knew that. Sitting at a desk all day was not good for anybody's figure. Even the station manager told him.

His hair was graying, the kiss of death in television for anyone his age. He had seen the hungry look on the faces of the new kids in the studio, the alleged interns who lusted to replace him. He went to a barber, a stylist who charged him an arm and a leg to touch up the gray and make it look natural. He had a nagging feeling that everyone could see that the color was not natural.

The phone rang. "Branstead, can I help you?"

"Hey babe it's me, we've got a problem," a female voice said He recognized his mistress, Judy Blackadar.

"Judy, we agreed never to bother me at the office. Did you forget that?"

"Hey, I never forget anything. I am only calling because I'm really scared. There's something really weird going on, and I..."

"OK, calm down. I've got a few minutes so tell me what's going on."

"Well, you know today I went out to the Giant grocery store for a few things. When I came back someone had been in the apartment and..."

"How do you know that?"

"Look Geoff, you're not the only smart one in this relationship and don't tell me that you don't believe in intuition, which I have by the way. I left stuff out on the dining room table. When I got back someone had taken a few things, I'm sure of it."

"Judy, what things to you think got taken?"

"Well, there were some bills, the ones with your name on them, the ones from PEPCO and of yeah, the water will."

"Shit," Branstead said, "That is really bad. What if my wife has some gumshoe checking out my place, I mean your place, and snooping for evidence?"

"My thoughts exactly, honey. Maybe we should get out of town. You know we could make a break for it."

"Judy that's not possible. I have a career here. I can't just quit and head off into some other town. DC is the center of my working world. Also of the cable business. I have to be here, not in some Podunk town doing house fires and drive-by shootings stories all day for peanuts."

Judy's voice was wavering. "Babe, I am scared, really scared. You know that we've been careful. We never go out where people will see us, that kind of carefulness. My parents don't even know we're seeing each other, and if they ever found out, it would be bad for me and for you too."

"You have to calm down Judy. Maybe you forgot where you put the papers, the missing ones. Maybe the wind blew them out the window. I don't know, but lots of things could have happened. Have you checked everywhere, even behind the chairs and the bookcase?"

"I'm not stupid Geoff. Yes I checked everywhere and I know they were here before I left and gone when I got back."

"Right, got it babe. Hey I gotta a show to do but I'll be home right after that, OK?"

Judy started crying. "Please come home as soon as you can, I need to hold you. You have you make everything all right."

"Got it babe, I'll be there before you know it. I promise."

"Just one more thing Geoff. You know that phone you got me, the cute princess one in pink. Well, it now stopped working. Can you call the phone company and tell them it's broken? I love that little phone. It reminds me of you. Can you do that please?"

"Sure I can, I'll call them right now as soon as I hang up and get that repairman over to check it out and get you a new one. See you soon. I love you." Geoff Branstead rubbed his temples after he hung up.

Someone knocked on his door four times. "Come in and shut the door behind you," he said.

A tall, stately woman came in the office. Grace Williams was the best looking woman in Washington television news and she knew it. Having risen through the ranks in broadcasting, she was idling at INN cable news until her big break came. There were water cooler whispers that she slept with the heads of the major networks to get interviews as their evening news anchor. No one confirmed the rumors but there was enough salaciousness to give them staying power.

Grace slid in and hoisted herself up on Geoff's desk. "How's that little piece of ass you're banging coming along?"

Geoff placed his hand on her thigh, and rubbed it. "Grace you're all I care about around here and I am your slave, now and forever."

"Bullshit Branstead. Keep it in your pants. I'd do you but it is not worth it career wise. I have loftier mountains to climb."

"Mount you mean?"

"Whatever. I can handle the truth no matter which way you slice it. I am here because I have a message for you from on high, from the top floor."

Branstead laughed. "There's only this floor darling, but I get the meaning. Do tell, what is the message?"

"Between you and me, seems that that tidbit you almost got, the one from that Senator, the guy from Massachusetts, was a ratings bonanza."

"And you took credit for it all I am sure."

"Maybe, maybe not, but that's not the point. Senior management wants you to move ahead here. That means a bigger role in the news reading slog. I see you've been to the beauty parlor to get that gray hair fixed. But dear Geoff I can tell you it looks like Shinola to me and to those new color cameras that we installed. Remind me to give you the name of my beautician, maybe she will have time to have you fixed."

"Cute comment Grace, but you know I'm on a limited budget here at the station. Maybe when I get promoted I can afford more glamour and a better hairstyle, maybe even a wig."

Grace smiled and crossed her legs. "You are a piece of work Geoff and if I wasn't already spoken for I might even consider taking you along for a nice slow ride. That might even include time on TV. But, enough small talk. I wanted to let you know that I have been getting calls from people claiming to know you. They've been snooping around and not even interested in talking to you."

Geoff frowned, and put his hand higher on Grace's thigh. "Well isn't that a fine kettle of fish as my dad used to say. I just got off the phone with my honey and she mentioned she thought someone had been going through the papers on her table while she was out. What do you make of that?"

"Well," Grace said slowly removing Geoff's hand, "Either you are about to be nominated to the Supreme Court or you've really pissed somebody off. Now they want to find some dirt on you, maybe for blackmail purposes. I don't know. Plus your little side action, Judy is it, is such a young thing maybe she's been hallucinating or something?"

"Age is just a number that's what I tell her all the time and she says…"

"She buys it because you're giving her more than just sexual pleasure. You're keeping her out of the food stamp line. And you're telling her that you love her. Better practice that lie before you use it again Geoff. The reality is that you're married, you're sniffing me up, and you're screwing some little chick on the side. I'd say that makes it hard to keep us all straight, wouldn't you?"

"I can do several things at once Grace. I have shown that I am an asset here at INN. Now I just wish things would move a little faster for my career."

"Take it from me, there's a lot of stuff happening these days and you seem to have that Senator, Cardozo that was that his name, well under your control. At least that's what I told them at the executive suite. If I were you I'd milk that cow some more until it runs dry. Just a hint, but take it from me, not an offhand kinda thing."

"Grace, a light bulb just went off for me. Do you think, or do you know whether any of this calling you and mysterious paper disappearing thing is part of the Senator's attempt to find out more about me?"

"Word on the street is that Alex Cardozo is a connected, some would say, a 'made man' in the mob. That being the case, I would not be surprised if he came after you. Maybe he has even put a hit on you." Grace laughed.

"Not a joking matter dear Grace. I hope that you're wrong. I will take the time from my busy schedule to call the good Senator and reintroduce myself as a concerned citizen."

"Now you're talking dear boy. Hey I gotta go, but before I do, give me a smooch." Grace leaned over and kissed Geoff full on the mouth, her tongue making slow exploratory circles. He was getting warmer, and not from the heater in the office.

"Geoff you are a good kisser. I will give you that," Grace said as she slid off his desk and rearranged her short skirt. "I have to go now but maybe later."

"I can only hope and dream Grace, that's my last word."

Geoff watched as she left the office and slid his hand along the desk top where she had been sitting. "Amazing Grace, that's what you are," he said softly.

CHAPTER 11

Andy Reid walked slowly up and then down the hill from the capital beltway, Interstate 95 or 495 depending on the road's location. A passing truck dropped him off at the Silver Spring exit. Wanda Brixton, his accomplice in the escape from somewhere to the north, was no longer at his side. She had told him she needed to 'take care of some things,' and that she would be in touch. Wanda dropped Andy at the Gaithersburg exit on Interstate 270. He found a gas station. He approached several truckers, finally finding one who was going to a location other than Northern Virginia.

Walking along the street Andy expected to see someone he knew. As he rounded the circle leading to his house. He noticed flashing lights in the distance, on his street. Breaking into a trot Andy was surprised to see the police in front of his house. As he ran to the steps he was stopped by a Montgomery County police officer.

"Can't go in there," he said gruffly.

"I live here, and that's my house, my wife…"

"There's no one inside this house except law enforcement. If you show me an ID I can tell you more."

"I actually don't have it with me, I was robbed and…"

"I get it mister, but there is a rule and I have to follow it. Can one of the neighbors vouch for you? I might be able to let you in if you can find someone."

Andy looked around and noticed a neighbor getting out of a car two houses down. Al Medberry, an older man with bad hearing and even worse eyesight stood looking at him. Andy was in a jam, so he yelled over to Al.

"Hey Al, it's me Andy. Can you tell this officer that I actually live here, and...?"

"What, what's that. Oh, it's you Andy, hey what's doing. You been arrested again?"

Al came closer. Speaking loudly Andy asked him to follow him to the place where the officer stood guard.

"Officer, this is my neighbor, Al Medberry, and he can vouch for me, can't you Al?"

"Hey this kid has lived here for a while, yeah. He and his wife, Nancy I guess her name is, spend time away but they live here in the winter at least. Yeah, Andy here is one of us, the good old Woodmoor group, that's what we call ourselves."

The police officer smiled. He shook Al Medberry's hand. The older man shuffled back to his house, hitching his pants over his ample stomach as he reached the driveway.

"Well, I guess you are the one who lives here, but as I told you before there's no one inside."

"I am at a loss to explain why no body's home." Andy said. "But can I go in? Maybe I can give the guys inside some help."

"Doubt that you can help but go ahead. Just don't touch anything, OK, it's a crime scene."

Andy stood there his mouth open. "Crime scene, what do you mean? What are you holding back from me?"

"Look, I just am assigned outside. I only heard from the guys inside on the radio. They said that the place has been tossed, as in gone over without sweating being found. Not a robbery I guess since all the valuables are all there. They were not touched."

"Where are my wife and daughter? They were home as of a day ago."

"A day ago? Where have you been? I guess we might need a statement from you on this. Stick around."

"I am going in now. Yes I can come back after to give that statement," Andy said.

The officer spoke into his walkie-talkie to alert the police inside of Andy's arrival.

The house's contents were strewn everywhere. The phone in the kitchen was ripped off the wall and then thrown in the sink. Beds were overturned, closed were emptied.

"As you can see," another officer said, "Your house is a mess. We'd appreciate you not touching anything. We're checking for prints. So if you don't mind, let's go room to room. If you see anything that seems not right to you tell me."

"Sure, but I am worried that my wife and daughter were here and…"

"Is this them?" The officer picked up a photo showing Andy and his family.

"Yep, that's Nancy and our daughter, all right. Her name is Alicia, by the way. She's in elementary school."

"When was the last time you spoke with your wife?"

"I called her yesterday, and we spoke for a little while…"

"On a business trip, is that where you were?"

"Actually I was coming back from a short official visit to West Germany. I got rerouted to another location."

"Another location, what does that mean?"

"Well, you see, I work for the government, the intelligence folks as a matter of fact. That means I go places that are not generally known to the public."

"Way out of my league, young man. You have to realize that I am just a county cop not an expert. I need to get more information from you. So drop the intelligence crap and tell me where you were."

"A place that I had never been to before, somewhere near the Maryland Pennsylvania border, I think based on the license plates that I saw when I finally got outside the perimeter."

"Perimeter, is that a military base? Can you tell me that?"

"Actually officer, it might have been at one time. There were a mix of civilians and military there. I guess they took me there to get me away from stuff. It was almost a nonstop interrogation that I had to go through."

"Wait, how did you see anything if you were always being interrogated, I mean how did you get away?"

"One of the guys took pity on me and let me go to a pay phone just outside the fence line."

"I do not suppose that you checked the area code or the phone number that you were calling from, did you?"

"Actually I did check that and it was area code 717. Is that a help?"

"That's quite an impressive memory, young man. But let me check," the officer said. "He keyed his mic and asked someone to check the area code. "Right, got it thanks," he said into the mic.

"The area code, 717, is part of southern Pennsylvania, Adams County actually. It's almost on the Maryland border, about 120 miles north of here. That's where you were."

"Hmm, Adams County, isn't that near Gettysburg? I see to remember that from my high school geography classes," Andy said.

"Could be. I can't add much to that. But how did you get there in the first place? Were you taken by car, plane or what?"

"Long story, but I was sitting on a Pan Am flight then hustled off in Germany and flown to the states on a military flight…"

"Are you some VIP? I mean getting a military hop, that's not a small thing."

"The Pan Am pilot indicated that with the president being shot at in DC…"

"Hold on, this is getting much too serious for me. I have to check in with my boss in Rockville to see if we need the Secret Service involved with this. We have an arrangement with them. We call when we need them, and in this case I think we need them. Can you wait here until I clear this up?"

"I'd rather find my wife and our little daughter, but at this moment I guess I have to stay here until we get some word that they're OK, and where they are. I guess you and I need to keep looking here. We'll need to see if they left anything behind. That's my first and only concern."

"Come with me and let's go room to room and see what we find," the officer said.

"What about the feds, the Secret Service? Are they gonna be mad that we've started to search the house without them?"

"Who knows and frankly who cares? I hate to sound like a careless little county cop but I've had enough experience with the feds, specifically the FBI, to know that they tend to see us as in the way. Naturally, I am happy to return the favor; I mean that. I tend to ignore them when we work together. That must be something you can relate to Mr. Reid. Weren't you a federal civilian or something?"

"Still am. I mean I have been both an Army officer and a civilian with the Department of Defense. My status is a little confused at the moment."

"OK please tell me what 'confused' means if you have the time. I have plenty. We have to wait for the feds to get here, even after we search."

Andy related his time in the Army, moving quickly over the incident at Stepping Stones and then his time as an undercover agent in Chatham. He glossed over the real purpose of the trip to West Germany, just mentioned that he'd been on assignment out of the country. The rest of the story he had already mentioned. The officer took notes.

"Well, I gotta admit that you've had a much more exciting life than me Reid. My life is one of just getting people on failure to stop, speeding and petty stuff. You've been at the intersection of some pretty amazing things. I never heard of that Cape Cod business, but then I never watch TV or read the papers. Makes me too agitated. So my girlfriend tells me."

Andy smiled. "You did hear that Reagan was shot, I assume?"

"Well I suppose that some of the news does seep into my brain, and certainly this did. Hell, every cop in the DC metro area got the call, even us off-duty guys. We had a stand tall order from the bosses in Rockville. I myself was called in to work the beltway exits. Big bosses figured that this was a conspiracy. Rumors and tips came flooding in. One good one was that there were a bunch of people involved, which apparently is not the case. So, yes I heard about it, made some overtime and lost some quality time at home."

Andy stood in the living room of his house. Every piece of furniture was overturned, and pillows were thrown around the room.

"Well, I have to tell you that I was in Germany when the shooting happened. That was the reason that I got whisked off a plane and brought back to the states by the air force. Then, as I told you, I was sent to this Adams County place, I escaped and here I am."

"Maybe the folks who trashed your house were trying to find you, or some hints about where you were? Did you ever think about that?"

"That thought crossed my mind, yes, but I think it's more likely that the two events are not linked. I barely had time to speak with my wife while I was held there. We had just one phone conversation that was so brief she'd barely had time to tell me she wondered where I was."

"Marital bliss, I am sure. Have you ever been AWOL before, I mean with your line of work and all that."

"Long story officer, a very long story, but yes I have. Sad to say that I've been a bad husband over the years. Thankfully she has seen fit to forgive me every time. I guess I chose the right girl many years ago. Now that we have a child, I might be guilty of taking her and our marriage for granted. But again, other than my disappearances recently I would have to say we're fine."

"Look," the officer said with a grin, "I am no shrink. I think you told me more than I need to know for this part of my job. But I appreciate your candor with a stranger. We all go through rough patches in our relationships. But let's get back to what we're doing here. See anything that seems unusual in here. Other than the mess? I suppose with everything tossed that might not be a fair question. But think, is there something that seems just not right?"

"It's really hard to tell given what I can see here. Let me look one place if you don't mind. My wife has this fetish for neatness, one that I don't share. She and I have a way of leaving messages where even I can find them. We have this little pad, the kind that you can write on and then erase with the back of your hand. We keep it in the top drawer of the dining room chest. That's where the dishes are stored. Can we look in there now?"

"I'll follow you," the officer said. They walked into the dining room and stepped around the overturned table and chairs thrown again the walls. "This the one?" he asked.

"Yes it is. Can I look in the drawer?"

"Be my guest."

Andy reached into the jumble of utensils and felt for the pad. Fishing it out, he picked it up and saw that someone had partially erased the message that was on it, hastily.

"Not sure what it says. But from what I can make out it says something like, 'see you there,' what whatever that means."

"Did you and the missus have a prearranged spot to meet in case of emergency, is that what it means?"

"We did not. Wait; there is one place that she could have gone if I had left a message. But that's really far. I know she'd have to get all the baby's things together for that kind of trip."

"Don't keep me in suspense where might that be?" the officer asked.

"A long way away, Cape Cod in fact."

Fog softened the pot holed asphalt streets of Chatham, The gray singled houses blended in with the light gray mist. Locals called it stainless steel weather, the time when both the sky and the ocean were the same neutral shade. Auto traffic was picking up, summer was not that long off. Shop owners were anxious to begin drawing the newcomers into their stores. One store on the main street, Mark, Fore and Strike, even washed its windows, though the weather was still iffy and the dust from passing trucks made the effort futile.

Harriet Rasmussen, head of the Hyannis FBI office, drove her easily spotted unmarked sedan into town. She parked along Chatham Bars Avenue, just down from the Squire. Her blonde hair was pulled back, but given her height and posture she was instantly seen by passing tourists and locals alike. Locking her car, she walked to the corner and looked casually left and right before crossing the street.

The Chatham Squire had just opened for the day. She entered the bar on the left and looked for signs that anyone was there at work. Finally, someone came through the swinging double doors carrying a box of beer bottles. He walked slowly behind the ten foot long bar and placed them in a cooler of ice.

Wiping his hands he spoke to Harriet. "What can I do you for kid? Need a little pick me up? I have the hard stuff ready too if that's your poison."

Harriet smiled and placed both hands on the polished bar. "Dear Alex, how long has it been? Seems like just yesterday that I was going over your file with the good folks at Customs. You know the one that tells me that you may be in the US illegally."

"Hey lady, I am not here illegally. I am a refugee and that qualifies me for this job and for my green card too."

"Alex, be that as it may, there is a time and place when even hard-working government clerks misplace or lose paperwork. In this case it could be yours, and as a sworn law enforcement officer I must do my duty and arrest that person who appears to be in violation of the US immigration laws."

"Lady, I have no idea who you are. I take your threat with a grain of salt. If you think you can pin that bogus lost paperwork shit on me, then I would gladly take it to the feds, you know the FBI. They're just up the road in Hyannis."

Harriet pulled out her FBI credential. "Welcome to the real world Alex. Now that we've had the foreplay let's get down to business. First I know that you do a little coke when you're off duty, maybe even when you're here. Second, I have on good authority that you have forgotten to put cash in the till when you're short yourself. Third, my sources tell me that you've been moonlighting in the no tax cigarette trade. I heard you've been meeting trucks from North Carolina over the bridge and then selling them to the smokers here. Does that about sum up your life of crime?"

Alex rubbed his bald head, wiping a bead of sweat from his forehead. He was a stocky, well-built man, and he had a reputation at the bar for ending fights with his fists, no matter who started the fracas.

"All right lady, so I do some things that may or may not be illegal..."

"*Are* illegal Alex, let me interject that thought here," Harriet said.

"*Are* illegal, OK, you made your point here. Give me a break willya? I am a hard working almost citizen of the United States. The bosses tell me that I am a good worker; at least that's what I here. Nobody complains about my work ethics or my time spent here. The customers, the paying ones, they are the ones that I help out, just ask anyone."

"Clairvoyant Alex, that's amazing that you'd mention that. I have a question but I want to be sure that you understand the ramifications of what I am asking and what you might answer. And, before I even ask, I want you to give me your word that what we say here stays here between us. Is that clear?"

"Well, yes it is," Alex said. "I might as well close the front door and lock it, since we get a lot of early birds in the joint. No use having them come in and check you and me out, is there?" He reached the door, locked it, and flipped the 'open' sign over. He drew the shades down on the door and the two windows.

Harriett spoke softly. "We can be private and that's a good idea. I won't take much of your time, this day, but I may need to speak with you again. That depends on what you say and whether I can verify your answers."

"Got it lady, I sure do. Now what can I help you with?" Alex perched on a stool and folded his hands. "By the way, you are especially good looking, you know that?"

Harriet reached over and quickly jabbed Alex in the chest with a practiced move that astounded him. He was gasping for breath, and said, "Hey, I meant no disrespect, and…"

"Shut up Alex, and let me do the talking, OK? Now, I need to know what you know and who you know that has anything to do with that jobsite over on Scatteree Road, just by the neck."

"Well lady, there is a lot to tell. I only know part of the story."

"I'm all ears. I have all the time in the world for your truthful answer, Alex."

"Well see, there is this kid, he's a regular here. He comes in and tells me that he and his uncle are working at that site. I get the impression that he has found something there, but he never says what he found. Anyway, later he comes in and tells me he beat up his old lady, and that gets me thinkin' he should get outa Dodge, I mean outa Chatham. I guess he's on his way somewhere, but's not the brightest of the bulbs in the sockets. That goes without sayin' since most of the family is so inbred…"

"Whoa, Alex, c'mon give me a name OK?"

"Weird name for sure, they are all part of the Billings family. Willie is the boss of the digging, I mean the excavation company. His nephew Chester is the woman beater, the one who comes in here. He actually paid for a beer recently, which was a miracle of sorts. Normally he runs a tab and never gets around to paying that off."

"Do you think that he might have come into some money, somehow?"

"Hard to tell since he gets a few bucks and then he is really flush for a little bit. But then he's flat broke most of the time. That's normal for a lot of the local drunks. We call them the townies. And that goes for a few of the summer types who spend most of their days here."

"Got that Alex. Small town drunks not paying for their booze. That's not a federal or even a major state crime. I can't get that to the attorney who might be willing to prosecute.

"Now, this is the big question. And please think hard about your answer. Did you or anyone you know go with this Billings character to see the site over on Scatteree? And if you did go with him, what did you see? Moreover, I hope that you'll think about this too. If Billings was ready to leave town after he smacked his girlfriend, did you give him any advice on where to go?"

Alex rubbed his forehead again and thought for a moment. He looked at the floor for a second, then said, "I guess that I told him to get outa town. I might have mentioned that he should ditch his beat up truck before he hit the road. But where he went I can't say. I know he's mentioned relatives up in New Hampshire, but can't tell you where they might live."

"I can check on that back at the office. Now tell me a little more about his truck, the make and model, that kind of thing."

"Hell, just a rust bucket for sure, like most of the wrecks that park out back. He did have a fancy plate though; let me see, I think it was spelling out something, maybe I can find that in my deep ark memory cells. Wait, now I remember it spelled 'DIGR' for digger, which he was."

"Clever guy. That should make my job a lot easier. I have to go but I may be back." Harriet got up to leave.

"Wait, you said that if you liked my answers there might be something in this for me, didn't you?"

"Well, yes Alex and thanks for reminding me. I'm not going to have you hauled in today for federal crimes or immigration violations, but if I find that anything you've told me is a lie, I will be back."

Harriet walked out the door of the Squire.

Alex waited to make sure she was really gone and reached for the phone kept under the bar. He dialed a local number and waited to be connected. "Dunlap, this is Alex. We have a new problem. Come see me as soon as you can."

CHAPTER 12

Interstate 95 might was designed by evil geniuses who decided that getting anywhere in a reasonable amount of time was not in the best interest of anyone who might have the misfortune of using the road. Nancy Reid and her daughter Alicia were in a major traffic jam on the Connecticut Turnpike. The road was famous for its tollbooths spaced inconveniently at intervals along its hundred and eleven miles. The last booth was the worst, with a series of trucks clogging both entrances and taking what seemed like hours to pay and go on. The last straw was when one large truck hit the tollbooth overhang and was wedged in. Nancy pounded the wheel, and looked at Alicia, who was strapped in a child's seat in the middle of the back seat. The little girl was almost asleep.

Nancy left home in a hurry after getting an urgent call that Andy was hurt in a crash in Chatham. He had called for her to come join him. She pulled out of town with just a hastily packed suitcase and headed north, an eleven-hour journey. It was uneventful until they left New York.

"Hey Alicia," Nancy said looking back at her daughter, "We're gonna see daddy soon. That will be fun."

"I miss my friends at school, Mom, I really do. When are we gonna be back at home?"

"Daddy wants us to see him at this new house, the one you've been to only a couple times, so he can give us a surprise. You know he likes to give you gifts."

"I'd rather be at home and playing with my toys mom," Alicia said.

"Me too," Nancy said softly.

The traffic jam eased and she was able to get the car up to 50 miles per hour, triple the speed she had been doing before. Up ahead the last toll-booth in the state loomed. There were no cars waiting at all.

As she entered the narrow lane to pay her quarter a uniformed Connecticut police officer stepped out of the booth. He waved for her to stop.

"What's wrong officer?" Nancy asked.

"Ma'am, I am going to need to have you pull over to the right and wait for me there, please."

"Is it Andy, my husband I mean, is that the reason for all this?"

"Please pull over so we can talk. I will explain everything to you. Can you do that for me?" He waived to the road's shoulder just beyond the tollbooth. Another police car was idling there.

Nancy pulled through the booth forgetting to give the attendant her quarter, and eased the car into the space behind the police cruiser. She rolled down the window and waited. The officer was talking on his radio, but she could make out what the conversation was. The officer gestured toward Nancy's car, then turned away, covering his mouth as he spoke.

"Mommy are we going to be arrested?" Alicia asked, a frown on her face.

"No dear, not today, looks like they just want to chat with us, maybe even help us get to see daddy, that's all."

"Good, but I still miss my friends. Today was supposed to be show and tell and I was really looking forward to that since it's so fun."

"I know that sweetie, and just think once we see daddy and we get some shells at the beach. We'll have lots to show and tell in school."

Alicia thought for a moment. "I still miss my friends," she said as her eyes filled with tears.

Nancy turned around to comfort the little girl, but was startled when the trooper knocked on her window. Rolling it down she asked, "What is the problem officer, is there something that I did wrong?"

"No Ma'am," the young officer said. Apparently this car is registered in your husband's name, is that correct?"

"Yes, but Andy, I mean my husband takes care of all that stuff for me, I just drive the car and let him fill it with gas."

The officer laughed. "Sounds familiar to me Mrs. Reid. But we had an All-Points Bulletin out for this car. And we thought might be driven by your husband. That's why we stopped you. And do you mind if I look in the trunk, just to tell the folks at headquarters that I searched the car?"

Alicia stopped crying and pointed at the officer. "Don't mess with my toys back there, I need them."

The officer laughed again, and said, "No darling, I will not mess with any toys back there, I promise."

"Mommy, please tell this man that my toys are *my* toys, and *not* his," Alicia said again.

"Promise that dear, I really do, cross my heart and hope to…"

"Ma'am not to worry, I will just lift the trunk lid and take a peek inside, nothing more. I will not even look for monsters in the trunk."

"You should be big enough to know that monsters live under beds mister policeman, not in car places," Alicia said with a knowing smile.

"I forgot that sweetie, I am sorry. You're right. No monsters in trunks, I need to remember that when I get off shift and see my own kids."

"Mister, do your kids have the show and tell at their school? I do. But I am missing it because we are looking to see daddy on Cape Cod."

The officer's demeanor changed from a smile to a frown. "Cape Cod, is that where daddy, I mean your father is?"

Nancy raised her hand. "Wait officer, Alicia knows that mommy and daddy sometimes go to Cape Cod in the summertime. Sometimes at different times of the year. That's where we're headed now."

"This young lady seems intent on being in class at her school not whipping up the turnpike in the middle of the week. Does that mean you're headed to the Cape for another reason, like seeing Mister Andy Reid?"

Nancy spoke in a low voice. "Yes, it does. I got a call that Andy was hurt and that I needed to get to the Cape as fast as I could. That's why we, she and I, are not at home and why Alicia is not in school."

"That changes everything," the officer said. "Let me escort you to the border. Then the Staties from Massachusetts can lead you the rest of the way. I do not need to check the trunk any more. So if you don't mind, follow me. We may go a little faster than many of the other drivers but I promise that we'll get you there safely."

Nancy sat there for a moment, reflecting on what just happened. "Hey sweetie, that nice man is going with us…"

"To see daddy," Alicia asked."

"Sort of, he's going to take us on a faster road."

The trooper motioned for Nancy to follow and he put his lights on, exceeding the speed limit for about a mile. She and Alicia were handed off to a Massachusetts State Trooper at exit one.

Chester Billings, man on the run, that's what he thought of himself. He had seen some of those James Bond movies. Now he was, in his own mind, on the run, escaping the bad guys.

He had gotten over the bridge from the Cape to the mainland and headed to New Hampshire in the stolen Ford. So far, no problems with the cops, even though they must have run the car's plate by now.

Stopping at a gas station he rubbed some mud on the Maryland number plate to obscure the numbers. Not perfect, but it would have to do until he put more miles between himself and Chatham.

Reaching New Hampshire took a few hours. Chester needed a break so he stopped at the State Liquor Store north of the border for a stretch and some shopping.

Another fellow traveler in the store's parking lot hailed Chester. "Hey Buddy, I see that you're a fellow 'Terp.' Where you from? I hail from scenic 'Bawlmore'."

Chester hesitated before he spoke. "Sorry, this here's a rental car and it's got tags from Maryland. I ain't from there. Where'd you say you was from?"

"Balt-tee-more, that's the official name but we call it 'Bawlmore,' sorta sounds better."

"Never been," Chester said. "Need to get there sometime."

"Since you're a native let me ask you a question. If I'm headin' south into Mass, will I need to worry about the state cops if'n I had a load of booze in the trunk? Heard that they, them cops, they lay in wait down there lookin' for evaders like me. Is that right?"

"Could be, they call it 'taxachusetts' you know."

"I hear that man, I really do. Say if I'm headed past Boston, where would you suggest I go?"

"Well, I am a native Cape Codder," Chester said softly. "I guess there's good and bad in that little place. Sometimes the bad is worse than the good."

"Do tell. Give me a little more about the place if you don't mind. I want to be sure it's worth my time. After all, I could just as easy bag the whole thing and start straight down 95 on my way back home."

"Hell, it's not a bad little place, the Cape I mean. Not really tourist season at the moment. You'll find fewer of those pesky folks to compete with. But, there's a problem, see since the tourists bring the cash and that means the stores and eating places are open. So when they ain't there in droves, then the stores are closed and most eatin' places are open only a couple hours a day. If you can stand that, then go ahead and cross that bridge, and head for the Cape."

"So," the tourist asked, "if you had to make a trip down there where would you go? I hear that Hyannis is a nice stop…"

"If you like tourist places like the Kennedy compound and that museum maybe, but otherwise it's not much in my mind. Head a little more down the road and go to Chatham, that's my hometown. It is a cute place to see.

"Ain't much of a Kennedy fan myself anymore, so maybe Hyannis will be dropped from my trip? How far is this Chatham from there, Hyannis I mean?"

"Half an hour, maybe more dependin' on the damned traffic. This time maybe with less folks headin' down route 6, give it a half hour."

The tourist reached out his hand to shake Chester's. "Thanks Buddy, appreciate the help and local knowledge."

"For sure, glad to help. Now I gotta get me some beer for the road. Ain't you goin' in too?"

"Changed my mind man after talkin' to you. I gotta head on down the road. I don't wanna meet any state cops as I cross the line."

"Hey, maybe they will get you, maybe not. Depends on what the donut shops are sellin' and if they got them some kinda quota."

The tourist slapped Chester on the back. "Good one buddy, hey see you later. Forgot to ask. Where are you headed?"

"Headed to do some fishin' up here. The season ain't officially started yet, maybe in some little lake where nobody can see me. I like to catch a few and maybe cook 'em up right at the lake."

"Good luck, and say I never caught your name," the tourist asked.

Chester hesitated, and then said, "Chester's the name, and I got the same last name as almost everybody in Chatham, but if you tell them you saw Chester then they'll figure out what's happening real quick. Somebody might even buy you a drink at the local watering hole. Who can say?"

"Well Chester, you are a good guy to run into. Most folks down in my hometown would spit on a stranger rather than talk to him. But that don't mean nothin' since we're all kinda homers, if you get my drift."

"Yep," Chester said as turned and pushed open one of the doors into the lobby of the New Hampshire State Liquor Store. He headed for the beer cooler.

The stranger from Baltimore waited for five minutes, walked over to Chester's blue Ford, and taking a small pad from his pocket, wrote down the tag number. He looked in the passenger seat of the car and saw that there were empty coffee cups and other paper trash on the floor. *Looks like Chester was on a road trip and stopped only for fast food,* he thought. Now he needed to get to a pay phone to report on what he had found.

Chester drove north with a trunk full of beer and a six pack of Slim Jim jerky treats in the front seat. He turned on the radio and found a country station, one that played songs that he knew. Life was getting better by the moment for Chester. He looked down for a second to check his stash of jerky. His car crossed the centerline. He sideswiped an 18-wheeler. The Ford careened off the road, rolling over. He landed in a dry bog.

Chester was thrown ten feet from the car and dazed. He heard the squeal of the truck's brakes in the distance and knew that the driver would come over and see if he was alive. He was losing consciousness and his vision was blurry. Warm, salty blood trickled from a cut on his forehead and his mouth. He heard footsteps and expected to see a trucker coming over the edge of the road. He passed out.

When he came to several people surrounded him. Keeping silent, he watched the tourist from Baltimore, the one he'd talked with in the New Hampshire Liquor Store's parking lot, walk toward him.

"Hey Chester, how's it goin'?" The tourist was different sounding than before; he had no Bawlmore slang now.

Chester kept quiet, trying not to throw up from the blood he was swallowing. His head hurt a lot and his vision cleared slowly.

"Chester, hey look, I can call for help. But first I think you have something that I want. Just give it to me and we can get you fixed up. Looks like you trashed that car, the one you stole down on the Cape. Guess the owners will never get it back, will they? What the hell were you doin' hittin' that truck like you did?"

Chester opened his mouth to speak and vomited.

"Shit man, this dude's gonna be dead in a minute. Why don't we just get into the car and see if he's got it hidden there. Let him die in peace," one of the other men looking down at him said.

The Baltimore tourist held up one finger and then pointed it at the fellow. "Look Herman, you idiot, we need old Chester here coherent for a few more minutes, see. He has that thing they want, we know that. But we don't know if he's got other stuff from that dig stashed somewhere, unless we can get him to spill everything. Is that clear enough buddy?"

"Yes it is clear, and thanks for the reminder, Bill. And don't call me an idiot OK? I may be smarter than you think."

The Baltimore tourist grabbed the other man by the throat and pushed him hard into the ditch next to Chester. "Looks like we got us a two-fer today. We'll just make sure it looks like a murder suicide. That'll throw the cops off my trail forever."

"Bill, hey we go way back. If the big guys thought you were trying to do me, I mean kill me, then…"

"What, you'd get a star without a name on some wall down in Langley, is that what you mean," Bill said.

"Hey, we were together in Laos and Cambodia, remember? Maybe even there were times that I saved your life," Herman Banks said, pleading for his life.

"Shit Banks, that's old news. We're mercenaries. And mercenaries are lone gunmen, they have no friends, just potential targets to destroy. Right now, you are a target of opportunity, and one less person to split the loot with once we get the payoff. So why shouldn't I just end it right here and now?"

"Cause you need an excuse, just in case anyone saw you jawing with old Chester in that parking lot. You mighta noticed that there were security cameras all over the place, even that lot, and you were caught on them from all angles."

"Part of the state's ID check, I guess." Herman Banks raised himself on his elbow and held out his hand. "C'mon help me up."

"Lucky for you I am in a generous mood, so this time…"

Herman reached up and hit Bill in the throat, crushing his windpipe and sending him to the ground.

"That's what mercenaries do," Banks said as he pushed Bill's lifeless body face down in the mud. "They kill first and don't ask questions at all. Your mistake buddy."

"Hey mister," Chester said weakly, "You gonna help me or kill me? If you're gonna kill me just do it. I feel like shit right now." He fell back in a prone position.

"Sorry Chester, you're gonna live to eat another day, but you and I, well we have some unfinished business that we've gotta take care of. For starters I need to know where the thing is, the one that you uncovered at the dig. Don't try to tell me you don't know what I am talkin' about either. We know that you killed a guy to keep that thing."

"He started it, buddy. I was just defendin' myself that's all."

"I am impressed a fat slob like you could even make an effort to defend yourself, I'll give you that. But, right now, I have the power and you've got puke all over you. Now who's in charge?"

Chester closed his eyes to let the pain in his head subside. "You gonna end it for me now? Hell, I can't go back to Chatham. I smacked my old lady and stole this the damned car, and there's probably a couple warrants out for me by now. You gotta know that since you know everything else about me."

That's the least of your worries Chester. You're gonna help me drag good old Bill's body closer to the car you wrecked and then we're gonna have us a nice bonfire, just like the one you did at Scatteree Road a while back. I need you for the time being. That is all you need to know. I may change my mind any day, any time, so you'd best be on your good behavior."

"Got it," Chester said, stumbling to all fours, and then got up. "Where we headed anyway? What about that truck driver I hit, ain't he gonna tell somebody?"

"Only if he had survived the accident," Herman said. "He had one of those seizures and he apparently was unable to survive the crash you caused, or should I say, the crash that our buddy Bill caused."

"You kill him too?"

"Collateral damage that's what we called that in Nam. Don't suppose you served did you?"

"Nah, flat feet kept me…"

"I would have guessed effeminate tendencies and alcoholism would have been enough. Flat feet that is as good an excuse as any for your physical to reject you."

"Hey man, I am a damned patriot, maybe even more than you will ever be," Chester said standing straighter.

"Chester, I have seen plenty in my lifetime and the last thing I need is a lecture from a useless piece of shit like you about who is patriotic and who's not. In case you forgot, the best patriots are sometimes our worst enemy. I could care less at this point, since you could say I've been through the wars for all sides Now the only thing I care about is who is the highest bidder for my services."

"I guess whoever's payin' you pays pretty good."

"Chester, yes they do. I was going to split the money with Bill here but he's not much help anymore. In fact he's dead or soon he will be."

Chester gulped, and then looked directly at Herman. You know you and me we kinda think alike. Maybe we can work out some kinda deal, just you and me, to get this all done?"

"Let me get something straight, and listen carefully. Bill was right when he said that you needed to stay alive long enough to be sure that we have the entire collection of stuff that our paymasters are after. I know you have no idea what you stumbled on. I want to keep it that way. But, you and me, we're heading back to Chatham and..."

"I can't go back there. I can't since they'll arrest me."

"Chester, that is a minor problem but one that I can easily handle, trust me."

"Do I have a choice?"

"Actually you don't have any say in this Chester. Let's get this car torched, dispose of the body, and head back south. I want to drive since you are pretty banged up, and just to be sure that you're playing the same game that I want you to, you'll be handcuffed in the backseat."

"Hell man, I ain't gonna do nothin'. I feel like shit right now. Maybe we could get one of them beers outa the trunk of my car, and..."

"Normally Chester I think you are the most clueless person that I've ever met but in this case you might have a point. Let's pour some of those beers over good old Herman's body, and leave some empties alongside you Ford. That way, even with the fire they'll think he was into drinking and driving, case closed."

"I guess that might work, but I can at least have one before we do that?"

"Chester, why not? You drive a hard bargain. In this case, I can't see much harm in feeding your alcoholic binges." Bill opened the trunk of the blue Ford. "Looks like the beer made it OK, good thing you got cans not bottles; else we'd be having you lick the glass for suds."

Chester straightened up. "I ain't no alcoholic. I just take a drink now and then, that's all. My old man, he was a drinker, that's what killed him, he was drivin'..."

"Chester no need to explain further. Here, take this beer, drink it up and let's do this. We got things to do and people to see. First you're gonna give me something that I want, something that you found at the dig site. I know it's with you. We're gonna check back at your little cottage for the rest."

Chester walked slowly to the overturned Ford and began to pull up the carpeting in the trunk, finding a cloth covered package the size of a small toaster oven.

CHAPTER 13

Police interrogated Andy Reid at the offices of the Montgomery County Police Department in Rockville Maryland. Officers walked past the Formica topped desk where he sat, most never stopped to notice he was there. A series of officers came, asked a few questions, and then left him to sit in silence.

At last he was almost ready to be released; at least that was what one detective told him. One excuse was the need to have the federal officers come in to assist in the case. It was more than two hours since the questioning began. The Secret Service, whose presence was required, never showed. It was all local cops, and questions repeated each time. Outside the smallish windows traffic piled up on Rockville Pike, as travelers headed somewhere to do something or perhaps just to get away from Washington DC.

It was late in the Washington DC spring but the daytime heat was starting, bringing the gray haze that enveloped the town, making people's eyes water, noses run, and their attitudes suffer. Andy was used to the heat, but the humidity was the killer for him and others. Starting in May the air conditioner was barely able to keep up, both in the car and in the house. At least Andy assumed the Cape would be cooler, maybe even cold.

"Mister Reid, you can go now. I want you to check in with me or someone here before you leave town."

"Well, I can tell you now," Andy said. "I'm headed to Chatham Cape Cod to find my wife and daughter."

"How do you know that's where they are? They may have gone there and then gone somewhere else. And you've told us that they never called you once they left Silver Spring."

"Call it intuition if you want to. I just have this feeling that I'll find them there and I don't know why, but I am determined to find out."

"We'll need to liaise with the Massachusetts folks just in case. Are you driving our flying there? We can take you to the airport if you need a ride. Maybe you want to get back to the house and get some clothes?"

"Thanks for the offer, but I guess you should know, I have a house up there, Cape Cod. It's full of clothes and even an old Mustang GT that somebody gave me. So, yes to the ride to the airport, that would be nice and no I don't need to go anywhere first."

"Reid I gotta hand it to you," the detective said. "You have led a charmed life. Now let's get you over to the airport."

The police dropped Andy at Washington's National Airport. He soon settled into a US Airways flight nonstop to Logan Airport in Boston. National was under construction again, thee seemingly endless rehabbing of the old airport, the one with the impossible flight path that followed the Potomac River like a crazed game of Pong. Pilots were judged on their ability to get into National without violating the highly enforced DC closed airspace.

Since the attempt on the president a few weeks before, there were three instances when Air Force jets from Andrews Air Force base, not a comforting site for pilots or passengers, met incoming commercial planes. US Airways flight 191 was an hour late leaving due to storms along the flight route, but Andy took the opportunity to fall sleep in his middle seat. After takeoff and the seat belt sign turned off, Andy wandered to the back of the plane to use the lavatory.

A flight attendant, a man who looked familiar, stopped him. "Andy is that you, how long has it been?"

"Well must have been a while since I don't recognize you, Mister…"

"Albert, that's me. We worked together for a time at the Pentagon, most of that time in the National Military Command Center."

"Albert Rosales, sure now I remember. You were a senior enlisted guy, made the coffee for us, now I remember you. Obviously you left the Air Force or you wouldn't be working here for the airline."

"Did my time, twenty years actually. I decided that the flying public needed my services more than Uncle Sam. How about you, are you still in the service?"

"Al, if I can call you that, you must have been away these last couple years. Got myself into more trouble than I ever wanted to, first by uncovering some deep dark secret, nearly getting my wife killed. Then I managed to get into the same mess again in the 1970s, this time chasing down, no never mind…"

"Sure sounds exciting Andy. I always figured you for a mover and shaker."

Andy laughed. "Shaker maybe yes, mover definitely no. I am headed to Boston and then down to the Cape. And hopefully to see my wife and daughter."

"Congratulations on having that kid, Andy, how old is she?"

"Just in kindergarten actually, and she and Nancy, my wife, have stood by me as I get embroiled in serious stuff, most of which never seems to go away."

"Man of mystery, that's you. Where on the Cape are you headed? If I may ask?"

"Chatham that's my final spot."

"Andy, if you can wait for me at baggage claim I am headed down there myself. Provincetown actually, for a weekend of fun and screwing. I can give you a lift to Chatham."

"P-town, isn't there a big gay community down there?"

"I won't tell if you don't," Alert said with a wink. "Different strokes for different folks, as the song goes."

"Weren't you married when we worked together Al?"

"Façade, Andy, she was a lesbian. So it worked out for both of us. The Air Force never suspected. For obvious reasons I never bothered to tell them."

"So, you're footloose now, I mean there's no steady out there?"

"Andy, my lifestyle is such that I travel all the time, and like the proverbial sailor, I spend time in every port and have a girl, in this case a guy, in every one of them."

"And in Provincetown too?"

"Not yet, but I have a weekend off before I hop on the bird again for a few days. Who knows what might develop? I might even find the true love of my life."

"I wish you good luck with that, Al, I really do. I have been less than one hundred percent faithful in my marriage, so I guess I am not the one to give advice on marriage or relationships. And yes, I will certainly take that ride down to Chatham. Thanks."

"How long are you there? I can pick you up after the weekend, and bring you back here."

"Thanks, but I am headed to Chatham for a while. I can't say when I might be back this way. If you've got a good phone number where I can reach you, let's keep in touch."

They shook hands and Andy turned to enter the small restroom. Albert put a hand on his shoulder, and whispered, "Watch out when you get off the plane, a little bird told me that you're a person of interest, meaning that they'll be tailing you at Logan. Act naturally and you'll be fine."

"Al, I would be very surprised it they weren't there ready to follow me. I guess that I am always on someone's radar. It's part of the thrill of being an international man of mystery."

"Damn, Reid, you are making me sweaty with all this talk of intrigue. Beats the crap we went through during those Pentagon days, doesn't it?"

"You mean spending time hunting down those rat-sized cockroaches and finding the infamous purple water fountain, like we did one time?"

"Fun times, yes they were. We had our share of people, some memorable, most forgettable, we worked with. What was that Major's name? I can place him, but I forgot his name."

"Ed Nicholson, is that who you mean? Actually he and I later met under less than favorable conditions, and he did not survive."

"God Reid, come back here after the bathroom and tell me everything, we have time before I need to get the cabin ready for landing. Want a drink? It's on me."

"Hell why not, I have had a horrible day, no I have had a horrible couple weeks, and now I don't even need to use the bathroom."

Andy sat in the small space at the back of the plane, the galley area. "Al, there have been times when I wished I was back in the Command Center, rather than what I've been through. I was on an assignment in Germany…"

Rosales interrupted, "See you are an international man of mystery."

"Hardly, but it was there that I met somebody else from my Pentagon days, a doctor named…"

"Bud Steinmiller, I suppose," Rosales said.

"How did you know that?"

"Doctor Bud keeps in touch, and to put it delicately, he enjoys my company and I well, I'm easy so…"

"He's gay, I mean Bud's gay?"

"Andy, he's bi, as in bisexual. That's fine. He's into *ménage a trois*, and other more kinky stuff. He also likes to watch, if you get what I mean."

"Al, I suppose I do, and that's a surprise," Andy said.

"What did he tell you about himself, I mean when you ran into him in Germany?"

"He never told me. But someone else did that he did time with the Agency, but mostly with me Bud was vague about when and where other than the time he was a Pathfinder in Laos."

"He actually mentioned that? I am surprised since most of those guys never speak of that time and place, or at least not while they're sober. But then he does like his double or triple Dubonnet on the rocks."

"Now that I think about it there was another person, a briefer, who warmed me about Bud. That guy, I think his name was Bill Leonard, he was the one who gave me that Pathfinder information.

"Bud seems more and more different that the guy I met over there, but I hardly know him. He keeps popping up, and after we had some time together in the little Bavarian village of Garmisch he showed up about to be seated next to me on Pan Am headed to DC."

Al Rosales handed Andy his cocktail. "Well, just watch out for the good doctor, that's my advice to you. While he has good mojo, as in good in bed mojo, I would not want him as a lifelong friend. Just my advice, that's all."

"Got it Al. I was going to say that Bud and I parted ways about that time. I got yanked off the plane, ended up somewhere back in the states, and have not really seen him since."

"Yanked off a plane, what did you do threaten to hijack it?"

"Cute, but no that's not the reason I got pulled off the big bird. The Pan Am folks told me that the president was shot. Then I and my bags were taken off, and the good old Air Force brought me back to the US. I wish I were making this up but it's all true."

"So, you left Steinmiller somewhere in the bowels of a Pan Am 707 in Germany? What did the assassination attempt have to do with you anyway? Were you a suspect? Was he? Actually I got see the Agency being involved in this kind of crap. "

"No idea, and to this day I can't figure out what the hell was happening that involves me. But then I always seem to be at the vortex of interesting events, and I never actually want to be."

Rosales nodded. "Want another one?" He pointed to Andy's empty glass.

"Yeah why not, I am not driving. One other thing. You know Doctor Bud wanted to come with me as they pulled me off, part of his Agency people shadowing thing, but the Pan Am folks were adamant that he stay on the jet. I guess he did since I haven't seen him again."

"Well, the day of the shooting it was chaos here at National Airport. We lost five hours flying time on departure that day while they tried to figure out if that kid, the shooter, acted alone. DC was an armed camp for a while. Maybe that explains why the folks over there, in West Germany, were so anxious."

"Could be," Andy said. "But I got hustled back here to a place up the road and then had to work my way back to Silver Spring, where I live. Once I got there, I found that my wife and daughter were missing and my house trashed. Not a good homecoming."

"Missing, what does that mean? You don't mean kidnapped I hope."

"Just what I said. I know from past experience that they would be headed to our house in Chatham if there was an emergency, which this was."

"Andy, can you be sure they're there, Chatham I mean, if they're not at home. Have you considered…"

"Considered kidnapping, of course I have, but I can't think about that just now. I have to hope that they're OK, and that I am on the right path to finding them."

Al smiled. "Andy, that's more like the old battle-hardened guy that I worked with back in the day. We'll get off this plane and then I'll get you to Chatham and then I'll reunite you with the family. That's a promise."

"Rosales, you are the man, thanks. I appreciate that. Now I think I need to use the facilities. Here's the glass, thanks for the drinks."

"See you at baggage claim Andy. I guess I should be working this flight, right. After all, that's what they pay me for."

Andy used the restroom and returned to his seat. As the flight attendants made their way down the aisles, Al Rosales whispered to Andy, "Don't forget, we've got a date at baggage."

"For sure, Al, for sure." Andy said and put his tray table into its fully locked and upright position, as the attendant requested. The plane descended into Boston. The day was clear and nearly cloudless.

The jet taxied to Gate 46 at Logan Airport, and the passengers all stood as one, jockeying to get out of the plane before their neighbors did. Andy waited for the most anxious passengers to push to the front with their luggage. As he finally reached the front of the aircraft, he noticed that Albert Rosales was not there, smiling and watching the departing passengers.

"Well I see that Mr. Rosales is not to be found, did he jump off the plane or something," Andy asked.

"Rosales, why is that name familiar," the pilot said with a wink. "We normally make him wait in the back, the aft as we call it, until everyone's gone. Only then will we release him to do a whirlwind check of the cabin. I hear that he's collected thirty gum wrappers, and about 12 cents in loose change so far."

Andy laughed. "Well, tell him that I say goodbye and I'll see him in the future, maybe down the road somewhere."

"Maybe I will do just that, and thanks for flying with us."

"Right you are, and see you all later," Andy said as he left the plane and took the escalator to the long hallway leading to baggage. The main portion of the 1950's terminal was dingy, poorly lit and overly cold. The windows were still closed and the overhead air conditioning was blowing full blast, ruffling the hair and clothes of huddled travelers who were sorting out gates and places. Many were tugging children along for another trip somewhere. Signs and posters were everywhere along the corridor. Graffiti artists enjoyed adding mustaches to the mostly female subjects pictured there. There was a gaggle of tourist gathered around a shop selling Boston merchandise.

"Gotta be a sale there, that's what it is," Andy said to a man in front of him.

"Sure is Andy, sure is," Albert Rosales said.

"Hey, how did you get ahead of me, I mean how did you get off the plane so quickly? I guessed that the pilot had you locked in the aft thingy."

"Andy, you already got the aircraft lingo down pat, were you ever a pilot?"

"Not willingly, no. I was a copilot on a small prop plane from Will's Air many years ago. That was on my first visit to the Cape. That was while you and I were working together in the NMCC, the Command Center."

Al stopped walking. "Will, yes I heard about him. Did you know that he flew air defense missions with the Brits in the days before we got into World War Two?"

"Nope, he was an old guy when I met him. Wiry and not at all stooped over, he even lugged my B4 bag into the hold without my help."

"Yeah, everybody has met good old Will. Folks said that he was a little touched in the head, but I can tell you up at Hanscom Field and even down at Otis on the Cape he was a legend."

"How so? I never pegged him for much more than an aging barnstormer or even a crop duster in the old days."

"One of my colonels in the Air Force, back in the '70's, told me that good old Will was involved in some black program we fielded, trying to understand the ability of the Nazis to reach our coasts."

"Well, they had that rocket under development…"

"The V-2, the Vengeance Rocket. It was used to kill lots of Brits and others in the last year of the War," Al said. "But there were other projects, some that no one knew about. I heard that Will got mixed up with ferreting them out and then reverse engineering them. At the end of the war he was part of a US and British group."

"I can't imagine him. What I mean is that when I saw him it was thirty years later and those years had not been real kind to him. He seemed confused at times."

"Andy, there are people out there who know what people like Will did and they would rather no one else knew anything, even today, in the 1980's."

"You think they did something to Will? If they did that seems kind of harsh doesn't it? Even for the US government."

"Well Andy, let me *tell* you. Let me give you my short lecture on the corrosive effects of too much secrecy. It's from my perspective of having served in or around these kinds of programs for many years. And, as an enlisted guy, for most of the scientists and officers I was just there to hold their doors open or get them coffee. They assumed that I was too stupid to figure out what was happening, but they were wrong.

"Back to Will, I heard that he was in Germany in late 1945 and that he worked on something called Operation Backfire, where we tried to launch some of the V-2 rockets to see what they could do, and how they could be improved. Most of them worked poorly, but that may have been because of the fuel mixture that was lying around. I heard the Nazis had more failures than successes on these rockets.

"While Will was there apparently he stumbled on some other stuff…"

"Al, I am all too familiar with German technology. Sadly. I was involved in uncovering two of their projects, and not willingly, over the last couple years."

"Ah yes the Stepping Stones incident, a name that will live in infamy, Andy, of course. However, about our good friend Will, if I can redirect here, Will was a pioneer in aviation, a real genius, kinda the Mozart of mechanics.

After the war, say in 1947 or so, I heard that he worked somewhere in Nevada, some test site, but nobody is supposed to know it's there. Will came back to Boston, got discharged from the Air Force and fooled around both here and Hyannis, eventually starting Will's Air."

"OK, that gives me the full dossier on our friend Will. But what in the world happened to him? Where is he now?"

Al stopped to think for a moment. "Last I heard he was holed up in some nursing home, somewhere near where you're headed, Chatham I think, or maybe Harwich. You can check when you get there."

"Right you are. But my first order of business is to link up with Nancy and Alicia, my family. Given all that's happened in the last couple days, I can't be sure of their safety, even in our Cape Cod rendezvous spot."

"Andy, it's really none of my business, but do you want me to come with you to Chatham and stay? Rather than just drop you off? I have no real scheduled Provincetown arrival time. A little time at the Cape's elbow would do me good."

"Sure, that works fine for me. I assume you know that Chatham is not P-town, it's a lot more…"

"Republican, I know, that's what Tip O'Neill always says, or at least one of his senior staff tells me he says."

"You do get around Albert, really you do," Andy said, slapping him on the back.

"I try to spread myself around, Andy, and always have. Just another service I provide to a public that is yearning to be free. Isn't that the line we always used?"

Andy and Albert walked out of the terminal after fetching Andy's bag at the Baggage Claim. They were stopped by a uniformed officer of the Massachusetts State Police. He asked that they follow him to a waiting unmarked white Econoline Van.

"What's going on," Andy asked.

"Your lucky day, some big wig wants to be sure you and your friend here get to Chatham with us a police escort. That's all I know. I just show up and do what they tell me."

"You mind if we check out your credentials," Albert asked with a practiced smile.

"You have to trust me. I have a gun. You don't so you're coming with me." The officer reached over and started to push Andy into the van.

Albert kicked the officer in the groin. He doubled over. Another chop to the back of the neck sent him to the ground, unconscious. Andy and Albert lifted the man into the van's back seat, and closed the door. If anyone was watching what had happened they made no move to interfere.

"Now," Albert said, "I guess we are like Bonnie and Clyde, you know, on the lamb, so let's get my car and head on down the road."

"Albert Rosales, you are one hell of a guy, you know that. I owe you big time, even if it means we both go to jail."

"Don't get me too excited about all those lonely guys in the slammer, Andy. You'll be my partner for the rest of this adventure."

They walked briskly to the employee parking lot, looking over their shoulders for anyone following them. Albert drove a new Camaro and was a fast driver. Andy knew they would be getting to Chatham fast if they weren't nabbed for speeding.

Wanda Brixton was not happy in the little village. Being one of the few African-Americans who were not employed as domestic servants in a seashore town led to many interesting and embarrassing moments.

At the Chatham Bars Inn she was told that the employment office was around the corner, since they assumed she wanted a position in house-keeping. On Main Street many people looked at her as if she were from another planet, which she might as well have been. But Wanda was on a mission. She hoped it would be successful.

She got in her rental car and drove down to the traffic light on Route 28, then headed toward Skunk's Neck. Reaching the large house she drove into the long driveway and knocked on the door. In about five minutes she heard a woman's voice and the door opened.

"Can I help you?" Nancy Reid asked. Her eyes were red as if she'd been crying, or was very tired, or both.

"My name is Wanda. I am a friend of your husband Andy, and I think we should talk."

Nancy hesitated. "Friend, as in how and where? I never recall Andy mentioning your name."

Mrs. Reid, I met Andy after he flew back from Germany. I was with him at that place where they kept him, and I actually helped him escape.

"I imagine that is possible," Nancy said, "But I am not really able to help you find him right now, if that's what you wanted me to do. I am hoping that he knows I am here. I assume that he's on his way to Chat-ham right now."

"I dropped him off not far from your house in Maryland, and I heard that you were gone. I also heard your house was trashed."

"Yes I left in a hurry, actually, I did not have time to write Andy, my husband, a note telling him where we were going. I never heard that the house was trashed, to use your term. My daughter…"

"Alicia," Wanda said. "Sorry, Andy and I had a lot of time together to speak about families, and stuff."

"Apparently, from what you already know about him. Before we go any further, do you know where he is?"

"No, not really, but I assume he's heading this way, and might even be here soon."

Nancy held the door open wider, and beckoned for Wanda to come in. "Well, it's cold out there so come in and let's see if he appears. I want to see his expression when he sees you."

"Why is that, Nancy?" Wanda sat down in an overstuffed living room chair.

"You are a beautiful younger woman. Andy has been a wanderer in the past. I forgave him once, and that may have been a mistake."

"But you have a daughter, isn't that a reason for him and for you to stay together?"

"Used to be, until Andy got called back into the government business I thought we had a nearly perfect life. We had a house, Alicia was getting into school full-time, and we loved each other."

"Mrs. Reid, trust me. Andy still loves you. Without going into details I can tell you that's he a faithful guy and he is faithful to you."

"Call me Nancy, OK. I am worried that Andy is easily tempted and easily forgets that he's married."

Wanda nodded but said nothing.

"So, where are you from and how did you get involved with this whole thing?"

"Long story, Nancy. Sometime when we have a lot of time we can chat about it."

A rattle of the dishes in the cupboard signaled the arrival of a car in the driveway. Nancy peeked out of the curtained window, seeing an unfamiliar smaller car idling there. Andy got out of the passenger side and a tall, handsome man shut off the engine, and then got out and stretched. They both walked to the door. Nancy pulled it open and hugged Andy, whispering there was a visitor.

"Wanda, what are you doing here?" Andy asked.

"Andy, you'll need me for the next couple days, I promise you. But for the time being how are you, and who's this?" she asked, pointed to Albert Rosales.

"Al, Albert, Andy and I go way back," Albert said.

"Nancy, this is Al. I think you may have met him when we both worked nights at the Pentagon."

"I do remember vaguely, and nice to meet you again. Did you and Andy drive up from DC together?"

"We flew into Logan, actually and I hitched a ride with him," Andy said. "He works for the airline and we reconnected on the plane."

Nancy frowned. "And Al, where is it you are headed, if I may ask? Heading to Chatham or somewhere else?"

"Nancy, dear, if I can call you that, I am a free spirit. I was on my way down Route 6 to Provincetown when your handsome husband corralled me into making an encampment here."

"Encampment," Nancy asked. "Does that mean you'll be overnighting with us?"

"If that's OK yes. I don't have another flight until Monday night so I am here for a couple days. Is that a problem?"

Nancy spoke up before Andy. "Not really, as you can see we have a mini-mansion here. It's complete with stuff and rooms that we've never used, so you and you too Wanda are welcome to bunk with us. Well, not really with us in the same room, but..."

Albert spoke up. "Well that makes it all good! I can easily lay my head on one of these pillows in the spacious digs you've got here, no problem at all."

"Wanda, you game?" Nancy asked.

"Don't rightly know as they say in the old time movies, y'all allergic to colored girls?"

Everyone laughed.

"I sure can stay here for a while, actually I got nowhere else to go so this works fine for me. Andy, how about you, is that OK with you?"

"Wanda, don't make me throw you out," Andy said smiling weakly.

"Never have and never will," Wanda said. "We go way back don't we Andy?"

"Yeah, at least a few weeks but not much more than that. Now can we at least devise a plan for the next couple days?"

"Let's let the guests get their rooms arranged first. I need to check in on Alicia who has been very quiet and then you and I alone need to go over the last couple of weeks, like where I've been and what I've been doing. More importantly let's chat about what happened. Just you and me." Nancy stood and walked to the doorway leading upstairs.

"Right Babe, I am ready, so let's do it after you check on Alicia."

"Andy, I thought you could reintroduce yourself to Alicia, since you've been gone for a while, and I'll tend to the Reid Motel here."

Andy knocked and then walked into Alicia's room. She was busy coloring a large piece of construction paper. Andy peered at the drawing and asked, "What exactly is that honey?

"Well, Daddy, as you know, it's going to be a picture. That means once I am finished with it. When it's done you can have it."

"Alicia, can you give me a hint at least?"

"Well," Alicia said, "It shows Daddy on a plane and he is going away from us."

"Where am I going on this airplane? Is it close to home, or far away?"

"It's the kind of place that you go to and you never come back."

Andy crouched down and got to Alicia's eye level. "Honey, Daddy is sorry that he was gone for so long and guess what: I came back and now I am here forever and ever for you and Mommy. So that's good isn't it?"

Maybe, maybe it is Daddy. But Mommy missed you very much. I saw her crying at home when you were gone. I know that she is really sad, and she wants a divorce."

Andy stood up and put his hands on Alicia's shoulders. "Alicia, I love your Mommy and you very much. I want to be a good father to you and a good husband to Mommy. So, I know that you and Mommy missed me but I will promise that it will never happen again. I have to cross my heart so you know that I am serious. See."

Andy crossed his heart and then clasped his hands together.

"Maybe Daddy, but I hope that you're not fibbing, because that would be a very bad thing."

"Yes fibbing is bad. And I know that you know that. Now you want to play outside? We can throw the ball to each other."

"Nope, I have to finish this. Mommy says I have to do my homework, since I'm missing school."

"Oh yes, that's right, you are missing school and your friends too," Andy said.

"Mommy says that it's your fault that my friends are not here with us. She said that you made us come here. I don't like it here without my friends to play with."

"Alicia, you are really a smart girl. That was the reason you and Mommy came here, but it's like an adventure. We are going to be living in a new place."

"I don't like these kinds of adventures Daddy."

"I know sweetie. I am sorry."

"Can I finish my drawing now," Alicia said.

"Sure you can," Andy said. "I'll let you finish now."

He watched as his daughter kept coloring, her head tilted close to the paper as if feeling the colors while she did them.

Nancy walked into Wanda's room. She closed the door. "Can we talk for a minute?" she asked Wanda.

"Sure, your house, your hospitality, and well, you know…"

"Wanda, I have to ask one direct question of you. Did you and Andy sleep together, ever?"

"No, not really…"

"What does 'not really' mean, that you sort of screwed him?"

"Nancy, please sit down. I was a paid employee of a place that Andy ended up after Germany. As the token black up there, I was the Girl Friday for those boys there, kinda the Little Red Riding Hood among the big, bad wolves. One of the chores they gave me was to titillate the inmates, I mean the guests. Andy was a guest."

"OK, exactly what does *titillate* mean? Any carnal stuff there, or was it just for show?"

"Swear to God, it was just for show. Andy was not even interested, I mean in going beyond the first stage, if you know what I'm getting at. He was a gentleman, he is a gentleman. He mentioned you and your daughter every chance he got."

"I have to assume that you're telling me the truth here, but if not, then I will have to ask you to leave this house, and…"

Wanda held up her hand. "Can I ask you a question, Nancy?"

"Sure, but I am not sure I can answer much more than I have already asked."

"My question is a simple one. What makes Andy Reid tick? Is he a devoted husband and father, or is he all that and human too? Men, not just Andy, are tempted all the time. Add a little liquor and judgment goes out the window."

Nancy sat at the edge of the bed. "You know Wanda that's something that I have been trying to figure out for nearly 15 years. Andy is a tightly wound guy. He can be completely focused, even to the point of forgetting that his desire to get to the bottom of something that leads him into trouble. He saw something in this little town and he never slept until he discovered what it was. That something almost killed me and him at the end."

"So I heard, and I am sorry."

"Don't be sorry. Andy was following a lead, a path nobody else wanted to follow or even cared about. His tenacity was a blessing in the end but it made him think that someone else, other than me, could be his soul-mate."

"Men," Wanda said with a laugh.

"Men are sometimes men who keep their marriage vows. In this case Andy forgot his. In the back of my mind, I can never forgive him for that."

'He would not be the first guy to stray Nancy."

"You're right about that. I know that deep down inside Andy is a good guy, someone who really wants to be a good husband. He's just a normal healthy male. He doesn't need to be tested by you."

"So, Nancy are we good then? Can I stay here and even be alone with Andy at times without you worrying?"

"Maybe, or maybe not. But for the moment maybe you could concentrate on Albert. He's not that bad to look at."

"Albert is a fine looking specimen but not at all interested in me or you, I can tell you."

"As in how and why?"

"Gay, and decidedly so. My antenna is fine tuned to alternate sexual orientation. It's not a look or a voice that gives it away, it's something else. Call it physic, or just intuition but I can tell."

"Wanda, I hate to admit it since I hardly know you. You are a good judge of character."

"You know my Dad always said the same thing. I was an Army brat, and had plenty of time being dragged from country to country and base to base. Along the way I met the good and the not so good, sometimes they were the same person in different circumstances. I was raped when I was a young teenager by a friend of Dad's. I never told him. It was my secret."

"I am so sorry Wanda."

"No pity Nancy, I live with the issue every day. I am not easily taken advantage of, especially now that I have been a victim of someone's sex power trip. I can handle myself."

Nancy hugged her. "You are welcome to stay here as long as you want Wanda. Forever, if you want to."

"Might just take you up on that, I just might."

Andy stood outside the room and listened. He felt a mix of relief and guilt about what Nancy had asked and what Wanda had answered. His brief time with Wanda was a good one, not exactly as innocent as Wanda described. She was a good-looking woman. Andy knew that his weakness was good looking women.

Nancy saw Andy when she came into the hallway. "Hey babe, are you checking on me and Wanda, or what?"

"Just snooping that's all. You really get a sense of her in there?" Andy smiled.

"She is a complex woman, and she seems genuine. Did you know that she was born into a military family?"

"I seem to remember that, yes. Did you get any other information?"

"Actually, I went in there to see if you and..."

"Did it? Is that what you wanted to know? You know that I have a history with good looking women."

"And Wanda told me that you turned down her advances, even more than once."

"Yeah babe, it was not quite as harmless as I wish it could have been. I was pissed, I was tired, and she was very lovely."

"I hope you're telling me that nothing happened."

"It could have, but it did not, really."

"OK babe. On another subject, how is Alicia?"

"She is coloring right now. She seems to think I might never come back if I leave again." Andy lowered his head.

Nancy held his hands in hers. "I was wondering the same thing."

CHAPTER 14

It was frustrating. Willie Billings was working hard at the Scatteree site, forcing the earthmover forward and backward as best he could. It was a long time since he ran one of these things, and the damn levers were stuck a lot.

For once, he wished that Chester, his nephew, had come back to the job. Chatham police had visited Willie's house a while back, checking on his whereabouts. Seems, according to the police, Chester had smacked Bonnie and smacked her pretty hard. Not a good start to the year for Chester. Willie told them he had not seen Chester in a good while, and they left.

As he turned over another shovelful of sand onto the back of the lot, a car approached. Alex Romanoff, the bartender at the Squire, got out and walked toward him, signaling for Willie to shut the earthmover off.

"Yo, Willie, got a minute?"

"Sure, Alex, what's up, somebody steal one of them ball point pens down at the bar?"

"Yeah, sure, that's what I'm here for. Wrong! I need to know what you know about your wonderful nephew Chester."

"He's fat and stupid, and lazy. That about sums it up."

"Yeah, that much I know from personal experience, but I was looking for…"

"Where he is, is that what you wanna know?"

"Sure, for starters, that would be nice?"

"Alex, well that's one thing I can help you with. Chester is M.I.A., as in gone and forgotten. Police folks want to know where he is as much as you do. In other words, I hate to say it, but I miss dear old Chester, kinda like you miss a hemorrhoid once it's fixed."

"Ha, that's a good one; I will have to use it once I get back to work."

"How come you are here and not over there pulling down beers, watered ones at that?"

"I've been given some time off for the morning, that's why. Got caught with a few dollars in my pocket that I forgot to put in the register, and…"

"Few dollars, for that they cut your hours, how cheap is that?" Willie said.

Alex lowered his head. "Well, it was more like a hundred dollars and I was kinda short this week."

"Shit man, they can afford it over there, ya know. Sometimes these piss ants what runs things…"

"I totally agree Willie. For one thing, I am their best bartender, even the folks what tend bar at other places know that."

Willie spat on the ground and wiped his moist stubble. "Hell can't change nothin' if they ain't gonna listen."

"Willie, my man, you should be glad you ain't from where I come from. When somebody does somethin' to you, and that somebody works for the man, the big man, you take it and you keep your trap shut. Otherwise, you can disappear, and real quick too."

"Hey, I forgot you're one of them communists, ain't you?"

"No more, not me, I am an American now, and proud to be one." Alex stood straighter as if at attention.

"But you came here, so what can I do you for?"

"Willie, I need to try and find Chester. He kinda spilled his guts to me before he left town, told me about hittin' Bonnie, and I wanted to see if he needs more help."

Willie Billings hitched up his jeans to the point just below his ample stomach. He took off his dirty baseball cap, surveyed it for a moment, and then put his back on his bald head.

"Somethin' wrong Willie," Alex asked.

"Well, hell, I am just cogitatin' here for a second before I answer. I am just wondering whether you and the cops are in this together, If'n you are, then I got nothin' to say about Chester or what I know."

"Willie, you know we pretty well. You probably know that I have had a few run-ins with the cops since I got here. I am not really that close to the officers at the PD. Other than that is there any way I can prove that I am on the up-and-up?"

"Free beer for life would be a nice start," Willie said with a laugh.

"Can't do that but I can just forget to add the second one to your tab if you're in when it's quiet," Alex said straight-faced.

"Sounds like a deal kiddo. Now, as for Chester, we got shirttail relatives up north…"

"Chester mentioned New Hampshire, is that where he went?"

"Nope, not New Hampshire, that was a decoy we used when we wanted to be left alone. Actually our kin folks live in Vermont, Killington to be exact, and one of them is some kind of big wheel at the ski resort there."

"Got a name, this guy at the resort," Alex asked.

"Ain't Billings, that's for sure. He's a shirttail like I said. His last name is Manchester, like the town. That's it his name's Andrew Manchester."

"Well Willie, remember our deal, free beer when I can pull it off, but only then. And as a favor, can I get you to forget we had this conversation?"

"You some kinda spy or somethin'?"

"Yeah Chester, that's me, Agent 007, secret agent Alex."

"What a bullshitter you are, and I sure will look you up downtown next time I'm in for a couple beers."

Bud Steinmiller strolled into the Agency's headquarters building and turned left, bypassing the turnstiles and the armed guards. He pressed the elevator button for the seventh floor and then used a card in his wallet to activate the doors.

Bud was not dressed like any of the others, the ones with the serious Brooks Brother's dark suits and wider repp striped ties. Bud was wearing old but pressed Khakis, a blue button down shirt and a hound's tooth jacket with no tie. The director's private elevator whooshed him to the top floor.

"Doctor, what a pleasure, how long has it been?" a security guard asked. He frisked Bud and then gave him a gentle pat on the back. "After the assassination attempt we've got to be more careful, that's all."

"Hey man I get it. Commies are everywhere and they'd love to get some Mole in here to do us all in. But to be more careful than we already are? Hell if we had any more security around here everyone's tongue would be removed and they'd be chained to the walls."

The guard smiled. "If you come by next week we'll consider that as a good suggestion and implement it. Now what brings you here, other than the need to see well-dressed employees hard at work protecting the nation from foreign enemies?"

"If I wanted to go to somewhere where that was the regimen this would be the last place I'd consider. You know that, don't you?"

The guard touched a small earpiece and nodded. "Right you are Doc, and they tell me they can see you now."

"Thanks old man," Bud said squeezing the guard's earlobe. "Catch you on the way out."

Steinmiller walked into the next set of rooms, and waited for an unseen person to turn off the alarm and electrocution system, so he could proceed. The green light above the door blinked three times before he could touch the handle and avoid a deadly jolt of direct electric current. Bud had once remarked that the geniuses in the technical department were a depraved bunch, real sadists. No one disagreed.

"Bud, welcome home, how long has it been?" a bearded man in a well-worn, older three-piece suit asked.

"About a week and a half, actually Norbert, but then you know exactly where I am at all times, and who are we kidding that you don't?"

Norbert Adams gestured for Bud to join him on a leather couch that faced the windows of his expansive office. Adams was a legend at the Agency, one of the vets who managed to stay on through the dissolution of the OSS, and live through several directors who had delusions of greatness.

He was a stocky man, with a full head of white hair and a white beard, almost Santa-like in his looks and his demeanor. Norbert was a man not quick to anger.

He was hard to dissuade when he considered a path the correct one. He alone argued that the 1962 Bay of Pigs operation, codenamed at the time Operation Pluto, was a disaster in the making. It was his dogged insistence in the pointing out the fallacies of the operation's planning and success that cost him a promotion to be Assistant Director. He was allowed to stay on after the Kennedy administration purges that followed.

Norbert Adams had no official title at the CIA. He was a freelancer, a man without portfolio. That meant that he could be involved in any project at any time without getting advance permission. This wide-ranging assignment did not sit well with the compartmentalists, as he called them; the fiefdoms created by elements within the Agency to hide money, or more to the point, to spend money lavishly on whatever could be bought.

"Bud," Adams said, "We go back a ways, back to the glory days in Southeast Asia, don't we?"

"Yep, I was a fairly young pup and you were…"

"A man with a mission, that's right."

"So, you called me Norbert, and I am here. Maybe after you give me some insight why, I can ask a few questions?"

"You can ask, but as you know I do not have to answer dear boy."

Bud stood and walked over to the window. "You know Norbert that one of the reasons these windows can't be opened is that in case of a major fire we'll all be incinerated along with our national secrets."

"Actually Doctor Bud, I presumed that it was to deter suicides by jumping, but your explanation is as plausible as any I've heard."

"Norbert, I'll apologize for taking up your time with drivel about windows. I just wanted to make small talk, which was the reason."

"Well, Bud you've given the listeners something to write home about, that's for sure." Adams picked up a small transmitter in his right hand and pushed a red button. Smoke rose from the nearest electrical outlet in the room. "Now we can talk, since they won't be coming to fix that while we're here."

Steinmiller nodded.

"I asked you to come today to discuss a matter of mutual interest. Seems you and some other person were in rural Bavaria at the same time a little while ago…"

"Andy Reid, our favorite person of interest. Yes that is true, we were there together."

"Reid is a lone wolf, and works for the Pentagon at times, then drops off our radar and he holes up in New England. Strange that he can do that, but then each of us has our idiosyncrasies don't we?"

"Steinmiller nodded that he agreed.

"As I was saying before I interrupted myself, Reid was involved in something in Bonn. Amazingly we're not in the loop on this program, but I am rectifying that. Whatever it was that we're not privy to, Reid was there, but then went to Garmisch for a little break. You met him there, and I am assuming that meeting was planned."

"Yes it was Norbert, I was vacationing in France, and the Bonn Chief of Station wired me to find out what Reid was up to. Even though this young man was at times good at ferreting out things, there is a suspicion in my circles that he might be a double, and working for the other side.

"By the time I got there to Bonn he was headed south, to Bavaria, so I followed him into the little town. I needed to smell that mountain air again. You know it clears the head."

"And what exactly was Reid up to?"

"Wish I could tell you that Norbert. As soon as I reintroduced myself to him, all hell broke loose. Some older gentleman, Werner Rasmussen, got ill. It seemed to be heart issues. I tried to get him to the hospital, but he died before I could."

"Doctor, I have it on good authority that Werner was killed, perhaps by his own son. Did you not know that?"

"Obviously not, since I had him prepped and ready for transport, and I was with him most of the time."

"Most of the time does not mean all of the time. I think that his son, what was his name, Hans, had been given instructions to have his father killed if it ever got to the point where he might be subject to anyone's questioning in a hospital."

"I certainly was not going to give him a list of questions to answer Norbert. He was in a great deal of pain when I treated him. Now that you mention it, he seemed overly anxious, even for an older heart patient, about his future."

"Well, Bud, there is a moral to this tale, and that is that people often betray their true feelings and concerns when confronted with decisions that can be life-threatening."

"Are you saying that Werner and Hans had some kind of death pact? Sure seems hard to believe."

"Yes that is what I am saying. Turns out that Werner was one of the lucky Germans, the ones whose ancestry might have included some non-Nordic types. His value to Hitler and the Reich was so great that he got a free pass from the Nazis."

"So, he came along with Von Braun and the guys from Paperclip then?"

"No, he was never even considered to be a threat, or ardent Nazi. In fact, he was given a citation by the new West German chancellor for his work to thwart the progress of Hitler's new secret weapons. So, you see Werner was a hero to us. He stayed alive with the Nazis breathing down his neck."

"Wow, Norbert, did you get to debrief him after the war, and if you did, what did he say?"

"I was a junior officer in the OSS, then stationed in London. To this day I do not know what happened. I was supposed to link up with a team in Berlin, and find Werner and have him interviewed, but…"

"What happened, did he disappear?"

"Hardly, he went right on doing whatever he was doing, and returned to one of the major universities to teach. He never looked back, and we never got the OK to talk with him."

"Who could have stopped you," Bud asked.

"It had to have been someone high up, maybe somebody in the White House itself."

"Well Norbert, that's interesting and frightening at the same time. Seems that the Rasmussen family is certainly an interesting one. Are there any other heirs?"

"The whole family tree and their provenance is shrouded in secrecy, not only US but the West German government's. We know that Werner's wife was killed in a bombing raid on Berlin, I think that was in late 1944. He apparently had two children, a boy and a girl, but with the fog of war we had lost track of one of them."

Bud scratched his chin. "I met the boy, Hans, when his father was nearing death, but how about the girl, do we have that name?"

"We have a team looking at the papers from the war. Especially the ones that deal with Werner's work for the Third Reich. We know that he was a rocket propulsion expert, and there have been rumors that he worked on other advanced projects."

"So how many of your folks are working on this thing?"

"Bud, with the budget being what it is, this is a low priority issue for the director. You know the Russian target always gets the biggest slice of the pie around here. I assume you now that the evil empire is among the top interests of the administration. As servants of the politicians we must acknowledge this fact in the Intel business.

"But we have a few good folks digging into Werner's past part-time. They're slogging along, I suppose, and maybe in about a year, maybe sooner, they'll have something to report."

"Well that's interesting, but you called me here for a good reason. Was this the issue you wanted to talk about?"

Norbert stood unsteadily. "Actually, I just need to stand up for minute. This damn arthritis is going to do me in. But you asked and here's the reason I called. Did you know that Andy Reid was an informal and off the books part-time asset of the agency about ten years ago."

"I've gotta ask, what exactly is a 'part-time asset' and what part of the agency are you referring to," Bud said.

"Back in the Nixon days, the Watergate days as the folks at the Post named it, there were a few rogue operations afoot here in Langley. Not all of them were beneficial to our core mission. One of them was run by a guy, a fellow now dead, and it involved Mr. Reid."

"After I saw him at the Pentagon and helped patch up his leg, I suppose. He never impressed me as much more than an overly inquisitive kid."

"You and he met in the late 60s. He was then a young officer in the army. His dalliance with us was a few years later. Reid was chosen to stalk one of the important Germans who came over during the post-war period. But they told him he was looking for deserters, the ones who left the US for Canada rather than serve in the army during Vietnam."

"Norbert, I know a lot of folks who left and then filtered back. Didn't Gerald Ford give them a pardon?"

"All of them got their papers back, yes. Andy was given the improbable task of being the coordinator of intelligence looking for these folks."

"When did this end, his job doing this?"

"Actually, no one is willing to tell me that it's either over or still being funded."

"I am not surprised. There are plenty of rocks and plenty of undesirable critters hiding under them. But then we never seem to eradicate the varmints do we? Once we uncover one, three more pop up. It's a never-ending battle around here."

"You are preaching to the choir, Norbert. I was part of one of those nobody-knows-we-are-here things for a long time. It's a strange world for sure. You get a stiff neck from looking over your shoulder all the time. I was supposed to be a courier once for one of these programs, but our airtight security was so airtight that the person I was making the delivery to never got the message. I ended up cooling my heels in an exotic locale for a few days."

"Bud, sure sounds like my kind of deal. Stuck in exotic locations with nothing to do, I mean."

"You would think it was. But tell me more about young Reid. That was where we started."

"Reid is no longer on that case, the one about the deserters. Most of the paper trail on his work for us has been 'lost or misplaced' according to our vaunted in-house record keepers. Reid is still apparently drawing a stipend, maybe one he will get for the rest of his life. But he was in Germany on someone else's dime, not on ours. He seems to sink into the background when he's not employed."

"Sure sounds like a special program to me. So where do I fit in this?"

"Bud, here's the deal. We need you to head to Chatham or Silver Spring, wherever Reid is at the moment. Make him your best friend, literally."

"I think he knows about my history, at least that's the vibe I've been getting when I talk with him. So, is it wise for me to be that close and that friendly?"

"What choice do we have Bud? Until the paper checkers find something we can use, which may be never, Reid is our target."

"I assume he has no connection to the Rasmussen thing, does he?"

"Most likely not, but then I've discovered over the years that people and places that seem dissimilar are often connected somehow. Maybe Reid knows something that can help us in this."

"OK Norbert, on the case. When I get to wherever he is do you want me to check back in?"

"No phone calls Bud. We know that most lines are being tapped, so use the post office."

"You most definitely are not in a hurry if that's how we'll communicate."

"Bud, I have all the time in the world. At this moment, my plate is full of meaningless chores and deadlines that are even more meaningless. Most of them I will never meet. So, anything you find about Reid and company, whatever they're up to, is interesting but not vital to my daily activities."

"Got it thanks Norbert." Steinmiller stood and shook hands. After he was gone for five minutes, Norbert Adams pressed a button and the guard entered the room.

"Make sure the boys down in tech got that all on tape," he said. "And get someone in here to reload the outlet's smoke maker. I may need it again."

Bud Steinmiller was hard at work getting his affairs in order before heading north to Massachusetts. The office he sometimes occupied was a deep cover one. The sign on the building referred to a construction company, a dummy corporation that had signs plastered on most building sites in the Washington area.

Most of the people entering and leaving the building, which was open to the public, wore jeans, tool belts and carried well-used hard hats. The workers were in fact electronics wizards. With their access to new construction, they were busy planting electronic bugs or splicing into existing cabling in buildings around the region.

Bud needed to get his work for this CIA contractor done first. That meant cleaning up the cutouts he had meticulously set up. He needed to arrange for someone to take his place, perhaps for a long while.

"Hey Jaime," Bud said. "Please get me the file on the current program, I need to convene a board meeting."

"Well Bud I guess that's possible. But you know just last week you told me never to get all these folks in the same room. How come the sudden change of heart?"

"Well, we have gotten new marching orders and I need to be absent for a while, maybe a long while and head north."

"As in how far is this going north? The north pole?"

"Nah. Much closer than that, about ten hours by car, that's all."

"Well, the great Doctor Steinmiller is not using the agency jet fleet this time is he?"

"Jaime, you are a great kidder, maybe the best ever. Actually this time I am a solo player. I am not actually sponsored by them, but doing something for them. Is that mysterious enough?"

"As always, a fog is descending over your activities. I am just here to maintain the appearance that someone cares. I shall be here upon your return."

"Jaime, do me a favor and check with the local cops in Montgomery County and see if anyone is still living at this Silver Spring address, can you?"

Jaime took the small piece of paper and left to make a call. She returned a few minutes later. Bud was dashing off a quick note to someone on his ancient manual typewriter.

"Cops tell me that whoever lived there is not there now. Actually, they tell me that the house was considered a crime scene, that someone tossed the occupant's belongings a while back."

"Anybody there, I mean anybody get hurt or whatever?"

"Not clear on that Bud. According to dispatch over there, the place was empty when they got there. Apparently now the whole house is yellow taped and off limits."

"That saves me from having to go over there and check on it, so thanks. Now let's get down to the board meeting. Where do we stand on the attendees?"

Jaime ticked off the names of many people, most in positions of power, who had already agreed to the impromptu meeting of the board.

"Senator Cardozo is the only person who has not responded," she said.

"We need him to be here, and until he is I can't go anywhere.

"I understand so let me try him at his summer home up there in Massachusetts."

CHAPTER 15

Andy Reid slowly walked around the perimeter of the Skunk's Neck's yard, deep in thought. For years, he had considered himself a lucky man with a great wife and now a lovely daughter. The dinner with Nancy and Alicia was great. However having both Wanda Brixton and Albert Rosales at the table made conversation difficult.

Wine flowed freely, there was a lot of laughter, and some gentle kidding. Andy was the brunt of most of the jibes, which seemed fine until Nancy and he exchanged glances. Married glances, the kind that signal a problem.

The pain was there, that look of betrayal, which he knew too well. After dinner, the guests offered to clean up, and Nancy announced quickly that she was going upstairs with a headache leaving Andy alone at the table with Alicia. Alicia wandered into the large living room to play with her Legos.

With no one to talk to Andy put on his coat. He made it to the front door, letting himself out. The cape air was warming, and there were signs that spring might actually be nearing. Some of the dormant shrubs had blooms on them.

He reached the far corner of the lot. He was staring at the near distance when Wanda tapped him on the shoulder.

"Lost Andy, or just wishing you were?" she asked.

Andy felt hotter than he had a moment before. His pulse was quicker. He felt ashamed. "Hey Wanda I thought you and Al were working the dishes over, what happened?"

"Al's a pro and I am well, just know that I am far from being domestic myself."

"So, you came out here to see me, is that what you're saying?" Andy hoped that his face did not show his embarrassment.

"Maybe yes, maybe no, it's your choice." Wanda placed her hand on his chest. She left it there. It felt warm, good, erotic, enticing.

"You know Wanda, I am ashamed to say that I listened in on you and Nancy before. I know that she suspects you and me of doing…"

"We didn't Andy, did we?"

"No Wanda, we didn't but we could have. She suspects that I have feelings for you. She wants to be sure it is not the case."

"Do you have those feelings Andy? Call it a scientific study, a search for ground truth. I am asking as a friend, that's all."

"Wanda, I'd be fibbing if I said that I didn't, you must know that. I am all too human. My willpower is sometimes not there."

"Is this one of those times?" she asked letting her hand wander down toward Andy's belt.

"Wanda, I need to be true to her, to Nancy, that's my goal. I can be a good husband, and it takes patience to be that. So, if you can just…"

"Take my hand away, sure I can. But just remember Andy that if things change."

"Wait, you told Nancy that you would never come between us, wasn't that what you said?"

"That's what I said, yes, but maybe I meant only half that."

"Maybe you should find some excuse. Just leave our house. I don't care what you tell Nancy. Whatever it is it might be for the best. You have to understand I am skating on thin ice here, and any hint of anything between us would be deadly for me."

"Andy Reid, you must know that I have some feelings for you. I can't say it is love, but it sure isn't just friendship. I have had plenty of Platonic relationships. Fine for most workplace encounters, but you and me, that's different."

"Stop for a minute," Andy said. "I have to admit we've had some harrowing experiences in the last couple weeks. I know that danger sometimes makes people feel closer to each other. Sometimes that gets confused with love, the romantic kind. Is that what we've got here?"

"Well, I find you interesting, and frankly the fact that you're married and have a kid makes that attraction even more for me. Call it perverse, but you push my buttons Andy."

"You've got nice ones," Andy said with a laugh.

"There's the fun-loving risk taker I first met. Sometimes Andy you have to let go, try something new."

"Been there and got in trouble over that."

"We can be very discrete Andy, and Nancy would never have to know."

"She'd know, I'd know. It would be on my face and in my lies. It makes no sense for me to play around."

Wanda embraced Andy. She kissed him on the lips. "That's for the next time Andy, if there is ever a next time."

"Wait a minute," Andy said.

"Yes. Had a change of heart?"

"Actually Wanda, I want to know what you motive is in all this? I mean are you interested in me for reasons that you're not telling me? After all, you show up at the most opportune times, not really by accident. Give me a small hint. What is really going on here?"

"Andy, I am who you see. I am in fact the person you think I am, no more and no less. I am working for someone, yes that is true. For your safety and the safety of your family it's better that you not know who that is."

"Overly mysterious Wanda. I'd say that you remind me of a lot of other women I've come in contact with. You want something but you're not gonna tell me what that is. I get it. But why the attempted romance, the dalliance you called it?"

"Andy Reid, do you take me for a shallow woman? I hope not. I was not kidding about the feelings that I have. I see you as desirable. End of story."

"But won't that interfere with this super-secret mission that you apparently have?"

"I am willing to take that chance. Trust me." She turned and walked back to the house.

Andy was ashamed. He felt weaker than before, emotionally and physically. He knelt down on the lawn and waited for the feeling to pass. It would not happen quickly he knew.

The sun set over the trees. A few large gulls laughed overhead and flapped their wings trying to get back to their nests before darkness set in. For the first time Andy could hear the roar of the surf in the distance.

The Chatham Police Department was never a hub of activity. Most days the police dispatcher was nodding off at the front desk. He worked nights at the A&P. His job was unloading the contents of the three trucks that arrived between two and five in the morning.

Flies buzzed against the Plexiglas window, trying to get inside where there were lights to circle and food to despoil. When a car pulled in front it of the department building it was usually a lost tourist. This was off-season and there weren't many of them around.

Officer Barry Eldredge, with ten years on the force and still not promoted above patrol officer was asleep. He'd learned to wake at the slightest movement. The new chief was a stickler for punctuality, for appearance and for professionalism. Chief Elmer Watkins told Barry Eldredge and two other officers they needed to drop a lot of weight or else be dropped from the force.

Barry was not that worried, since his uncle was one of the selectmen in town and the chief served at his uncle's pleasure.

The phone rang, startling Eldredge awake. "Chatham police," he said stifling a yawn.

"Is the chief there? This is New Hampshire police dispatch calling.

"Nope, I mean no, chief ain't here at the moment. He is out at some conference in Boston. Maybe I can help?" Eldredge pushed aside his Coke and looked for a pencil and paper.

"Maybe you can, officer. You had a BOLO on a man named Chester Billings did you not?"

"We did, domestic battery, fleeing the scene, that kind of stuff. Have you got him there?"

"We have his body. We found the Billings ID on a body alongside the road, just north of our station. Can you give us a physical description of Mr. Billings?"

"Yeah, Chester is a fat guy, about five foot ten or so, scruffy lookin' if you get what I am sayin'…"

"I get it. Thanks for the help."

"Wait, the chief's gonna ask me questions so maybe you can give me some details on what happened to him. Was he dead of natural causes, or somethin'?"

"Actually looks like he was shot in the back of the head, according to the medical examiner's initial report. He might have been involved in a traffic accident as well. Maybe one in which he hit or was hit by a large overland tractor trailer."

"Damn, two pieces if bad luck I guess. Do you want somebody to get you a photo of Chester to make an ID for sure?"

"Sure, officer, can you send us a fax?"

"I think I can. See, the chief well, he usually makes the fax machine go, and I've just watched him, but I'll bet I can figure it out."

The officer sighed into the phone. "See if you can, and if not call me back at this number." He recited a ten digit number. "When is the chief coming back, by the way?"

"Should be back here tonight. Gonna leave him a note, that's what I'll do."

"Thanks officer…"

"Eldredge, Barry Eldredge, that's me. Glad to be of help."

"Well Chester my boy you are officially no longer wanted by the Chatham PD, I just took care of that," Herman Banks said. "You know an idiot named Barry Eldredge down there on the force?"

"Yeah, he and me we go back aways. We were both in high school together. But then I moved on to trade school I started working for my uncle Willie. Old Barry, he joined the police after some time in the Army, I think he was some kind of MP, you know a police guy."

"Got it Chester. Can he be trusted to tell the Chief down there what I just said? I mean he seemed stupid. Is he really that dense?"

"Hell, Eldredge is no better than the average cop down there, and that's not just me talkin.' Gotta be common knowledge ya know?"

"No I don't know and that's why I asked in the first place. I asked Barry Eldredge to fax something to this phone booth. That'll never work. I wondered what he'd do then, that's all I need to know."

"He don't know a fax from a fart, and that's the truth. He's afraid to even change his own oil in his personal car, that's what a dufus he is. So no way is he gonna do a fax, whatever that is."

"Good to know, Chester. That means we can start back home to the Cape pretty soon. Maybe we'll wait until it gets dark."

"You sure that we oughta head back," Chester asked. "I kinda hope that all that stuff is over. Bonnie, my girlfriend, she may not be ready to forgive me. Hell, I may not be ready to forgive her either. But, just for old time's sake, maybe I'll check in on my uncle. You got a dime so I can call him collect?"

"Chester we're not gonna be calling anybody just yet, so hold your horses," Banks said.

"Geez, I didn't mean nothin' by askin' and I just was thinkin' I haven't checked in for a while, that's all."

"Chester, how many times do I have to tell you? The problem is that when you call down there or anywhere, there's a good chance that some-one is gonna hear you, maybe they have the phones tapped, but that's a chance we don't want to take. Right now, you're dead as far as the police know."

"I was thinkin' maybe I was dead a while back with that truck and all, but now I got me a new lease on life, right?"

"That depends. It depends on what you can give me once we get back south of here. If all goes well and I get what I was looking for then you can be sure I'll consider letting you go."

"Consider, what does that do for me? I want assurances. I ain't stupid you know, and I know that you're a hard core kinda guy. What chance have I got to make it alive once we're there? "

Herman Banks grabbed Chester by the tee shirt and held him close to his face. "Look, you fat slob, I am going to say something, and I hope you understand what I am saying here. You are only valuable to me as long as I need you, and not one minute longer. You know my name, and you saw my face, so that makes you a real liability to me. See, I normally am an anonymous soldier of fortune, and that means no one gets to know me, to remember me. Got that?'

"Yeah, I got it. What if'n I was to tell you that I got me a piss poor memory for faces and places. No matter what I would never remember anything you said or your name or face. Would that be good?"

"Chester," Herman said releasing his grip, "I am sure that you could be trusted, but why take a chance, that's my motto. So, let me see how you behave and then maybe, but only maybe I'll consider your fate. Not now, but after we're able to get the rest of what I'm after."

"Hey, I gave you that package, the one that I snarfed up at Scatteree, so what else you want?"

"To be technical I found it. You didn't give it to me. I got to be sure that nothing else is laying around that you missed, or worse yet, that you conveniently forgot about and you're keeping from me."

"Why would I do that, mister? I swear, on my mother's grave, rest her soul, that there ain't nothin' else back there that I know of."

"Chester, it's the fact that you don't know that makes me suspicious that there are more things back there. Maybe you even ran over something with that dozer of yours and buried it even more into the mud."

"Sand, that's what we got us a lot of, pure Cape Cod sand, not much else. I know that we moved a lot of debris, but like I said…"

"Enough, we're getting in the car and we're heading back down there, so get yourself together and let's move."

It was a slow day in Wellfleet, like most of the days in the offseason in the smaller towns of the Cape. Karl Wallace looked out the plate glass window of his jewelry shop, bracing himself on the windowsill. He could see his reflection in the glass, a handsome man in his later years, snow white hair, good posture, not heavy, but not thin either. His posture was as good as it was in 1939, he knew that. Only the color of his hair, which everyone said made him look much more distinguished, changed.

"Dad, are you feeling dizzy again?" His daughter asked.

"Well, just a little, you know. I think it must be the blood pressure medicine that makes me so," Karl said. "You worry too much about me darling. After all, I have a lot of good years ahead. Even without your mother here to correct my faults."

"Well, we can make a trip to see that doctor of yours, maybe we can just close up shop early, how would that be?"

"Holly, if I was very sick then maybe I would consider this. But as you can see I am fine now. There is no need to go to the medical office." He straightened up and nearly fell forward, righting himself with effort. Karl Wallace grimaced and slowly opened his eyes.

"You know dear, that I am not that young anymore, and these kinds of things happen to older folks like me. I am not that bad, considering my age."

His daughter laughed. "Dad, you are indeed a man of many talents but making excuses is far from your best talent. I can always tell when you are telling me a lie, like you are now."

"Holly, it is a good thing that your mother, may she rest in peace, is not here to hear you accuse your father of being untruthful."

"Mom would have said the same thing if she were. She always warned you that you were about to kill yourself. You work these long hours. Not to mention the amount of chemicals you've inhaled over the years when working at your bench in the back of the shop here. I guess we'll never know how much sulfur you've ingested since the 1940's."

"Well, working with precious metals in never without risk. It is like the alchemists turning lead into gold, do you remember that from your school days?"

"I do father. Some of your work is indeed magical. But you are over 75 now and you should consider slowing down. Why not give your assistants more of the work…"

"They are all dilettante's daughter, and I will not have my reputation sullied by presenting inferior work to my clients."

"Suit yourself father, but I did warn you. I am going to the bank to make a deposit and then I will get us some lunch. What can I bring?"

"My hunger is not so great just now. Perhaps just get me a small half sandwich from that place down the road, whatever it is called."

"Arnie's Deli, is that the place?"

"Yes, he is a good cook even for a Jew," Karl said.

"Father, you should not say things like that in the shop. What if some-one overheard you, and then reported it? Please try to remember that if you can."

"What would they do? Scold me for speaking my mind. When I was a boy in Germany I learned early that speaking out was a dangerous thing. When I came here to the United States I rejoiced in my ability to speak freely. That freedom of speech is guaranteed. I read about it in my citi-zenship class. I will not stop speaking my mind now."

"There is a limit to that freedom Dad. I am just saying that you should be careful when you speak of other people in derogatory terms."

"I know that darling, and yes I will be more prudent in my choice of words. But you know he is a Jew, I have seen the numbers on the inside of his arm, the ones they got from the camps."

"Dad, that's for him to know and not for public broadcasting, so you best forget that you saw that."

"*Ja* that is right, you are always being more correct than I am, dear Holly. That's why I let you boss me around here." Karl laughed and clapped his hands together. He smiled and waved for her to move along, to take her time and bring back his lunch.

Holly put on her coat and walked out of the shop, looking down the street for approaching traffic. Karl sat down at small bench and placed his head in his hands. The headaches were more frequent now; they kept him up at night. He had problems with his normally exceptional vision.

Sometimes things were unfocused; the other day he could not see through his ten power loop and had to ask an assistant to finish a small welding piece for him. The assistant was smug, Karl noticed, and actually completed the work with an acceptable level of competency. Karl never told him that, since that would be tantamount to giving the man a false hope that he might someday be a fine goldsmith.

Karl sat alone, his breathing slowing, and he felt he might be dozing off. It was not good, he thought, to fall asleep in the middle of the day. His eyes were getting heavier and his daughter would be gone for a while.

The phone rang, jarring Karl awake.

"Hello, this is Karl Wallace Jewelers, how can I be of assistance?"

The line was static-filled and hard to tell who was calling. Karl almost hung up.

"Hello, is this the Karl Schultz who worked with my father in the war," a woman said.

"I do not know what you are talking about madam. Would you be thinking perhaps of someone else?" Karl's forehead glistened with sweat.

"My father Werner, he was a good man, and he spoke kindly of your contributions to the cause."

"I must confess that I do not have any idea what you are speaking of madam. Perhaps you have dialed in haste, and you have reached the wrong party?"

"Perhaps this will jog you memory Karl. When you bailed out of a plane after the camera apparatus failed, you saw to it that my father would be safe, is not that correct?'

Karl was speechless.

"I guess that means that I have not reached the wrong number given your response. Karl, are you there? Please say something."

"It has been a long time madam. I was sure that no one would ever call me back. That is the only reason for my hesitation, that and nothing else. You must know that I spent years, no I spent decades waiting for this call. But, I must ask, why now, and not before?"

"My father passed away recently of natural causes. That generated a series of events which led me to you. Father was a stern man and he kept his secrets. I do know some of them, but it was not until he left us and I was summoned home to hear the full story that your name was mentioned."

"Madam…"

"Harriett is my name, but it was Helga you can call me Harriett for the time being."

"Helga, thank you that clarification. I would remind you that I am a man advanced in age, nearing 80 in fact, and that my physical condition is not the best. Just a warning, that is all."

"Karl it is your mind that we need, not your body. It seems that there is an item that we need. You alone are one of the few people who can identify it. Moreover, if that happens then you can tell us if the passage of time has rendered it unusable. Is that a task you would be up to doing?"

"If this means I am back on the path of work that I started long ago, then yes, certainly I am ready. I have papers that will be helpful in this quest. But, you have not told me about what location I will be checking. I am located on Cape Cod, the little town of Wellfleet, and not really much of a traveler these last few years. So…"

"Not a problem Karl, we can send a car to pick you up. Would you mind being on call until I can call you back? I need to check one thing before I can establish a firm time for your activation."

"That would be fine Helga. I must tell you that it makes me proud to know that the project your father and I worked on will be restarted, and this time brought to fruition. He was a great man and a great scientist, perhaps in the opposite order, but you know what I mean."

"Yes I do, he was a good man, and dedicated too. Now let me call you back soon. In case you are not in when I call I will use a code word to alert you to my reason for calling."

"Ah yes, the old intrigues," Karl said.

"Since you make jewelry of the highest quality I will tell the person who answers, if you are not there, that I am calling with regard to a Platinum diamond ring, will that be good?"

"*Ja*, that is excellent. No one will suspect the ruse is really more than a call about a fine ring."

"Karl, it has been a pleasure to finally speak with you and I look forward to a successful adventure. Until we speak again, then."

"Yes, until then. I await the call." Karl hung up, smiling. Suddenly he felt a sharp pain in his chest that radiated down his arm. He nearly passed out. After a few minutes Karl slumped in his chair, slowly regaining his composure.

He looked at the lamp on his bench. The light was flickering it seemed, but then it became very bright like the sun. Karl blinked and shielded his eyes, just as if he had seen a nuclear bomb go off. He needed to avert his eyes.

Karl fell face first on the hard wooden floor breaking his nose. He was laying in his own blood and sweat. It was as if he was back on board the Horton jet, cruising over the North American continent, working for the Reich, the greater good, and the advancement of science. Next he was standing tall as a much younger man with close-cropped blonde hair, standing tall as the leader of the Nazi regime pinned a medal on his chest.

His wife was there, her eyes downcast as if deep in prayer. That little Austrian weasel, Adolph Hitler, stood before Karl. Hitler averted his eyes. The next man in line was Werner Rasmussen, his mentor and his best friend. Hitler's hand trembled as he fumbled with the pin on the back of the medal.

After Hitler left them, Werner leaned into Karl, and said softly, "We are making history now and in the future. It is our honor and privilege to do so."

Karl grasped the hand of his good friend Werner, with tears in his eyes, and nodded yes. The vision ended. Karl was now asleep.

Outside the jewelry shop, a few passersby looked in the window but did not stop, preferring to head for whatever they needed to do. Karl was behind the counter, his life ebbing away.

Holly Wallace, Karl's daughter, waited at the Deli in a long line of customers, an unusual event for an off-season weekday. Glancing at her watch, she decided to ask to use the phone to call her father at the shop, to tell him why she was taking so long. The owner gave her the phone and she dialed. There was no answer.

Leaving her place in line Holly ran down the street four blocks to her father's shop. She pushed open the door, and heard the familiar bell. Her father was not at his desk and he was not standing by the counter. Holly walked over and checked the workbench. Her father was sprawled out on the floor, his face bloody.

She leaned down and saw that her father had a pulse. She used the shop phone to call the fire department. Five minutes later the local EMTs arrived and transported them both to Cape Cod Hospital in Hyannis, a forty-minute ambulance ride.

Along the way, Karl awoke. He grabbed at his oxygen mask and told Holly about the call he'd gotten while she was out.

"Darling, this woman had a very important message for me. I need to be ready to complete a task for her. Can you please assure me that the doctors will keep me only a short time? Other than my face being very painful I feel actually fine. I am not making this up darling. I really feel fine."

One of the EMTs leaned over Karl and asked him to put his mask back on, and not to talk. Karl tried to sit up, but fell backwards on the gurney, his eyes closed.

"Lady, your father needs to rest, and not to talk. Please try to stop him if he tries again," the EMT said.

"Dad is a stubborn old German, but I will try to make him quiet. He is a man who does not take orders very well. I will certainly try."

"Please do, Ma'am, we've got another half hour before we get to Hyannis, so it's really important…"

Karl arched his back, as if in severe pain, and stopped breathing. The EMT called the ambulance driver, telling him to pull over. He got out a small Epi Pen and jabbed it into Karl's chest. The old man began to breathe again.

"Dad," Holly said, "You'll be fine. Yes, I can make sure that you're back at the shop quickly. First you need to be a made better. We can deal with the call from your friend later."

Karl nodded that he understood, closing his eyes.

The ambulance driver pulled back onto the highway lights on and sirens blaring. Most of the traffic pulled over.

CHAPTER 16

Wanda Brixton walked toward the center of Chatham. She was still being noticed by the locals. That was good. She went into one of the many storefronts to peruse the goods. After a few detours she walked to a pay phone in Kate Gould Park. Dialing slowly she put in four quarters and waited for an answer.

"Yes," a man said.

"Plan underway, and I will call later," she said.

"Complications expected?"

"You know me, sometimes there are. But most times there aren't any." She hung up.

Nancy and Alicia Reid were walking down Chatham's two lane main street. Alicia was interested in skipping over the cracks in the sidewalk, reminding her mother that it was very bad luck to step on any of them. Nancy smiled. It reminded her that own mother told her the same thing. Alicia was a precocious child.

It was not good, Nancy thought, to have her pulled from her school in the middle of the year. But Andy and his intrigues put them so far away. Once things were sorted out, Nancy would need to decide if they would be living in Chatham full time or just during the summers.

They took the short detour up one wide step and into the Mayflower Shop, one of the older shops that never closed in the offseason. The place was old-fashioned store, complete with a small post office annex in the back and lots of stuff in the front. Kid friendly things were always on the lower shelves so that smaller people could handle them.

Alicia picked up a red stuffed Lobster toy, and looked at it thoughtfully. She held it up for Nancy to admire.

"We'll see if we can buy it honey, but Mommy wants to look for something first. Is that OK?"

Alicia grasped the toy tighter. "Maybe Mommy. But I really like it, I really do."

Nancy thought it might not be a good time to mention all the stuffed toys that Andy had brought with after his visits to West Germany. Alicia now had twenty Steiff bears and other animals in her room in Silver Spring.

Nancy looked over the racks of magazines, checking for the latest issue of Newsweek. The cover featured a black and white photo taken outside the Washington Hilton where the president was shot. It was grainy but the shocked look on the president's face gave the picture extra emphasis.

She picked up the magazine to thumb through it. She heard a loud crash. The store's front plate glass windows exploded into hundreds of glass shards.

Nancy dropped to the floor. She pulled Alicia toward her. Glass was everywhere. Nancy heard an approaching siren. Staying low, she waited for anyone else to say something, but there were no voices, no cries for help. The sirens got closer and then stopped. A uniformed officer came to the door and stepped through the now glass-less frame.

"Anyone in here?" he asked drawing his gun.

"We are. We are back here. By the books and the magazines, officer," Nancy said.

"Stay where you are Ma'am until I check on the clerk." The officer was silent for a long time.

"What's wrong," Nancy asked.

"Dead body Ma'am, that's what we got here. Poor lady never knew what happened I'd guess. Shot in the back of the head. Maybe hit by sharp glass, can't tell which."

Nancy felt a chill, and hugged Alicia closer to her. "My young daughter and I are back here, I don't want her to see this."

"I understand Ma'am. How about you and you daughter head out the back way. I have the front secured, so check and see if the aisle is clear? I will have another officer meet you there. Will that work?"

"Maybe it will, let me look," Nancy said, craning her neck around the corner of the shelves to the back entrance. "Looks clear we're heading out."

"Mommy, can I have the toy," Alicia asked, her voice trembling.

"Sure baby, they can do with one less little toy I guess. We'll pay for it later." She walked slowly and carefully to the back of the store and pushed the wooden door open. The sun was shining and there were two older cars parked in the small lot. A police cruiser pulled in and the Chief of Police, Elmer Watkins stepped out.

"You two OK?" he asked.

"Fine, say could you let my daughter Alicia sit in the police car? She's never had the experience," Nancy said with a wink.

"Sure, honey let me open the door. You can sit inside while I talk with your mom, is that good?"

Alicia clutched her toy. "I guess so, Mommy, please don't go anywhere. I'm scared." She sat in the front seat of the police car and showed the toy lobster all the special things in the front seat.

The chief stood with his back to the Mayflower, and looked over his shoulder at Alicia, who seemed to be calmer.

"So what happened just now? Was that a gas explosion?"

"Ma'am, I don't really know. We need to get the crime techs down here from the State Police. I think we had a shooting, that's my opinion."

"A shooting, what kind of ..."

"High caliber automatic weapon would be my guess since the windows were blown in with a lot of force. My officers tell me that the clerk who was standing there took a bullet in the back of the head. She's not gonna make it."

"A shooting right here in Chatham? This is such a quiet town, I find that amazing, if not hard to understand. Is there a reason this happened?"

"Wish I knew Ma'am, but we've got carnage and damage in this building to deal with. One of the things the state cops can do is give us a sense of where the shooter was, trajectories of the shot, that kind of thing."

Nancy stood quietly and watched Alicia as she played with her new lobster toy. "You know," Nancy said, "It might be that I was the target. Have you considered that?"

"What do you mean?" the chief asked. "Are you telling me that you're able to know this, or that you feel this in your bones?"

"More than that chief. Maybe we have not met. But your predecessor and my husband had quite a few adventures together over the last couple years."

"You're Andy Reid's wife? Wow, I apologize for not making the connection. I sure had a ton of information dumped on me by the former chief, not all of it complimentary to your husband.

"In Chief Kennedy's last conversation with me before he retired and moved to Florida, he told me that Reid, I mean your husband, sorry, was a decent guy. But he also said he seemed to attract trouble, but that he always got out of it."

"Chief, Andy and I have been coming to Chatham for a long time. He and the former chief's daughter..."

"Janet, yes I know that part of the story all too well."

"Andy and Janet were lovers, but that's over. I've forgiven him, we've moved on. Now we have a child, and…"

Another police car pulled in and idled. The chief excused himself and walked over to the car, speaking to the officer inside. He came back and spoke to Nancy.

"Mrs. Reid, I am going to take you and your daughter back to your house in my car, is that all right?"

"No. I parked my car down the street and I can follow you home if you drive us to the car."

"Not a good idea. My men think that someone may have tampered with your car. It has been broken into, and there a suspicious package on the front seat. Out of caution, we're having the bomb disposal guys come down and check it out. We've cleared two blocks of Main Street just in case."

"God," Nancy said, "This is amazing. Here I was just trying to get a little quiet time in town and all this happens. Why me? What could anyone possibly gain from all this?"

"Maybe they, whoever they are, were sending a message?"

"They failed to deliver that message if they were. I am still here and so is Alicia. I guess maybe they had more ideas than just a message, more like actually killing us. If that's the case, well…"

Nancy broke down sobbing. The chief held her for a minute then braced her. "Stay strong if you can, if just for your daughter's sake. We'll get to the bottom of this and get the people responsible too. That's my word, and my word is…"

The chief stopped mid-sentence and fell forward into Nancy. He was bleeding from the center of his chest. Another shot hit the cruiser sending shards of Plexiglas from the lights everywhere.

Alicia was screaming at the top of her lungs for her mother, asking her to help her. Nancy jumped in the front seat and pushed Alicia down and toward the floor of the vehicle.

"Honey, we'll be safe, trust me. These policemen will keep us safe, they have guns and know how to protect people like us."

Alicia was still crying, and Nancy covered her as best she could with her body.

"I want daddy, where is he, why can't he be here now?" She asked in between sobs.

"I don't know. I wish he was too." Nancy cradled her child in her arms and cried.

The Chief was not moving. The shooting had stopped for the time being. It was an eerie quiet. Nancy feel more afraid.

Over at Andy and Nancy's Skunk's Neck house, Albert Rosales was fussing in the kitchen. He was making what he called 'the best dinner bar none' for that evening. Andy Reid stayed away; knowing that there were too many sharp knives and hot pans to be around.

"Where is Wanda?" Andy yelled standing at the kitchen door.

"Said she was napping, which may mean she's really doing that or not," Rosales said.

"You aren't sure?" Andy asked.

"With women, I am never sure, Andy. I was married but as I told you it was a marriage of convenience for both of us, just to keep me in the service. If you ask me about men I could fill several books, but women are a complete mystery to me. Must be a gay thing, I don't know."

"Well, my family is downtown. Maybe I'll head over there and see what they are up to. Are you under control here?"

Al dropped a large frying pan with a loud noise and yelled several obscenities. "Maybe that will wake up sleeping beauty upstairs," Albert said.

"Maybe so, Al. I am off to town. Need something?"

"Nope, I've got it all here. Just leave and when you get back all will be in order. No snacking please. This is going to be a major feast for the eyes and the stomach too. Just go."

"On my way," Andy said, grabbing the key ring for his ancient Mustang. He walked outside and glanced back at the house. Wanda was looking out her bedroom window. She did not wave.

Andy was halfway out of the long drive when two cars came in followed by a state police car. Both cars blocked his way. He turned off his engine and waited in his car. Both officers came over and asked him if he was Andy Reid. He reached for his wallet but when they reached for their guns, he put both hands in the air.

"Let me get that sir," the state police officer said reaching for Andy's wallet. "Just in case, I am sure you understand." He reached in and took the wallet.

"All too well, officer, all too well," Andy said. "Can I ask what this is all about?"

"Yes, and I see by your license you are indeed Andy Reid, as you've said. Thanks." He handed the wallet back to Andy. "Seems there has been an incident in downtown Chatham. We're here to check on you and also escort you to the police station."

"Why, is my wife involved?"

"She and your daughter are fine, Mr. Reid. I know that since I just saw them with the Chatham police. They are a bit shaken up but otherwise…"

"What the hell happened and when? I never got a call from anyone," Andy said.

"Sir, with the chief being shot…"

"Damn, let's not do any more explaining. Get me over to the station."

Andy climbed into the state police car. The trip was short, they sped into town. Andy left the back seat of the car before it came to a full stop and ran inside the station.

Alicia and Nancy were sitting on a weathered wooden bench, looking at him, but not saying a word. He rushed in and held them both.

"What happened?"

"Not in front of Alicia, Andy. Let's just go back to the house and we can talk, OK?"

"Sure babe, we got an escort right here." Andy pointed to the state police officer standing in the corner.

"Actually sir, I am going to need to ask you and your wife a few questions before we go."

"Can't it wait? As you can see both of them are not really that coherent at the moment. I'd rather that we delay the questions."

"Tell you what," the officer said. "I'll drive you three back to your house. We can speak there once your daughter is safely inside the place. Will that work?"

Andy looked at Nancy, who was still dazed. She nodded that was acceptable, so they stood and walked to the cruiser.

A small crowd from town and the firefighters from the adjacent fire station gathered to see what was happening. A Chatham police officer walked up to them and put his hand on Andy's shoulder, as if to show sympathy for them.

Andy smiled weakly and mouthed his thanks.

Within ten minutes, they were back at Skunk's Neck. In another five minutes Alicia was in her second floor bedroom. She was animated and talking to herself.

Andy and Nancy sat down in the den. The state police officer faced them. Both Wanda and Albert were out of the way. The room was theirs alone

"Mr. and Mrs. Reid, I guess I need to tell you that we are looking very hard for the person or persons who did this. We'll find them. That much I can promise you."

"Nancy gave me some details but why don't you start at the beginning," Andy said, squeezing Nancy's hand. Nancy looked down at the floor but she was not speaking.

"You know I think my wife is going into shock. Have you got a way to get a medic over here to look at her? No sirens or lights, OK?"

The officer reached for his shoulder mic and spoke into his two-way radio, asking for an ambulance. They sat in silence, and Nancy blinked several times, fighting back tears.

In a few minutes, the rescue squad was at the entrance to the driveway. Two paramedics came in. Nancy reclined on the couch. The paramedics asked her a few questions, then did a physical check. She never responded to their questions, and they looked over at Andy and the officer. They took her pulse and showed a bright light into each eye.

One paramedic walked over to Andy and said, "Mr. Reid, she is not in shock as far as we can tell. I think she just needs to process what happened. It's like the guys I served with in Vietnam, we called it shell shock, but these days there is a new name for it, post traumatic something or other."

Andy looked at Nancy, then at the medic. "I think I get it. Nancy had a terrible time when we got to that Stepping Stones place years ago. She was almost killed. It took more time for her to heal mentally than physically."

"Sir, I would recommend that she get a lot of bed rest for the remainder of the day. And if possible she is not to be bothered by anyone or anything. Can she do that? If she can, then I see no reason to transport her to the hospital. They will basically do the same thing as you can here."

"What if she can't sleep or she gets agitated?"

"Call 9-1-1, that's what we're here for," the paramedic said. He and his partner packed up their bags and left, backing out of the long driveway.

Andy escorted Nancy to the master bedroom, and put her to bed. She closed her eyes, and was instantly asleep. He watched her for a minute, and then walked down the hall to Alicia's room. Peeking in he saw that she was also asleep, curled into a fetal position, her right arm covering her face.

"Well, they are both asleep at the moment," Andy said as he came back into the den. "What happened?"

The state police officer checked his notebook. "From what I have been able to piece together but your wife and daughter were in the Mayflower Shop and there were shots fired…"

"Fired at them?"

"We assume so, but I can't say that officially. Someone with a long rifle fired one or maybe several shots in the direction of your wife and daughter, killing a female clerk there. She was in the line of fire, and being there must have saved them, your family."

Andy sat motionless. "Who could be so cruel as to target my family? No matter what I may be or may have done, there's no reason for anyone to try to kill them."

"I understand Mr. Reid. We are working to find the killer, the motive and get you those answers. But there's more…"

"More than that? God, that's enough isn't it?"

"Yes sir, it's quite a bit to digest, I'll admit that. But the perpetrators then took another shot at your wife while she was talking with the Chatham Police Chief. He had responded to the first shots being fired. He died there at the scene."

"So you're telling me my family had two attempts on their life today, Jesus, what else can happen? I mean, I really can't even think of life without them." Andy put his head in his hands.

"Mr. Reid, I can only tell you that finding those responsible is my and my department's number one priority. We've made a call for additional assistance, and they will be contacting you soon." And there's more. Your car, your wife's car was broken into. There was a package on the front seat, the bomb squad was called…"

"Stop," Andy said. "I get it somebody wants me dead and my family too."

"Too soon to make that assumption until we investigate everything. Now as I was saying, we've requested additional assistance from." Andy looked up. "Who did you call?"

"Sir, I called and requested the assistance of the FBI."

"What? Why on Earth? Is this a federal thing?"

"Might be sir. I got Boston's permission to make the call for them."

"So, who is gonna be calling? Do you have a name for this FBI guy," Andy asked.

"Not a guy Mr. Reid, it's a lady. She's Harriett Rasmussen. She heads up their Hyannis office. Never met her but I heard she is a real pro.

The man driving had stashed his scoped rifle in a green duffle bag. After wiping everything clean with a towel, he threw the bag and rifle into the ocean behind the unoccupied house where he'd parked. Getting back in his car he drove slowly to the gas station at the corner Stony Hill and the state highway, about five blocks down the road.

"Got a pay phone?" he asked the bored teenage clerk.

The clerk pointed to the small glassed booth behind the building, an old-fashioned one. It was the kind that was getting more and more uncommon except in these kinds of places.

Throwing in two quarters, he dialed and waited for three rings, and then hung up. His quarters came back so he reinserted them and dialed the same number again. The call was answered on the first ring. He was asked for a situation report.

"The target was acquired, the work on her car done, but there was some collateral damage," he said.

"As in what kind of collateral damage?"

"See, there was a clerk in the window and she was blocking my shot."

"So you killed her? Is that what happened?"

"Yeah but the woman and the kid you mentioned were not hit. I added a little improvisation when they left the store where I saw them. They were in the back parking lot and I plugged the guy they were talking to. Good shot if I do say so."

"Who was that?"

"Some cop, I guess. He got out of a black and white."

"Look, we're not paying you to be a mass murderer, got that? I just hired you to get to them, to scare them. Not to kill them or somebody else. That's over and done with. What's your next move?"

"Lay low, that'll be my plan. I'll wait for your next call. I am here for a while and you know how to reach me."

"Yes I do know how, and I will be in touch. Are you sure that no one saw you, or maybe remembered your make of car?"

I am a professional. Pros like me never screw up. No one saw me or even can figure how I pulled all this off so neatly. I even made sure that I got all the shell casings from my shooting perch."

"Except that there are at least two people dead and there were supposed to be none."

"Like I said, the clerk was in the way and the cop, well he was an inviting shot. You know I hate cops with a passion. Call it a gift from me to you."

"I do not need these kids of 'gifts.' I want you to stay as far out of sight as you can until the whole thing is over."

"Hey wait, you asked me to toss that house down in Maryland. I did that remember? Now I figure I got a pass since no one saw me. Cops are still wonderin' how that happened."

"Old news. We need to concentrate on this assignment, and the next, if there is one."

"Right. Love working with you all. But when can I get my other half of the payment," the gunman asked.

"Meet me at the usual place in about fifteen minutes and we'll make sure you get it."

"Good, that's good. I got me a plan, and it's gonna require cash money, so sure, I'll meet you there."

He hung up and walked out of the phone booth. Checking around, he saw that someone left the normally locked bathroom door open. He decided to take a leak. After all, he thought, it would be easy to get to that meeting place in ten minutes, even going well under the posted speed limit.

The gunman looked at the trees just starting to bud. Heading toward the adjacent village of Harwich, he was thinking that down in Florida, where he was headed, it would be summer soon. He smiled, and pulled a cigarette out of the pack in his shirt pocket. He told everyone he never smoked but that was just a little lie. He knew that this employer wanted a nondrinker and a nonsmoker. Fat chance, he thought.

Fumbling for his lighter, we swerved across the centerline and nearly hit a fish truck. The driver laid heavily on his air horn, then gave him the finger. He downshifted and continued down the highway toward Chatham.

Normally the gunman would have chased after the truck and taught the truck driver a good lesson, but not today. Today was payday after all, and paydays were good. A few miles later he pulled into the library parking lot in Harwich Center, and waited. He chewed a little Doublemint to be sure that his smoker's breath didn't betray him.

A black sedan pulled into the empty lot and idled. The gunman straightened his shirt and tie and walked over to the car. The electric window slid down silently. He was face to face with his employer for the first time.

"Got the payment?" he asked looking at his watch.

"I smell smoke on you. You told us you never had been a smoker. Did you make that up?"

"Nah, just that someone at a gas station where I made that call from was puffin' away and I guess I caught it all second-hand. Now about my payment."

"Paid in full," the driver said, pointing a pistol at the gunman's head and firing once. "We're even now."

The car's window closed silently. The driver headed back toward Chatham.

CHAPTER 17

Karl Wallace was doing well in the Cape Cod Hospital. He got a clean bill of health from the ER docs. They wanted to keep him overnight for observation. His daughter Holly was there, holding his hand, stroking it gently.

"You know father you gave is quite a scare."

"Holly, there have been times in my life when I was much closer to death than I was earlier today. This was just an attack of the flu or something like that."

"Dad, the doctors tell me that you may have had an anxiety attack. They think you might have had one of those silent heart attacks. I need to remind you that your doctor in Wellfleet told you to cut down on coffee and sweets."

"Well, it might as well be a death sentence if I have to do that. What co these medical people know anyway? Some of them are not even Americans; they look as if they just got off the boat from Africa or Asia."

"Dad, you've got to keep your voice down, and I really wish you would not make those kinds of remarks. You can think that way if you must, but can't you keep your thoughts to yourself. Just remember that it is not 1942 anymore. You're an American citizen now. These people are doing their best and it's not for you to judge them on where they were born or what they look like."

"Daughter, my old habits die hard. I can tell you that from my long experience there is a need to maintain values that I learned as a young person. If you stray from those you have betrayed your elders and your parents. That is my belief."

"I am not going to argue with you today. I want to have you get some rest. Before I go and get a cup of coffee is there anything that I can get for you?" Holly asked.

"Do you remember that I told you? About the fact that I had a call from someone who wanted me to do something?"

"Yes I do, and you said it was a woman that you never met. What is her name, do you remember that much?"

"It was Helga, no, she told me to call her Harriett. She was the daughter of one of my colleagues from during the war."

"But father, you told me that you were in the United States at that time, I mean during the war."

"Technically yes, I was in North America, for at least part of the time. It is a long story and one that I must tell you sometime."

"How about telling me now," Holly said. "I have nowhere else to go and I want to hear all of this."

"My darling, what are you doing, preparing a book of my life?" Karl asked with a grin.

"No father, I am not preparing a book. But I could since I know virtually nothing of your past, other than you were born in Germany. You did not fight for the Nazis. You've told me that several times.

"Until now I was content to have that be what I needed to know. You are a good father and a good husband too, mother always said."

"Ah yes, your dear departed mother was a saint, and I am grateful for the time we had together."

"Dad, I need to press a little harder here. You are a captive audience. What did you do during the war and where did you do it?"

Karl shifted in the hospital bed and then closed his eyes. "Can you get me a glass of water dear, please," he asked.

Holly poured the water. "Now here it is. Once you've quenched your thirst please tell me about that time."

"Well, you see what I was and who I was is a state secret…"

"Dad, I have to interrupt. A state secret, but of which state? I assume you mean the United States, is that right?"

Karl looked relieved. "Yes darling, I was an in-place espionage agent for the Americans during the war. In fact, Colonel Donovan, the head of the OSS, personally hired me because of my German language skills. I was attending MIT in the 1930s and I was studying there with other Germans from the Physics Institute in Berlin."

"So, when the war started you went back to Germany and worked there as an American agent? Wasn't that dangerous? You could have been found out and shot."

"It was always in the back of my mind, Holly. I have never told anyone else of my role. In a bit of irony Hitler himself hailed me as a hero of the Reich. He once gave me a medal."

"You have just blown my mind, as the teenagers say father. I must say that I need time to digest all this. Maybe when we are back in Wellfleet we can talk more about all this. But you mentioned that you had a call earlier, before you fell in the shop, from someone. What was that all about?"

"That call and my background are both interconnected my dear. This woman, the one who called, told me that she needs to have me investigate something, an item from long ago, that might be hidden here on Cape Cod."

"But she does not know that you were an American agent does she? How can you be sure that she is not coming to seek revenge for what you did during the war? Old hatreds die hard, father."

"She is someone who knew my colleagues. She is on a mission. I will give her what I think she is after. It may be something she thinks is valuable but I know it is not. I am not so foolish to give away my own secrets. Those I will take to the grave."

"Father, Cape Cod, that's a long way from Germany isn't it? Mind telling me what the connection is?"

"Yes dear. I will but I need to have a few minutes rest if you will allow that. You see I am tired now and I need to close my eyes. Please have the nurse come in as you leave. I think I will take that pain medicine that she offered me earlier."

"Are you sure, because I can get the pill and bring it in to you. Is that all right?"

"Actually I want to see that beautiful buxom nurse, the one who was here earlier. She makes me feel good," Karl said.

"Father, you are getting better I can tell. Let me get her and I will go to the cafeteria for a small snack. I can be back in a few minutes."

"Take your time Holly, please. I am here and going to be here as you can see. All these wires and tubes have me tied down to the bed. So please go and enjoy a respite. Perhaps even get a small bite to eat?"

"Perhaps, but hospitals have a reputation for food that is not the best, as you know."

"*Ja*, I know but you need some food. Go there. Be slow in coming back, I will be fine."

Karl closed his eyes, and fell into a fitful sleep, muttering in German.

Holly walked down the hallway past the nurse's station. She stopped to tell the charge nurse where she was going and how long she would be gone. The nurse nodded but she was staring intently at a page full of handwritten notes. If she heard she did not seem to say.

The cafeteria was uncrowded. It was an odd time of day. The lunch crowd has cleaned out much of the hot food. What was left was overly wilted and steamed. It looked unappetizing. Holly got a candy bar and a cup of very strong coffee. She sat down at one of the tables near the window. Pulling the candy bar's wrapper down she felt the presence of a tall woman standing nearby, over her table. She seemed anxious to say something. Holly turned and faced her.

"Are you by any chance Holly? The daughter of Karl Wallace?" the woman said. "Pardon me for interrupting while you're eating. If you would like me to come back later I can."

Holly waved to an empty seat at her table. "Please sit down, and yes I am his daughter, how do I know you?"

"I am a distant friend, if that is the correct way to say it. My father, Werner and your father were former comrades long ago. I'm Harriett Rasmussen by the way." She thrust out her hand.

"Nice to meet you. How did you happen to know that my father was here in the hospital? He arrived by ambulance less than three hours ago, and I assumed that no one knew where he was or why. We did not tell anyone else."

"Holly, if you don't mind me calling you that, I called your father at his shop earlier today."

"Well, that is a real coincidence. He told me about the call when we were coming here in the ambulance. He also said that you had asked him for help. I wasn't sure exactly what you needed or what you wanted him to do. Can you tell me?"

Harriett looked out the window at the traffic jam building on Main Street. "Actually I would rather speak with your father, since it's a sensitive matter. I guess you'll have to trust me on this."

"Harriett, I am willing to trust you. But in my opinion and also the opinion of the doctors, my father is not able to have visitors at the moment, and might not be for a while. Can't this wait?"

"Holly, yes it can wait. Let me give you my card, and when your father feels up to it then he can give me a call." She stood to leave.

"Wait, I see you're with the FBI? Is this some kind of national security thing? If it is and my father is in trouble I'd like to know about it. And I want to get a lawyer before I say anything else.

"Don't you folks need to inform people that you're feds before you start a discussion? I have to tell you I am not at all pleased with what's happening here, Miss Rasmussen."

"I understand that you are under a lot of strain right now. I must tell you that your father is not going to be arrested. He is not implicated in any crimes. I just wanted to speak with him about the good old days. No other reason at all."

"That'd ridiculous. Why would an FBI agent merely want to chat with a stranger? I am not going to say anything more to you. I suggest, Miss Rasmussen that you go through proper channels before you try to interrogate my father or me. Please wait for my lawyer's call."

"Holly, wait. It was not going to be an interrogation…"

"And, another thing. How did you find me and him? Were you doing some kind of undercover thing in Wellfleet and here too?"

"That's not our style Holly, not at all. J. Edgar Hoover is long gone and it is a new decade. We're good for America and mindful of the Constitution as well."

"Save that speech for someone who believes it," Holly said. "As I said, if you have any more questions take it up with our lawyer. Here is his name, I'm sure you can find him given your resources."

Holly stood up and left her coffee and the candy on the table. Harriett held out her hand but Holly refused to shake it. Heading for the nearest phone, she called her attorney.

Harriett Rasmussen smiled and continued to look out the window. There was plenty of time to make this all work, she thought. Just a minor setback, nothing more. Holly was hot-headed, under a lot of stress. She would eventually see the error of her ways. Harriett considered making her less comfortable, and dismissed the idea as premature. After all it had been decades, so what did a few more days matter? She sat at the table and waited a few minutes. There were hospital personnel who would let her see Wallace. All in good time.

Holly walked back at her father's room. She was surprised to see that he was now fully awake and he had regained some of his color. His nurse was inflating a blood pressure cuff. Karl was protesting that she made it too tight.

"So dad, I see that you're back to your old self," Holly said.

"As soon as this mean-spirited woman leaves I'll be a lot better," Karl said glancing at the nurse.

"Mr. Wallace, you are a fine specimen. You are getting better by the moment. I wanted to ask if you were single?" the nurse said with a wink.

Karl blushed and stammered, "Well, I, no never mind. This is a trick I know just to get me to behave. It's not working, I can assure you."

"Come now sir, after all we've meant to each other. Please tell me you are just kidding."

Karl smiled. "You must be one of us, based on your excellent behavior."

"*Homo Sapiens*, yes I am one of *us*, I mean one of them," the nurse said releasing the pressure and deflating the cuff.

"*Nein*, I meant you are German also, I believe. There are so few of us here on this island."

"Not an island, just a state of mind," the nurse said with a wink.

"May I ask your name?" Karl said politely.

"Edith Goldfarb. That is my name. I thank you for asking."

Karl looked down at his feet and said nothing.

The nurse turned to Holly. "Well, that was a short conversation, I must say. Hope that I didn't say something improper."

"No, in fact you did everything well. I'll fill you in on my father once we're outside the room."

"I can wait, certainly. In the meantime Mr. Wallace, please keep getting better. We will have you out of here in a jiffy. How is that?"

"Fine," Karl said without looking up. "I am not pleased with the hospital at this moment."

The nurse patted him on the arm and left the room.

"Well father, you were rude to that woman, and she was being nice to you, even flirting." Holly touched her father's shoulder.

"She is not like me. I do not feel that she would be a worthy person to be with," Karl said.

"Why, because she has a Jewish sounding name, is that the problem?"

"Holly, please understand that I have made it my life's work to avoid these kinds of people, and..."

"Avoid them? Hardly, father. You have made it clear that you have no use for them merely because they are not like you. What if that nurse were not actually Jewish. That is possible you know. Many people have names like hers but are not."

"It makes no difference to me Holly, none at all. I make my decisions based on my perceptions, on my feelings. No one has the right to change my opinion of what I think or what I do."

"Dad, please understand that my primary concern is that you get better and that you come home soon. We can try to live a normal life, whatever that is. Is that so hard to understand?"

"I am an old man, and I am not that well. What I do is what I do. I never apologize for what and who I am. My life is lived, and my race is nearly run. That is my final remark. Now when can I go home?"

"I'll check and let you know what they have to say. I hope it will be soon. One of your employees has promised to come pick us both up when you are ready."

Karl nodded and turned away. "Can you leave me alone now Holly? I need my sleep." He closed his eyes.

"We need to continue the discussion about that woman, the one who called. She cornered me just now down in the cafeteria. I felt that she was rude, and I told her so. So, if she calls again she will need to go through our family lawyer. I told her that."

Karl nodded that he understood. "She might be persistent, I should warn you. Her call has given me a reason to live. I need to go home and get on with my plan."

"You need to get better. You need to rest. I need to go home."

Holly walked out of the room, and spoke to the nurse for twenty minutes. The nurse patted Holly on the back, telling her she understood. She was familiar with geriatrics, and the patients she dealt with were far more difficult that her father she said.

Harriett Rasmussen was back at her home in Osterville. She called her brother Hans in Germany. It was an expensive thing to do, but she justified the call as necessary.

"Is Hans there?" she asked, trying to filter out the static.

"*Einen moment bitte*," a man said curtly.

"This is Hans, who is this?"

"Harriett this is your dear sister. I am calling from the States."

"Based on the time of day back there you must have important information to impart. Do you wish to call me back on a more secure line?"

"No, I think we can accomplish what we need to without doing that. I am at home now. It has been a strange day."

"How does this change the plan? Not at all I hope."

"It presents just a small change Hans. However, I would like to discuss a new strategy to get where we want to go. You will recall that we heard about father's long lost friend. We heard that he is still here? I have found him and spoken with him by phone. He is willing to assist in the object's identification, which is the good news."

"Wait," Hans said." Is there bad news that you are about to give?"

"Yes and no, actually, since the older man had a health emergency, He is currently in hospital."

"And he is expected to recover I hope. We need him."

"Yes he is doing better I hear. His daughter, a woman named Holly, is the problem. She and I met. She became suspicious of my motivation and has contacted a lawyer now."

"But you are also a lawyer, and you can fix this, I assume?"

"Yes, but it will take time. I do not want to confuse the old man. I know that the longer we wait for his assistance the harder it will be to get the information we desire."

"You should continue on the path even with this new problem. The result has to be the same, regardless. I will brief the committee here and let you know if there are further questions."

"Thank you Hans, I will continue to provide status reports, and call you tomorrow if that is all right."

"Yes, please do," Hans said. He hung up. "Gentlemen," he said to the three men listening in the same room, "We have a problem."

CHAPTER 18

Bud Steinmiller stood at the head of a long polished Mahogany table. He pressed a button on the speakerphone, waiting for a beep that signaled the unit was on. The room was full of people summoned from both the Washington DC area and other locations on the east coast.

"Senator, are you still there?" Bud asked. He leaned closer to the phone.

"Yes, I am, in fact I am on the Vineyard at the moment. I am dealing with a constituent," Senator Cardozo said.

There were a few quiet snickers around the table. The Senator's lifestyle and romantic liaisons were well known. Someone once said that it was required to be a democratic senator from the Bay State.

"Good, wish we were there too," Bud said. "Now we need to discuss something, and I hope this meeting will develop an action plan. I have already briefed folks here about my temporary absence from the program."

"Excuse me, but I came in late," Senator Cardozo said. "Why exactly are you leaving?"

"Sorry, Alex but I was given a specific task by a senior agency person, and I think you may know who I mean, and I need to head up your way for a special project."

"Bud, I sure hope this senior person, whomever that is, knows that we are in the middle of a constitutional crisis. God, we can't be sure the attempt on the president was not done as part of a larger plot by the communists. We have to be ready to respond to whatever they have in mind."

"Senator, I know that our group's mission is tantamount. I never forget that. You and I are cut from the same cloth. We both appreciate what America has done for us. We would both give our lives to protect that freedom that we enjoy.

"We both see the dangers of the new world order, the one that those damned Russians are behind. We know that there are spies everywhere, and only by being in a tight knit group can we work our best."

"Easy Bud," the Senator said. "I was not assailing your patriotism, just making a point about priorities, that's all."

"Senator, as a man who spent years in a rotting Southeast Asian jungle, I can tell you that I have always had priorities in mind, and in everything I have done since. I need not apologize for anything that I have ever done. It was always with my country in mind, but not always at my side."

"Bud, let's start over. I get it. Now please tell me what I've missed."

"Well," Bud said loudly, "I need to go north. North as in Massachusetts. I checked on our person of interest and he and his family are not in Maryland. Someone unknown tossed their house. I might be gone for a while. I've left messages at the normal drops for our clients. Most know the chain of command. We have that contingency down pat. They have the option of either going dormant or using alternate methods."

A hand went up at the table. "Bud, I know you can't tell us how long you'll be gone, but is there at least some way we can contact you if we need you in an emergency?"

"Good question and here's the deal. I am on an assignment where I am completely divorced from anything to do with you all. I need to be scrubbed, to use the vernacular, of all ties. I have Jaime working on my phone records as we speak so our good friends at NSA don't stumble on me for some reason.

"I've also enabled my newest clean address protocol. After the meeting I can give you each one of them, the addresses I mean. I will call in if I need help, so we'll need each of you to take a shift watching the gray phone."

Some members of the group groaned. Another weekend ruined by this new assignment.

Bud cleared his throat, and spoke quickly. "We need make sure that our program continues without me. Right now I'll need an oral status report from each of you on where we stand? Let me know if there are any issues that I can work on before I leave."

Each of the members gave a short summation of his activities. No one had any problems to report. Bud nodded as each took their turn.

"Senator, you must have something to report?" Bud said.

"Well, maybe this is not the venue, but here goes. I had an issue with a reporter, a fellow named Branstead, a while back. Seems he got wind of something we were doing, God knows how. I had a good friend work on him, and hopefully he's been neutralized."

"Did you have him whacked?" Bud asked.

"Doctor you have an evil sense of humor. Were I not as tolerant as I am, I'd be offended by that hateful remark about me and my ancestors."

Bud laughed. "Well Alex, when in Rome, or in this case Sicily…"

Everyone around the table laughed.

"Calm down folks," Cardozo said. "I merely asked my friend to make sure Branstead was put off the trail. I have not seen his byline recently. And to put this to rest, he never appeared in the Washington Post obituaries. So I have to assume my friend solved the issue."

"Maybe," Bud said, "We'll send a party out to that little network and see what he's up to."

'No need. One of my friends, a woman with whom I have had dealings, is on the case. She tells me that he's got a lot on his plate. His mistress is giving him all kinds of shit. Did I mention he's married, not that that makes any difference. He's been worried about his hair color ruining his career. Yes that's what I said, his hair color. Grace, my acquaintance, keeps close tabs on Geoff Branstead for me."

"Amazing Grace. Let's hope that she is as good as you say. No blow-backs on us. I assume you know we need airtight operational security. If word ever got out about what we were doing it would not be a good thing. For most of us it would mean jail time."

"I know that Bud, but thanks for the reminder. Mr. Branstead is or was a minor irritant, as most members of the press can be. I needed to put him on a different trail. I threw him a bone and he ran after it. And to make sure I kept his attention focused elsewhere, I had his life become a little more unsettled."

"We're off topic. What did you do?"

"Bud, you ask the most interesting questions. Branstead is screwing some young chick, Judy somebody. She is half his age. He is also happily married. The young woman was the best way to get to him. We made sure that her normally tranquil life as the whore was more unsettled. That's all."

"Wonderfully done, Alex. Remind me not to cross you. I assume you had a quid pro quo for all this, I mean friends do things for friends, don't they?"

"Bud, what my action man wanted was a very minor favor for a small gambling, no I mean *gaming* concern. Got to get that new word in my head, sorry. Anyway, the *gaming* concern was being hounded by the Feds, specifically the FBI. I just called in a chip with the Assistant Director and we've hopefully solved the problem."

"Solved as in how?"

"Well, Bud, before I can answer that I need to get this cleared up. Then we can chat about how. You know the old saw: It ain't over 'til it's over, and it's not quite over."

"Ok, I got that; we got to keep ourselves on task. That I know. You get a free pass on this one," Bud said. "Now, we need to go over a few other things."

"I might have to cut you off, my constituent needs something," the Senator said.

A female giggled in the background.

"Got that straight, Alex, so go ahead and take care of her, or him. I'll be in touch if we need more." Bud disconnected the speaker phone.

"Well folks, the Senator seems to need time alone with a voter, maybe insert himself in her voting booth, and who are we to interfere with that?" Bud slapped his thigh.

A hand went up at the table. "Bud, are we done here, I need to do some public service."

"Well, aren't we the group of good people?" Bud laughed again. "Let's call it a day. We need to head off to that job we've been doing so well, so long, and keep the faith y'all."

The room emptied out, and Bud gathered some papers, putting them in a manila folder and then stuffing them into his briefcase. He locked the case with a key and then placed the folder in his office safe, spinning the dial five times.

Geoff Branstead held his head in his hands. The day had started off poorly. His mistress was done complaining about the things that were happening to her. In her schoolgirl's handwriting she left him a note that she was leaving. In the note she mentioned that she had told Geoff's wife about their arrangement. Branstead tried to intercept the mail but forgot that Judy Blackadar had his email address at home.

Geoff's wife confronted him. She told him that she would kill him. She tried. He hit her. The police were called. Geoff now had a record of an arrest. The big boys at INN called him in and fired him on the spot. Geoff tried to speak to Nancy but she never returned his calls.

He walked to the Metro station and jumped in front of an oncoming subway train.

Andy Reid waited at the house on Skunk's Neck. The plain sedan arrived and a tall, shapely woman in a very expensive looking outfit got out, straightening her skirt. She walked to the door and rang the bell.

"Harriett Rasmussen, Special Agent FBI, Mr. Reid, glad to meet you," she said shaking Andy's hand.

"Come in and meet the family, Miss…"

"Harriett is fine, and is all right to call you Andy."

"Yes. Harriett, this is my wife Nancy, and our daughter Alicia."

"Nice to meet you both," Harriett said to both women.

"Miss Harriett, do you have a gun," Alicia asked.

"Well honey, I do but I guess it is pretty safe around here, and so no I do not have a gun with me."

"Do you have one sometimes?"

"Yes dear, I do, but not now. How old are you?"

Alicia held up all her fingers. "This many," she said.

"That is lovely my dear. Would it be OK if your mom and dad and I had a chat, maybe just me and them?"

Alicia sighed. "I suppose that would be good, I have things to do in my room," she said. She headed up the polished stairs to her bedroom.

"What a gem she is," Harriet said.

"Sure is. So you may have heard that the least couple days have not been normal, in fact they've been shitty for her and for us too," Nancy said.

Andy added, "Yeah, Nancy and I are tired of being targeted for no good reason. You may know that this has been going on for a long time with us, over a decade. I feel I am in some kind of time warp, the kind where you can't get out."

"Yes, I get that, Andy and Nancy too. I wish I could tell you that it's going to get better, but…"

"But, that is a word I hear a lot these days. I don't like the sound of but," Andy said, and Nancy nodded she agreed.

"The however I was going to mention is that there are forces at play here in little Chatham that might be canceling each other out, I can't be sure. You and your family are caught in the middle."

Nancy spoke, "Are you telling me, are you telling us I mean, that what's been happening is not really specifically aimed at us? You heard I am sure that the incident downtown nearly had my daughter and I killed? I would call that more than an accident."

"Mrs. Reid, I concur that they, whoever they are, are people who use whatever means they can to get their way. Violence is their favored tactic, and that's why we're seeing this carnage."

"I don't get it," Andy said. "If we are at home in Maryland we get the house tossed, as if someone is looking for something there. We come here and the violence follows us. I'd say that makes us the target."

"Mr. and Mrs. Reid, let me be clear and at the same time a little evasive. What we've got is a national security issue here. That is as far as I can go without getting myself and you in trouble. It is of major national importance, I can assure you, and were I not sworn to secrecy…"

"Pardon me for stating the obvious Harriett, but that's pure bullshit! I have been a victim of this so-called national security crap for a long time. People hide behind that curtain to do very bad things sometimes illegal things. I've seen it happen many times. I hate to admit it but I have been a willing member of that group too."

"Point made and taken. We're in a hot period in the so-called Cold War just now. I can tell you that the shooting of President Reagan put us all on high alert."

Nancy interrupted. "But they have that kid in custody, the one who did it, so what is the big deal? He was a loner from what I hear."

"Maybe, or maybe not. He seems to be a lunatic, a fringe player. I would remind you that Lee Harvey Oswald fit that same mold. We are in a forward in the foxhole mode right now. Everyone's worried there are others out there with similar motives. Copycats.

"What I am trying to get at is this. Shooting a chief of state is never a small matter. When it happens there is a look back at all the leads that precede the event. We know that the Russians have cells here in the US, most of them dormant. Key events can bring them back into play."

"You think this was a Soviet plot to shoot the guy? Well, that is a new enemy that I never thought I'd be facing." Andy laughed.

"Let's get down to your level, the Reid family if we can. I'll leave the national scene to my higher ups. My sources, and there are many, tell me that there is a contract out on your life Andy. What they can't tell me is who is making that offer, and who gets paid if they are successful. Is it the Russians? Maybe. Maybe they are using a cutout, a third party, to get the job done. We always suspected that the KGB was behind things, but that they never did anything that could be traced back to them. That way, when an operation falls apart and the bad guy or guys get caught, their hands are clean."

"Still seems far-fetched," Andy said.

"Andy, I know that this is a very sensitive subject. If I could make this all go away I would. You have to trust me. I can and will get to the bottom of this. I've got one other thing to mention. Seems that the folks at FBI headquarters have taken a real, some might say obsessive interest in you and this little town. Normally here on the Cape we get the run of the mill stuff."

"Like beat up home mail boxes?" Andy asked.

"No I meant the occasional bank robbery, actually."

"Well," Nancy said, "We know less now than when you walked in the door. I for one want to figure out who is behind these attacks. I really want your assurance that they'll stop."

Harriett listened patiently, "In law enforcement just like life there are no absolutes Mrs. Reid, and that's a fact. Nonetheless, I want to get to the ground truth here and put somebody in cuffs before too long."

The door opened and Wanda Brixton came in, smiling,

"Did I hear someone mention handcuffs? Wow is that a way to check in on a conversation or what? If you folks want some alone time I can just go upstairs. By the way I can scrounge up a few pair in various sizes and colors."

"Wanda this is FBI agent Harriett, what was your last name, I forgot?"

"Rasmussen, Harriett Rasmussen, pleased to meet you. I know you hear this a lot but have I met you somewhere before, maybe it was overseas? You last name is?"

Wanda grimaced. "Wanda Brixton. It might have been that since Dad was an Army lifer. We lived all over."

"Germany perhaps, maybe that was where?" Harriett said.

"Lived outside Stuttgart for a while when I first started college. I was only there on my holidays."

"He was stationed at Vaihingen is that right?"

"Yeah, that's right. How about you, are you an Army kid too?"

"No Wanda, my Dad, who was a native German. He worked near there. Place was called Wiesengrund, I think."

Wanda grinned. "That's interesting, I've never been but there are lots of places in good old West Germany that I need to see sometime. Maybe even East Germany, if they ever tear down that wall."

"Hopefully that will happen in our lifetimes. Our president seems to be challenging the Russians at every turn. Maybe it will come, and hopefully without too much turmoil." Harriett stood to leave.

Andy said, "Are you leaving? You just got here. Isn't there more that we need to discuss?"

"No, I have other cases, though as I mentioned this is number one. My pager just buzzed. I need to get to a phone to call headquarters."

"Harriett, we have phones here," Nancy said. "Use one of ours if you'd like."

"Thank you Mrs Reid, but I need to make this a secure call and unless you have a phone that is, I must get back to Hyannis."

Andy smiled. "We used to have one back in the day. The line is still there. They removed the box after the second Stepping Stones debacle. It's a long story, but the Agency put it in. Then they unceremoniously took it out. The tech guys from the air force banged the door jamb going in and coming out."

Nancy stood and followed Harriett over to the front door. "Nice to meet you, but as you can imagine, we're still pretty shaken about what happened downtown. I have bad feelings about our future too. I don't want to make our daughter part of that. So, anything you can do would be great. I'll show you out."

Harriett Rasmussen walked to the door and said farewell. Wanda watched Harriett get in her government car and drive away.

"You know folks, that woman is a fraud," Wanda said.

"Nancy and I saw her FBI credentials. That's hard to fake."

"Andy, what I am saying is that she might be an agent but she's not telling the whole truth, not even part of it."

Nancy said, "And you know this how? Is it intuition, clairvoyance, x-ray vision, or something else?"

"All of the above Nancy. Did you notice her reaction when I asked about Germany? Her hesitancy after the question I asked and the answer she gave is the clue."

"Well," Andy said, "Clue me in if you will. I can't recall anything unusual in what she said."

"OK, here goes, Andy. She mentioned about her dad being a German citizen but not much more. It was a half-truth. If he indeed worked at Wiesengrund he might be or have been a war criminal. That place was used by the Nazis for slave labor, and they sent undesirables there to help build Luftwaffe airplanes."

"Wanda, that's a big leap even for you. He might have been at Nuremburg and not found guilty for all we know."

"Right Andy, but here's the kicker. What is her last name?"

Andy looked at the business card she had given him. "Rasmussen. Hey, that's the same last name as the fellow that I tried to save in Garmisch. But there must be plenty of Rasmussen's in Germany, like Smith around here."

"You recall that his son, according to what you told us at the site, was able to be alone with his father. And that the son seemed nervous that you might not give him time with his father?"

"That's natural. Especially since the old man was almost gone," Andy said.

"Full disclosure Andy and Nancy too. The entire Rasmussen family has been on our radar for the last two decades, since the 1960's. They are…"

"Wait," Nancy said. "Exactly who is the '*our*' in *our* radar? Can you be a lot more specific?"

"OK it's come clean time for Wanda. We are part of a task force that operates to find unrepentant Nazis and other war criminals. These Nazis are a dwindling bunch. Due to their advanced age we have little time left to bring them to justice. A complicating factor is that some of our own government types in the immediate post-war period decided that the best and brightest, no matter what their crimes, should get out of jail free and not pay the required two hundred dollars."

"Wanda, when I first met you near DC you were part of an organization, right, the one that made life miserable for me. Was that the same one?"

"No Andy, I was just a plant there and a good one until you got there. I was sent to investigate the depths of the conspiracy…"

"Slow down, please. What conspiracy," Nancy asked.

"The condensed version is that I was given access to the site by a person who shall remain nameless, but Andy knows the person. He, that person, was able to bypass the usual background checks and get me in. You know that fellow, Bill Leonard, the interrogator you met and who escorted you outside our facility to make the call home?"

"Yeah, I do remember him, was he in on this?"

"Sort of, and I am being vague on purpose here. See, we always compartmentalize in my group. We never know who is really with us and who is not."

"Go on, yes I remember him, Leonard I mean."

"His boss and my boss was a randy old Colonel, a man named Jackson, who was the guy I was looking into. He knew my dad from the Army. I was sure he was a paper shuffler who managed to spring a lot of Nazis during those hectic days after the peace came in 1945."

Andy said, "What was his motivation? Was he following orders? Was he a closet Nazi?"

"Dear old Jackson, Andrew Jackson ironically, had the simplest of motives, He was in it for the money. Seems that Jackson discovered some of the German scientists got paid in stolen art during the war. Remember that Hitler looted the galleries of occupied Europe. He intended to build a museum of fine art in Austria. He even had Albert Speer work up a design and a model. Pure Nazi grandiose style of course.

"In exchange for these felons getting a free pass Jackson accepted some of that art work. It was hectic after the Reich fell, stuff was shipped back to the states by ship. No one thing cleared customs. With the right stamps of approval this art could have ended up anywhere. My bet is that Jackson still has the art stashed somewhere. When he finds the right buyer, someone who wants to have it and not be known, he'll live an excellent lifestyle."

"Good old fashioned greed. At least that makes sense. Where is the good colonel these days? In jail I hope."

"Nope Andy, he's still in place at the site up at the Pennsylvania border. I mean we have to find a trustworthy attorney at the department of justice to bring him to trial."

"That might be hard." Nancy said. "Seems that everyone who is involved with this mess, hopefully excluding you, is a potential double agent. Have I gone mad or is that true?"

"Nope, you're not mad, you are just suspicious like I am. My dad instilled in me the need to trust but verify. I have never forgotten that edict. He died trying to right wrongs, and I guess I feel that I am following in his footsteps."

Andy spoke up. "You think Harriett is in on this Nazi protection thing?"

"Who can say? In my book everyone is a potential target. She may be FBI but that means little to me."

"Wanda, so back to Harriett. What do we do next?"

"Glad you asked. I think we need to set a little trap. You game Andy?"

"Sounds like I don't have a choice," Andy replied.

Bud Steinmiller waited smoking outside the Hyannis Airport, He was tired but ready. He checked his watch. He wondered where and when his car would arrive and who would be driving. A series of airport drive-by lookers passed by, hoping to catch someone just out of baggage claim. Bud had everything he needed in an overnight bag. It was a practice from his army grab and go days. As he turned to go back in the terminal for a second, someone honked and waved him over to their car.

"Hey buddy," the driver called out through a mostly closed window, "You lost?"

"Nah, just waiting for a ride that's all," Bud said looking to his right and his left.

The driver slid down his window and pointed a very large pistol directly at Bud. "Guess then you'd better be comin' with me, old friend."

Bud walked slowly to the car, and finding the rear door locked slid in beside the driver. "Hey, you have the upper hand. Mind introducing yourself?"

"Names are nothin' Bud old boy. They're just ways to catch folks and you ain't gonna catch me so let's do without 'em OK?"

"Whatever, but where are we headed. I was going to…"

"Same place I am old fiend, dear old Chat-Ham as the natives refer to it. Do I have to cuff you to the door or are you gonna behave?"

"Docile and a man of compassion, that's me, mister unknown name. Docile as can be."

"I like that buddy, so let's motor on down the mid-Cape to your final destination.

The car pulled into the traffic circle and they headed east toward the village of Chatham. Bud discretely pulled at the catch on his watch and depressed a tiny button, sending an SOS to his group that he was in trouble.

CHAPTER 19

Karl Wallace was restless. He was waiting for his daughter Holly to go outside. He secretly wanted her to leave him alone. He'd been on bed rest for a few days after his trip to the hospital. He knew that he had to complete at least one more mission, even if that caused him bodily harm.

He sat up and made sure that Holly's car was gone. Dressing slowly and painfully, Karl stood at the edge of his bed. He searched for his spare set of keys, the ones that Holly never knew about.

He walked slowly to the garage door and with effort pulled it up. His chest hurt a lot from the effort but Karl was stoic. He held onto the doorjamb for a second and let the crushing feeling pass. He was perspiring heavily, something that he almost never did. He wiped his brow.

Getting in his car Karl had difficulty turning the key, and he cursed softly, knowing that the engineer in Stuttgart who designed the ignition was a fool. He should have known that older people also drive these kinds of Mercedes.

Backing out of his driveway, he was distracted by the sun in his eyes and ran over his own mailbox. There was a scraping sound as Karl inched forward over the wooden box, leaving it shattered on the street.

"Later," he said, "I will deal with that later."

Karl drove off, the car spewing a cloud of white diesel exhaust and loud rattling. The car lurched forward. He knew where he had to go and what he had to do. He needed to get there and do that before anyone else found out.

Route 6 was not crowded. Karl drove faster than the posted limit. He was nearing the Orleans merge when a police car pulled up behind and turned on its flashing lights, signalling him to pull over.

Karl was normally a rule follower. In this case he knew that stopping for any reason, even for a citation, would be dangerous. It might derail his plan. He pulled over and waited patiently in his car until the officer was nearing him on foot from behind. Pulling the Mercedes into reverse, he backed up knocking the officer to the ground. Karl screeched out of the parking lot and continued on his quest.

The officer crawled slowly to his car. He pulled himself up to the door handle. He called in a description of the car with a partial plate number before he collapsed again. He was bleeding and passed out. Cars drove by not bothering to stop, headed for something, somewhere.

Karl's large car headed down Route 28, the two lane road that connects Orleans to Chatham, about 11 miles, most of it hugging the coastline. There were few cars. Karl drove in the middle of the two lanes to gain speed.

He felt dizzy and pulled over behind a weather beaten boatyard to rest. A convoy of local and State police cars roared by in the opposite direction, the one from which he had come. He waited five minutes until he could not hear their sirens any more and then pulled out again.

His final destination was less than five minutes away, but over forty years in fruition. It was the culmination of many things. Karl felt relieved and enthused that he was back on duty.

"We are nearly there, Werner," Karl said to no one but himself, "Now if we can remember the location, we will make good on that promise that I made you long ago."

He coughed and the wiped his eyes. He narrowly missed an oncoming car. The other driver, seeing the old man, merely gave him the Cape Cod wave: hands just slightly off the wheel, signalling no malice intended.

Karl pulled slowly into the smaller street, the one with the Indian name, Scatteree. What an odd name, he thought then as now. He stopped in the middle of the street. He closed his eyes and slouched down. He began to dream.

Maps from American mapmakers were not clear about this elbow of land, this part of Massachusetts. Memories flooded back.

Spies sent in the newest U-Boats to reconnoiter the coastline had more luck measuring the depth of the shoals and judging the quality of the sand for a potential amphibious landing. Measuring inlet widths was beyond their capability.

It was Werner who suggested that some kind of overflight, perhaps in a manned but unarmed plane would do the best job of mensuration of these ground targets and features.

One of the most ambitious, but technically unskilled people that the Nazis brought in suggested making a faux American airliner from scratch. Karl pointed out that with the war in full swing very few people had the luxury of getting on a plane in America. He pointed out that the majority of air travellers were now government or military personnel.

Ironically, it was that idea of using an airliner that began the mission. An intermediate decided to turn to the Horten family. They had worked on advanced projects, most of which were designed but never built.

The team developed a blueprint for a radical new design. The plane was transported in a disguised freighter to North America, then launched in secret from an ice covered Canadian runway to overfly the United States.

Karl Schultz and Werner Rasmussen were hailed as saviours of the Reich. They were the men who would finally bring the allies to their knees. It was a grand send-off from the factory near Stuttgart, even though the top tier of Nazis decided not to attend.

Perhaps, Werner mused, they were not willing to give credit for the mission to the two scientists unless and until it was successful. It was the way of the Nazi regime and to be expected. It was the standard in the Third Reich—do nothing that is risky. Always appear at the moment of success to claim credit.

Werner and Karl met the third member of their mission, their pilot. Karl had long forgotten his name. He was a poster boy of Reich aviators. He had been flying the ME 262 *Schwalbe*, the two engine jet nicknamed 'the Swallow' that was about to become operational. He had actually pulled the new Horten out of a potentially deadly stall on his last check-out flight.

Standing tall before they headed via train to the north coast, the three men had different worldviews. Karl recalled it as if it were yesterday.

He and Werner were playing a dangerous game, a tightrope walk between keeping the Nazi brass enthralled with the potential of their work, while at the same time, feeding their contacts within the underground information that could blunt the efforts.

Werner was a pragmatist. There was science and there was politics. He left the politics to Karl, but asked frequently what was going on. Where they intersected there was bound to be conflict.

Karl was also a realist. His time in the United States strengthened his belief that the Nazi's were fools, albeit very dangerous ones. He never told Werner that he was a plant, a double working for the OSS. Werner never asked. To speak about these things, they both knew would be certain death if overheard. Maybe, Karl mused, Werner knew.

Karl knew that Werner was a scientist at heart. He at one time feared that Werner's love of progress had no moral compass. In addition to all his other tasks relayed from the Allies, Karl knew he had to keep Werner focused on the larger task, the need to ensure that whoever won the war, they would not be punished or deported.

Karl contacted the SS commander at the forced labor camp near Stuttgart where the plane's slave laborers were. He told him to round up the pilot's young wife and children and keep them at the camp until the mission was complete.

Taking the young flier aside, Karl told him that he had better comply with whatever he, not Werner, told him or his family would die a painful death.

"What would you have me do?" the frightened aviator said.

Karl placed both hands on the man's shoulders and said, "You and I are going to be players in a grand drama. My good friend. Werner is not quite as willing as I am to put on a false face. I fear that he might actually do what the Nazi's want us to do. I do not think that is a good idea, do you?"

Bewildered, the pilot agreed. He said nothing more.

"I am a man of the world, young man. I can see the value in what we are doing but I fear that it will tip the scales in favor of these Nazi fellows. They are not nice people as you know."

"But you seem to accept their accolades sir, if I may be allowed to comment. You use their SS henchmen too."

"Point taken young man, yes I do. My ultimate goal is survival of my family and myself. I have made provisions for them, and for me. This mission is part of that plan. Do you understand what I am saying?"

"Clear as can be sir. I am concerned that I will never see my family alive again. That is my only concern," the pilot said.

"You are doing a great service for the Reich and for science by taking this on. I will not ask you to demonstrate your allegiance to the National Socialists, nor do I care. Your allegiance for the near term is only to me, not to them. If you follow my instructions to the letter then your family will be safe and you will be reunited with them." Karl sat down in the mocked up cockpit of the Horten.

"Sir, I pledge that I will follow your orders, I really do. I am a German citizen. But I am not a political one. I had to join the party to get into the Luftwaffe. That the extent of my affiliation. You must understand that I grew up with Herr Hitler's words in my mouth but not in my heart."

"No need to grovel, young man. As you know it is dangerous to have these kinds of thoughts anywhere in Germany. I need your assurance that you will never speak of this to anyone anywhere. If you hesitate and cannot give me that assurance I will have to deal with your family," Karl said with no emotion.

"I swear on the honor of my family that I will never speak of these things."

"Good, now you must show me the controls of this aircraft since I will be your copilot."

"I was not aware that you had training in these jets," the pilot said.

"I have learned many things in my life, young man and this will be another for me."

The pilot blanched. "You mean you've never…"

"Never flown an airplane, yes. That is what I meant. But, my faculties are all in wonderful shape, I have an idetic memory, and besides, how hard could this be? I am an accomplished designer of advanced weaponry so I have had much interaction with pilots and weapons engineers. This is not that foreign to me."

"No offense sir, and no need to convince me," the pilot said. "I was merely commenting that the plane is designed for two pilots, and there are few of us in the Luftwaffe with experience in these new jet type engine aircraft. Since we have no tail the plane behaves unlike all other aircraft in the Luftwaffe. It sometimes seems to want to do things I do not want it to do."

Karl laughed. "You, young man will be astonished at the degree to which I can learn about the plane and its characteristics. I am a quick learner. I designed many of the rockets that the fatherland used on the British people. What the Nazis do not know is that I also made sure the final guidance mechanism was slightly off target."

"I am even more impressed now," the pilot said giving Karl a salute.

"Now, let us begin my indoctrination, and then in a few weeks we shall begin our mission."

The pilot nodded that he agreed and they opened a large sheaf of blueprints.

Karl awoke from his dream. He was startled awake by a knock on his car window. "What," he said loudly.

"Hey Mister, just checking to see that you're alive. Sorry that I startled you," a uniformed young man said. "You know we can't be responsible if someone rear ends you almost in the middle of the road. Want to pull the vehicle off the road?"

"*Ja*, I am sorry officer," Karl said. I was dozing off."

"Maybe sir, you'll want to show me your license and registration then sir. Please stay in the car, if you don't mind."

"But officer…"

"Eldredge, Barry Eldredge. I am sort of acting chief of police around here, and you are?"

"I am a jeweler. I have a shop over in Wellfleet. My name is Schultz, I mean Wallace. I am a naturalized citizen and sometimes, due to my age, I even forget my name."

"Sir, have you been drinking? Reasonable folks don't forget their name, do they? How about I give you a roadside sobriety test? It won't take long." Eldredge put his hand on the Mercedes door handle.

Reaching into his pocket Karl pulled out a small flashlight type object and aimed it at officer Eldredge's chest, sending a strong electric pulse directly into his chest. The policeman fell to the ground convulsing.

"Sorry my good friend, but I am on a mission. Most likely you will awaken in a few hours and have no memories of my being here," Karl said to the still convulsing officer on the ground.

Driving off he rolled up his car's window. Now it was time to look for the marker that he had left years before. Driving into Chatham's outskirts, Karl was pleased to see that he remembered the code that he had used to recall where the special item was.

He counted the telephone poles along Cedar Street, and then pulled into a small clearing; one that had been mowed recently, and cleared of most of the invasive small trees and brush. A wooden sign suggested that the land was for sale and inquiries were invited.

Karl left his car. He pulled the sign out of the ground. "This is not for sale, now or ever," he said. He stepped on the sign.

He walked thirty paces until he found a small depression in the ground. Using only his hands, he scooped at the sandy soil, looking for that box, or what might remain of it.

CHAPTER 20

Nancy and Alicia packed their car. She waved goodbye to Andy. This after a series of tender hugs and explanations to their young child that Daddy needed to do something. Andy told Alicia he would see her soon. Alicia did not cry but hugged her Steiff bear very tightly, Nancy buckled her into the back seat of the car.

"Babe, it won't be long and with the help of these two folks, I think we can flush out the people who want to do me harm," Andy said.

"Andy, this is déjà vu, you know that. We've had this conversation twice since we've been married. It gets harder every time to believe you. Just me thinking out loud, and you know that I say what I mean, and I don't hold back," Nancy said.

Andy held her tight and whispered, "I can't guarantee much about our future. But I can tell you I love you and always have. I know that this is dangerous but I want to end this crap now and forever. You know that you only get so many chances to make things right, and I guess I think this is my chance.

"I never choose to be involved. My life seems to be the jump from problem to problem. I am sorry for that. I hope you understand. And I never want to leave you and Alicia ever again."

"Andy, I sure hope you're right. I guess being from German stock I am naturally distrustful, and sorry that I am. I see the world as absolutes and you see shades of gray. But that makes us a good couple, right?"

Alicia stirred in her car seat. "Mommy you said we were leaving. Stop kissing Daddy and let's go. My bear is having a nervous breakdown."

Andy smiled. "Where does she hear these things? God she is one funny and very bright kid."

"Not from schoolmates since she got pulled out to come here. Maybe from watching TV?"

"Guess we'll need to unplug that too, she might be having Sesame Street nightmares," Andy said kissing Nancy hard.

"I'm off. I'll call once we get to where we're headed. I love you even though you are a terrible husband." Nancy pinched Andy on the arm.

"Later my dear and I promise we'll get this over with and soon, so fret not, OK?"

Wanda Brixton and Albert Rosales watched them from the second story windows of the Skunk's Neck house. Wanda turned around and looked at the wall facing the ocean.

You know Wanda you need to get Andy Reid out of your head. He is married with a kid. He's trying to get through this. The last thing he needs is you complicating his life."

"Albert, you are a wise man. Being wise does not mean that you are right. I have feelings for him, and don't know why they are so strong. I will try to control myself. Andy seems receptive sometimes…"

"Wanda, go and take several cold showers, will you. You are a beautiful woman, very sexy and definitely more than a little sultry. Quite a catch I'd say if I were interested, which by the way, I am not."

"Albert, I have to admit that I have and had feelings for Andy. I tried, unsuccessfully I'll admit to make some progress with him. But he seems happily married, and he told me that once, back at that place we had him corralled."

"What about here, you must have had some chances to get him aroused here in town, maybe at the house while Nancy was away?"

"Yep, that happened I will admit. Again he seemed not really receptive."

So," Albert said, "We've got a contract that you'll keep yourself under control? Promise that and we're good to go, whatever happens."

"I promise," Wanda said crossing her heart and smiling.

"OK, now let's get crackin' as we say in the airline business, or at least I do," Albert said, slapping Wanda on the behind.

Andy, Wanda and Albert sat in the living room. Andy was rubbing his forehead. His headache from getting worse. Wanda stood and began to walk over to sit next to Andy on the couch, but Albert pulled her back, so she sat opposite Andy.

"All right, we have a plan of sorts, don't we?" Andy asked.

Wanda shifted, pulling one leg under her, a message for Albert that she was going to stay put for a while.

"Andy, first we need to get word that Nancy and Alicia are safe and sound. Then once we know that we'll need to see where Harriett Rasmussen is and keep her at bay. Maybe I should do that?"

"Nah let me handle her, "Albert said. "My job is customer service and she looks like a sucker for my charm and good looks."

"Good enough," Wanda said. "Andy, you and I will need to work independently to get over to Scatteree and see what we can find."

"What's my thing?" Andy asked. "I am stupid about these operational things. Just ask anyone who's had to clean up my messes. Damn it, I was hoping that you two could be the front men and I'd just be in the background. Like the dummy."

"Hey buddy, you're not stupid at all. We're gonna need you to brush up on your acting skills, maybe with the help of a little makeup, so we can fool a bunch of folks."

"You have the 'con' dear Wanda, and yes I will be a willing participant. Right now I need an aspirin for this throbbing headache. Soon as Nancy calls, get me right away because I am gonna lay down in our bedroom."

"Sure Andy," Albert said, "Wanda and I need to confer anyway."

Andy walked up the steps and went to his bedroom. He closed his door. He waited for a call from his family.

Wanda stood and walked to the front door. Pushing open the screen she looked left and right, then sniffed the air. "Hey Albert," she said, "I think we may have some problems downtown, based on what I am smelling and not hearing."

"Do tell, what exactly is going on, super sleuth?"

"Well, the street out at the main junction is obviously barricaded since no cars have gone past us in the last ten minutes, and there is faint chemical odor in the air, something that may be dangerous."

"Since I don't have a gas mask you're gonna have to be more specific dear girl."

"Well, call me inquisitive. It seems someone is using tear gas in the area, or at least something smelling like tear gas."

"And guess what, you're going to say, nothing smells like it, isn't that right?"

"Not in my experience, that is for sure."

"So what next? Please help me Wanda," Albert said with a smirk.

"Not another Beach Boys song title joke. Do you know how many of them I have heard in my lifetime?"

"Plenty I am sure, but now tell me what is going on, as far as you can tell?"

"Nothing good I can assure you. Let's get lover boy out of bed if we can. We all have work to do."

Albert smiled, "I don't want to get him too excited so you better do it"

Wanda walked upstairs. She found Andy passed out on the bathroom floor.

Noreen Caruso and James Dunlap stared at the muscular-looking stranger in their office. He was holding a large revolver and pointing it at them. The windows of the Chatham Permit Office were shuttered and the door to the office was now locked.

"So, my undercover friends, at long last we meet," the stranger said waving the pistol back and forth.

"We are at a loss here, sir. If you introduce yourself maybe we can settled whatever this is about without bloodshed," James Dunlap raised his hands in surrender.

"My name is not important, but you can call me Bud, that's my *nom d guerre* this week. Let's just say that we've been looking for both of you for a long time. I must admit that we were searching everywhere and found you in this little hamlet out in the ocean. Isn't that bizarre?"

"Why us, what have we done?" Noreen said.

"Other than being active clandestine agents for the USSR, you mean?" Bud Steinmiller said.

"Preposterous. Both this lady and I are proud Americans, you can check our records. We are certainly not Soviet or Russian agents," James said.

"According to my sources, God I love saying that, sounds like I am Dan Rather or something. They tell me you Boris and little Miss Natasha here are plants. You are deep cover Russians in a sleeper cell. I hear that you were just activated for a search mission here in the village."

"Pure fantasy, Bud, if I can call you that. We're coworkers and nothing more," James replied.

"And comrade Dunlap you're screwing this little comrade too, I suppose for the good of the mission and the motherland? Don't deny it, your spouses may or may not know and I am certainly not going to tell them. You can do that if you wish before going to Boston and speaking with the federal authorities there."

"We're certainly not going to be deported are we? Even if what you say is true, we are owed due process," Noreen said.

"Love those legal defenses you guys mount as if you actually thought they applied to you. For starters we have enough evidence on you to get you on the next plane to Russia. Aeroflot, that masking taped together airline of yours, can whisk you out of New York back to Moscow. That is after we make a swap."

"Swap of what, or whom?" James Dunlap asked.

"Not your concern comrade, you just need to know that the folks in DC and Moscow see you as trade bait, that's all. By the way, people tell me that other Russians have been trailing you. They've heard you make a few unpatriotic comments. That being the case, you might want to make final arrangements before heading home to Soviet justice. Just a small warning."

Dunlap and Caruso looked at the floor, saying little.

"Well, no confessions? No they-made-me-do-it excuses?"

"Shoot us now please and get it over with," Noreen said. "We'd be better off anyway. We'll be tortured in Russia. It will be a slow and painful death."

"That's too easy. It violates my sense of propriety, sir and madam. We are in the same business, you and me. There's an unwritten rule—the spies work against each other but we never shoot to kill, just thwart, and if that results in death, then so be it. I'd rather see you both rotting in one of our federal prisons, ratting out the others in your ring, but that's not my call. You will be featured in all the papers as soon as we get to Boston so you might want to be presentable. Put on some make up and all that," Bud said waving them to the door.

James Dunlap jumped and reached for Bud's gun. It was an easy move for Bud. He killed Dunlap with a shot to the center of his chest. Noreen did not try the same thing. Bud turned and shot her in the forehead.

"So much for those alleged spy versus spy nonviolence accords," Bud said pushing the two bodies to the center of the room.

Picking up the office phone and dialing 911, Bud held a handkerchief over the mouthpiece, and excitedly reported about hearing shots at the Chatham Permit Office. He then placed the gun in Dunlap's hand.

Wiping off anything he had touched he walked outside the office, closing the door behind him.

CHAPTER 21

Chester Billings and Herman Banks hid near the Scatteree dig site. They were hoping that the darkness would give them some cover. They first had stopped at Chester's house. They found nothing but old moldy food in the refrigerator and a mess in every room. Chester's girlfriend Bonnie never came back to the house. That much was clear.

"Well, Chester my friend, you've got a clear shot at greatness now. Dear Bonnie done cleared out. Seems you've got a nice house, sort of. Now you are going to give me what I want. And you're gonna forget that you ever met me, aren't you," Banks said.

"Yeah sure, my memory is piss poor about faces and names must be all that diesel that I inhale all the time."

"Not to mention all that booze," Banks said.

"Man like I said, I ain't gonna spill no beans, now or never."

"I get it, Chester, and if you play along, you'll do well," Banks said.

"I am a man of my word, you ask anybody, anywhere."

"Chester, I got the picture. Now it's your turn. It's dark enough. I have a flashlight, so let's get moving OK? You show me where you first saw the thing and then we can get you back home to whatever it is that you do daily."

Chester walked cautiously to the grader and bent down. Banks was holding the flashlight and did not see Chester pick up a large baseball bat and swing it at the flashlight. It flew out of Banks's hands. Banks reached in his waistband and found his pistol. He pulled it out and shot Chester once, Chester held the bat up and swung again. This time Chester hit Banks in the head and he fell onto the sandy soil. He was bleeding. Chester took two steps and then fell face first into the same dirt.

An older car pulled into the lot at that point. Karl Wallace got out. He walked unsteadily toward the two bodies, and pushed at them. The fatter of the two moaned as he did. Karl pulled out the electric shocker flashlight shaped device. He held it against Chester's skull. Chester heaved up and down then fell silent.

Karl walked to the tree line at the edge of the lot and sat down against a tree. His heart was pounding, he needed to rest, and soon he was asleep.

"C'mon Andy get up, please," Wanda said as she shook Andy Reid. He woke for a moment then slumped back, almost hitting his head against the toilet. Wanda called down to Albert to come quickly.

"So, he's actually dead?" Albert said with a grin.

"Nope, I think he had a vasovagal episode and he fainted."

"Now you're a doctor too," Albert said.

"I am a little bit of everything dear boy, and can make elementary diagnoses like this one."

"Point well made, Wanda, well made. Now what do we do?"

"Andy just needs to come out of this and it will take a minute to get his faculties back. Hold him up and forward so his head is forward."

"Is he going to be able to function once he comes out of this?"

"Al, I don't know if he can. We may have to do some adjusting to get our plan in place. Can you stay here while I make a call for assistance?"

"Sure, but what kind of help, is it medical?"

"Nope Albert, it is from another source, and I hope I can raise him."

"Boss is off somewhere today, can I help you," the long distance voice said.

"Yes, this is Wanda calling, where is he at the moment," she said.

"Wanda, as in Brixton, is that you?"

"Yes, who is this?"

"Bill Leonard, that's who, wondered where you got to. I got the run around here every time that I asked about you."

"Secrecy is its own reward, Bill, that's my motto. Hey, we can catch up later. Now I need a favor if it's a good time to ask."

"Go ahead," Leonard said.

'I need you to run down the family of a former client. Her name is Harriet Rasmussen…"

"Helga is really her name and she is on the most wanted list right now. But go ahead."

"She's FBI."

"Was that is what I mean. Seems she's AWOL at the moment. She may have headed for Canada."

"God Bill, you are so far ahead of me on this. I am ashamed that I bothered you with this. Now I hear she had a brother, Harold, and I am sure you know that."

"Detained by the West Germans, actually. They managed to get him in the act of conspiring with a bunch of other clients, some real ones and the rest strap hangers, at a place in the FRG."

"So, now I can relax I guess, is that right?"

"Not really. Do you remember the case that we heard about, the one with the supposedly deceased client, a fellow named Schultz?"

"Vaguely, yes I do."

"We hear that he is alive and on the move, maybe near you up there on the Cape."

"I won't even ask how you knew where I was calling from, but how old is this guy? He must be pretty well into or past middle age, so why worry. Was he a major war criminal?"

"It depends on who you ask. Operation PAPERCLIP never handled him. Heard that it was alleged he died on a mission. It was a mission that I can't talk about over this phone. Let's just say it involved an airplane overflight."

"I've got it. So what else do you know?" Wanda made some notes on a piece of scrap paper.

"Helga, I mean Harriett contacted him. We know that from our NSA's friendly phone taps. She visited him when he was hospitalized with a heart condition. Karl's daughter Holly had words with Helga and they parted not the best of friends."

"Got that much Bill. But where is our client Karl now?"

"Wanda, he apparently is leaving a trail of death and destruction. He started out in Wellfleet, got stopped by a local cop. He used some device to kill him. Then he headed your way, maybe to Chatham. We have a tracer on his car, but he must have found it. The signal is now dead. Tech is working on a solution. I doubt he could have yanked it out of the wheel well."

"At his age I would assume there's not much yanking going on in his life," Wanda said laughing.

"He knows physics backwards and forwards and some of his discoveries were world changing. I can tell you that much. I would not put it past him to have squirreled away some whiz-bang thing to protect him and hurt anyone else around him."

"Right, armed, ancient, dangerous, does that sound like him?"

"Sort of, but there is one other thing I should mention."

"Bill, don't hold back now," Wanda said.
Remember that fellow Bud Steinmiller?"

"Sure do, but why?"

"He's afoot somewhere, along with his little band of miscreants. You know the ones with the patriotic fervor and the lack of regard for the constitution. All of them are keeping mum about where."

"We have an inside source, don't we?" Wanda asked.

"Yes, but the problem is that the source has been cut out of most big meetings. He was even late for one when Bud announced to their band of sunshiners that he was heading out of town."

"I understand. Can you call here and leave a message with Albert, one of my housemates, when you hear more about Bud?"

"Albert, is that the name? He sounds very rich and very old."

"And he is gay, also young, buff, and handsome you must know, Bill."

"Whatever. Yes I will call and leave a message once I have something. Bye for now sweetie." Bill hung up the phone.

Wanda went back upstairs and found Andy walking around slightly winded and still very sweaty. Albert held him by one arm and gave Wanda thumbs up.

"Are we better now?" She asked Andy.

"Yeah, I must have fainted. For the life of me I can't tell you why. I was washing my face after I took that aspirin, and…"

"Wait, let me see that bottle."

Andy went back into the bathroom and returned with a small glass bottle in his hand. He handed it to Wanda.

Opening the cap, she smelled the bottle and then checked the cap.

"Andy you may have been poisoned with this crap. Where did you get it?"

"We got it downtown at the drug store a couple years back…"

"And the house was vacant for a long time wasn't it?"

"Yes, but there was a caretaker."

"Every day, someone was here?"

"No, not every day, just from time to time."

Wanda frowned. "So you can see how someone might spike an aspirin?

"What good would it do if they had Nancy take it and not me?"

"It was a scatter shot approach Andy. Trust me the folks who have it in for you do not care if you are the target or one of your family members."

"Damn it! Thank God no one else uses this," Andy said as he threw the bottle down on the rug.

"Hey that's evidence Andy, so keep it in once piece can you?"

"Sorry, really I am sorry. Do I need a doctor?"

"Have you had a glass of water since you took the pill?"

"No, I have not, why do you ask Wanda?"

"Put your finger down your throat and throw up, that's why. I guess that will work unless you have a relapse."

"Are you kidding Wanda, really?"

"I never kid Andy; you should know that by now. Now go barf in the bathroom and we'll wait out here."

Albert listened at the bathroom door.

"He's getting to it; I can hear the growls starting."

Wait for him and make sure he really does it," Wanda said as she went to her room.

Opening her suitcase she removed and assembled a rifle and scope, connecting them with a practiced click.

Nancy let the phone ring four times, and then hung up. Andy was probably doing something outside, she hoped. She hoped he was not getting into trouble. On an impulse she dialed the Skunk's Neck house again, and this time the phone was answered on the second ring.

"Reid Residence, "a woman said.

"Wanda, this is Nancy, where's Andy?"

"Recovering from a little fainting spell, sorry. He passed out in the master bath, Elvis style, but he's fine now, just a little groggy."

"Drinking was he?" Nancy asked.

"Nope, he might have had a blood pressure drop, I don't know, but we felt his pulse. He seems to be fine now."

"You know Wanda, his family on his mother's side had had a lot of heart issues. I should have told you that before. I have been on him to have more blood pressure checks but he's stubborn and won't listen."

"I get that, the stubborn part. I wonder if that might have had something to do with this?" she asked, hoping to sound nonchalant but convincing at the same time.

"Well, can he talk to me, or is he too zonked?"

"I'll check," Wanda said. She put the phone down and waited two minutes. "Nope, he is still groggy, almost asleep. So can you call back in maybe an hour?"

"Sure, but please tell Andy that I love him and that we're here safe and sound. He wanted to know that."

"I'll pass that on Nancy. I will tell him that you'll call later." She hung up the phone.

"Who was that?" Andy asked, holding onto Albert's arm.

"Your better half, kiddo. She wanted to tell you that she and Alicia are safe and sound. She'll call back in about an hour. I didn't give her the blow by blow of what really happened since I figured she had enough excitement for today."

"Right, got it. She'll call back soon?"

"About an hour, she said. How are you doing?"

Andy stood up and let go of Albert's arm. "Better than before but I am still not one hundred percent."

"You upchucked didn't you?"

"Well, let's just say that I am not hungry. I will never, never be bulimic, that is for sure."

"Hardly a worry," Wanda said. "Albert, are you ready to do some snooping with me?"

Andy stood unsteadily. "Me too lady. I have gotta get some time in the field, this is personal. I will be fine, really I will."

"Wait and talk to Nancy in about an hour, and the darker it gets the better for me," Wanda laughed at her inside joke.

CHAPTER 22

The wind picked up. Bud Steinmiller wished he had brought a heavier jacket. He watched from the doorway at the Epicure liquor store across the street for ten minutes. Finally he heard sirens.

Chatham Rescue and Fire Department personnel pulled in, breaking the door down to the town offices. A solitary cruiser arrived. The police officer had a hurried conversation with the fire and ambulance personnel. Bud saw him reach into his cruiser to call someone, maybe the state police. All this in hushed tones. Going to his trunk, the officer pulled out his roll of yellow tape and roped off the area. Tourists strolled by and seemed not to notice.

"What happened," Bud asked another officer who drove by and parked next to the storefront where he was standing. "Murder Suicide is what I heard, town employees likely. You see anything?"

"Nah," Bud said, "just walked down from the Squire. I was on my way home. I stopped when I heard the sirens."

"Right sir. But if you recall seeing anything just hop on over to the station and tell the guy at dispatch. This is not an average crime here in little old Chatham."

"Apparently not, and I understand, yes. And thank you," Bud said bowing humbly.

Turning around, Bud made a mental note of the officer's description, and filed it away for possible future reference. He needed to call in and see if there were any further developments. The nearest pay phone was in the lobby of the Mayflower Inn. The place was virtually empty at night.

Reaching for a quarter he dropped the coin in the slot and then dialed a local number. Letting it ring once he hung up and waited. The phone rang.

"Bud here," he said, not sure who he was going to reach.

"Alex Cardozo, Bud, old boy, as you can see I've got the phone detail tonight."

"Wow, even power players get to stand in from time to time Senator," Bud remarked.

"Right you are. We're in recess downtown on the hill. I decided to man the hot line, for the good of the republic and all that."

"Impressive, I must say. Now let me tell you where I have been and what I've done."

"Can I record this call? My scribbling is hard even for me to understand"

"Why not? If we're caught, I'll tell them that it wasn't me on the phone just somebody who sounded like me."

"Best of luck on that one, Bud. Go ahead."

"Well, I found the two Russian sleepers we had surmised were here…"

"And you're bringing them back for questioning I would hope?"

"Actually, a body bag will be their mode of transport. The two of them were uncooperative. I was forced to use extreme measures. They are in that great commissariat or luxury dacha in the sky by now. I made it look as if it was a murder suicide thing. They were screwing each other and married to someone else, so it carries some weight.

"The ME here in Barnstable County is a lightweight; almost flunked out of medical school for using hard drugs, but his daddy called in some favors, he went to a secret recovery center in New Zealand and then finished school."

"Nice to know. Can you track him on this case to make sure?"

"Senator, you read my mind. I will make sure that the good doctor is aware of the tryst angle and that he sees all the evidence, which I planted as part of my concerned citizen act. I'm good at that."

"Yes you are Bud, and well known around the world for that. Give me your exact location there. I might need it in the future."

Bud recited his address of the motel in Chatham where he was staying. "I'll check in later, but here's a question: What do we hear about Andy Reid? He's been off the radar for a while."

"Let me check, and when you call back I'll have that information," Cardozo said.

"Good. I assume that the issue with the FBI lady in Hyannis is now not a problem either?"

"It is already taken care of, Bud. No worries there either."

"Well, then I can rest here in Chatham until I get more information from you or I need to call back in."

"Right you are. I've got to catch another line, so until later if you don't mind."

Senator Cardozo reached for the intercom and pressed a button, summoning an aide. It seemed like it took a long time for anyone to respond. He was irritated. At last someone answered.

"Get me Angelo DiSalvo can you? It's important, He needs to call in right away." The aide left the room and returned soon with a message that DiSalvo was on the line.

"Angelo my friend, when we last met there was an issue with a Hyannis lady who was interfering in your business. I just wanted to confirm that she is no longer a problem, isn't that right?"

"Alex, old friend, you have some juice, I gotta tell you. FBI lady vamoosed She is not around no more, so yeah, we like the outcome."

"So, now in the spirit of camaraderie, I have a favor to ask, dear friend."

"Senator, your wish is my commandment, as the sayin' goes, what'ya need?"

"You certainly have heard of Ben Steinmiller; he works with me from time to time?"

"Yeah, rogue agent in the CIA last time we crossed paths, why?"

Cardoza paused, then said softly, "Here's where you can find him, kill him as soon as possible, No need to call me back unless you have problems."

"Your wish is done, sir," Angelo said. He hung up.

Senator Cardoza smiled and returned to reading the Style section of the Washington Post. There were a few concerts at the National Theater that he might have to attend.

CHAPTER 23

Andy spoke with Nancy for half an hour. He was waiting for his head to clear. Hanging up he walked to the front door. He looked for Albert and Wanda. Their car was there but they seemed to be nowhere in sight. Switching on the large overhead mercury vapor street light, he saw two figures at the end of the property line, carrying something. They walked into the light and waved to Andy.

"Out for a walk," Albert yelled. "We'll be in now that you're up and ready."

Andy waved back and waited, holding the door.

"So, Nancy is all right, we hope?" Wanda said.

"Yeah sounds like she is and she's with folks that I trust. That's as important to me as her being out of here."

"Good news. Now that it's another good dark and stormy night, let's head over to our hunting grounds," Wanda said. She picked up a large scoped rifle.

"Hunting time. Are you sure ex-Nazis are in season right now?" Andy asked. "I thought you were going to being them in alive."

"I have something for you to carry too, old buddy." She handed him a semi-automatic pistol.

"What are you Albert, a conscientious objector?" Andy said.

"Nope, got me a nice knife right here," Albert said unsheathing a large hunting knife.

Andy smiled, and checked the pistol. "I suppose it is loaded and ready," he asked Wanda.

"Guess so. It might be a test of your restraint. Maybe we can get this fellow alive. I want him to stand trial. Maybe he'll get what's due. You on the other hand might be interested in what he is after over here. After all wherever he is going is important to know about."

"I suppose I can be the backup for you Wanda. Albert can always be the guy who takes up whittling later in life."

"Sure Andy. Now we need to get over to that part of the village and check on Karl, our client, as we refer to these fellows and in some cases, these girls."

"Lead on Wanda. I am just an observer with a piece, and Al's a guy with a knife," Andy said.

Locking the front door Andy climbed in the back seat next to the rifle. Wanda drove fast through the dimly lit streets, high beams on and not stopping for traffic signs.

Bud Steinmiller was almost asleep in his motel room when he heard a knock on the door. Getting up, he reached for his pistol and approached the door from the left side. There was no peephole.

"Yeah," he said to the closed door. "Need something?"

"Mr. Steinmiller, you have a phone call in the office," a voice said.

"Can't you transfer it down here?" Bud asked.

"Could have yeah. But the caller told me to come get you. He said not to transfer any calls."

"Shit man, do you ever take any initiative in your job? Might be a radical suggestion but how about you transfer the call and then I won't need to get dressed to walk over there?"

"OK mister, but the caller, he's gonna be mad at me, I know," the voice said.

Bud was about to say something when a hard push splintered the door, and a man wearing a mask walked in, holding a large pistol.

"Doctor Steinmiller, I presume," the intruder said.

Bud leveled his gun at the man's chest. "And you are?"

"Name's Angelo. I am a friend of the Senator's. He sent me to speak to you," the man with the gun said.

"So, he sends you to break down my door, come in with a gun, and maybe kill me, is that it?"

"Hey man, just following orders. Nothing more than that. See, me and Cardozo, we are sorta blood brothers. We grew up together, his Nonna and my…"

"I got it Angelo. There's no need to do the Italian genealogy thing for me. So, what's it gonna be? See who can shoot first and then who can drag the other's body to your car's trunk?"

"Maybe that happens in the movies Bud. I actually thought The Godfather was one hell of a movie. It made me proud. I even shed a tear or two. That Puzo fellow knows his shit."

"So now can we see who the better aim is and get this over with? I need to get some sleep after I whack you," Bud said. He cocked his gun.

Angelo slowly holstered his gun and put his hands in the air.

"What the hell, you're not going to test my aim?"

"Bud, I had orders to kill you from the man, the Senator. But I ain't in the killin' mood today. I need to keep my affairs clean. I told Cardozo that I would do this I owed him a favor. So can we call this a pow-wow, and just forget that I came here?"

"What about Cardozo? I mean he's gonna figure this all out since he has friends everywhere."

"He's got friends but he's made tons of enemies along the way, including some powerful ones in the FBI. His little caper calling the deputy director over there sent those gumshoes into a rage, and they called me in to…"

"You Angelo do not strike me as an FBI agent, either in looks or demeanor."

"Between you and me Bud and I trust you not to tell anybody about this. We've been working for the same organization for a long time but our paths never crossed."

"Bull Angelo, I know every operative in the US. You are not on that list that I have seen."

Well, here's a clue for you. Remember the time you were a Pathfinder over there?"

"Yeah so what," Bud said. "You could have heard that from the Senator. He's not known for keeping his mouth shut."

"Nope we were scheduled to replace you when the roof fell in, Congress got involved, the bastards. The program was scrapped. Your code name was Rambo, and you worked with a guy at NKP named Jerimiah who was from Cleveland."

Bud lowered his pistol. "Angelo I still don't see you as one of us, but what the hell. I am willing to give you the benefit of the doubt." Bud reached out his hand to shake his hand but Angelo chopped Bud across the throat, and he fell to the floor.

"Sorry Bud, I hate to mess up a room. It takes too long to clean it up. You'll just need to take a little ride with me over to a bridge here in town. Maybe you will go for a swim."

Angelo hoisted Bud on this shoulder. He lifted him in the trunk of his black Cadillac sedan. After he dumped Bud's body in the water Angelo called in. "Done and done," he said softly, then hung up.

CHAPTER 24

Karl Wallace watched for signs he was being followed. He had good vision for a man of his age, everyone including the eye doctor told him. What he failed to mention was that he was part of an experiment during the war, one devised by some of the best Nazi medical personnel, to accelerate the amount of focus in low light for the human eye.

There were painful injections in his cornea. Karl suffered temporary blindness. But the doctors told Karl he would notice the difference once his vision returned. In about two weeks, he was still not able to see very well, but he could read by the light of a single candle held over twenty feet away. It was almost a miracle he thought at the time and one that he now took for granted.

His hearing was also exceptional and he attributed that to avoidance of jarring noises for most of his life. While on missions over enemy lands he wore a special headset that blocked all external sounds.

"I need to make sure before I leave," he said speaking to the empty lot. The two bodies had not moved since he stunned them. If they were dead that was good. One less complication. If they were to awake while he was there he would up the flashlight device's voltage and kill them. It was a necessary thing.

Karl stood unsteadily, waiting for the pain in the center of his chest to subside. It was getting less painful he thought, but just to be sure, he pulled out a small metal vial and unscrewing the top, he put a small white Nitroglycerin tablet under his tongue.

A car approached. Three people got out, a black woman and two white men, all dressed in dark clothing. The woman was carrying a rife with a scope. Karl could see that it was a powerful weapon. She was not carrying it to shoot rabbits or squirrels. He moved back further to the scrub pines that still bordered the plowed field.

"Two dead ones over here," the first man said. The woman nodded and put her free hand around her ear. Looking left and right at first she walked toward the hiding place where Karl was standing.

Karl reached for his stun weapon. He set it at maximum distance, waiting for the woman to turn directly toward him. He had never used the weapon at this range. Given its age, he hoped it still had the reserve power to work. He had faith in the super weapons he and others had developed, he reminded himself. It would work, he thought, or else.

The woman scanned the tree line and then pulled her rifle's sight to her face, looking though what appeared to be a green-tinted eyepiece. "I've got something showing to the left of the third pine near the road," she said loudly.

"I'll check it out," the first and taller of the two men said.

The second man pulled out a large silvery pistol, and cocked it.

Karl decided to take matters into his own hands. He stood up, hands in the air. "Do not shoot, please. I am an old man and I am not armed."

Wanda pulled the rifle's trigger. Karl fell to the ground.

CHAPTER 25

"What the hell?" Andy yelled. "We were supposed to take this guy alive, and now you killed him."

"I winged him that's all. With my excellent aim," Wanda said. She walked slowly toward the prone figure and felt for a pulse. "He'll make it."

"God, this guy's no spring chicken, Wanda," Albert said as he crouched over Karl.

"Cool off you two, I know my medical stuff and this guy's only dinged. He'll survive."

"Thanks Doctor Brixton, that makes me feel much better," Andy said as he watched Wanda bandage up Karl's arm.

"You'll be fine Herr Doktor, I am here to complete the task you started long ago," Wanda said.

Karl said something inaudible and Wanda reared back, shaking her head violently. "No, that is not true, never, never!"

"Karl smiled, then using his good arm, pushed the stun gun against Wanda's chest, throwing her backward, unconscious.

Albert and Andy rushed to her side as she started to convulse. She was having some sort of fit. It took all their strength to hold her down.

Karl stumbled to his feet. His one arm was dripping blood. Using his good arm he pointed the stun gun at them. Both men raised their hands in surrender.

"You both are going to be my safe passage out of here, gentlemen. I trust that having seen what happened to this black female you'll cooperate. To protect myself I will sit in the back seat of your car, and watch both of you. Rest assured that I will not hesitate to kill whoever is driving, if there is a misstep."

"Well, Karl or whatever your name is, we will be very meek. You can be assured of that," Albert said.

"Good, but now I must find what I left here years ago. You will need to give me a minute."

"How can you see in this darkness?" Andy asked.

"Miracles of ancient science, young man. I will leave it at that."

Karl looked hard at a metal box that was wedged under the seat on Chester Billing's grader. He pulled out what looked like a metal Thermos. He checked it for tampering and then placed it under his right arm.

Andy put his hands down. "Karl, looks like you've got something very valuable there. May I ask what it is?"

"Not that I mind sharing this information. As a layman it might be too difficult for you to understand and equally for your companion."

Albert straightened up. "Well sir, seems you are not holding all the cards. You are an arrogant person as well. No offense, just commenting."

Karl shot a wave of energy from the Stun Gun that dropped Albert prone on the ground, writhing in pain.

Andy made a quick move and grabbed the stun gun, turning it around as Karl pressed the switch. It failed to do much to Karl, but he appeared dazed and confused. He fell to his knees dropping the Thermos.

Wanda rose behind him. She knocked Karl forward. He fell face first into the sandy soil.

Andy was surprised. "Wanda, he was not going anywhere. Why did you do that?"

"Just a safety measure Andy. Just being sure that our good friend here was not going to pull some other stunt like the one he did on me again."

"What are you going to do to this guy?" Andy asked.

"I am afraid that you'll never know, Andy my friend," Wanda said, She hit Andy over the head with a rock, knocking him out.

CHAPTER 26

Nancy Reid walked into Andy's hospital room in Hyannis. She was carrying a small plant in a ceramic vase. She placed it by Andy's bedside. As she had done for the last two weeks since he was admitted. Nancy waited for some sign that he was going to wake up from his coma.

Today, like all days, the monitors beeped and the lights flashed, sometimes bringing a nurse to reset the machine and other times, just stopping, resetting on their own.

The doctor on duty told Nancy that there was no change overnight. She mentioned that in all likelihood it could be weeks before Andy woke up.

Nancy held Andy's hand and spoke to him, hoping Andy could understand. "Hey there darling, Alicia wishes she could be here to see you but the hospital won't let her in. Some silly rule about being at least 16. Anyway, she tells me that she is going to make you a present. When I left her with the sitter she was using crayons and drawing something."

A nurse came in and checked the monitors, then left smiling at Nancy.

Nancy spoke directly to Andy. "Well, let me see what else is going on. There have been a lot of phone calls to the house. I had a friend check our mail at the place in Silver Spring. They've put it all in a big box and are mailing it to Chatham. Might be here in a week or so."

Andy's eyes remained closed, his breathing was steady. The bandages covering his head were removed the previous day. His bruise and swelling looked almost normal.

"Oh I almost forgot, you had a call from a guy, somebody named Bill. I wrote the name down. Yes, it was Bill Leonard that was his name. He seemed to know a lot about you, but he was not going to give me his phone number, just said that he would call back.

"Do you know him, or is this a crank call?" Nancy asked.

Andy's eyes opened for a moment, as they had in the past. His mouth moved, as if he were going to say something.

Nancy pressed the call button to summon someone. A nurse and a doctor came in, looking at the screen on his heart monitor.

"He was trying to tell me something," Nancy said, her eyes filling with tears.

'With this kind of transient global amnesia, patients have subconscious reactions, we don't know why, to stimuli from either words or colors or movement," the Doctor said.

"Andy, can you hear me?" Nancy said, squeezing his hand.

"Damn it," Andy said pulling his hand away. "Who are you and why did you do that?"

Author's Note

"Secrecy both protects and thwarts moral perception, reasoning, and choice. Secret practices protect the liberty of some while impairing that of others. They guard intimacy and creativity, yet tend to spread and invite abuse."[1]

I recently read Ben Rich's memoir, **The Skunk Works**[2], a mid-90s reporting of the Lockheed advanced airframe and airplane manufacturing facility located in Burbank California. Kelly Johnson, Ben Rich's mentor and founder of the facility, agreed that security for security's sake caused delays and added costs to these special programs. That got me to thinking about the core principles of security, some of which are grounded in reality, but many are not.

Scatteree began as a third in the series of events centered in Chatham. I reached back to this locale in two previous novels, **Stepping Stones** and **Skunk's Neck**. For those who have not read these books, the first is set in the late 1960s, about the time I first met my wife and visited Cape Cod and the Village of Chatham. Stepping Stones Road, one of the streets in the village was the place that the protagonist, Andy Reid, discovered and then investigated.

Looking for another locale within Chatham, the name of Skunk's Neck Road came to mind, so I placed Andy Reid there in the early to mid-1970s, and gave him another shot at being killed or being a hero. Once again the Stepping Stones facility was at the center of the problem and the novel.

---

[1] Sissela Bok, **SECRETS: On the Ethics of Concealment and Revelation**, Pantheon, New York, New York, 1982.

[2] Ben R. Rich and Leo Janos, **Skunk Works, A personal memoir of my years at Lockheed**, Little, Brown and Company, New York, New York, 1994.

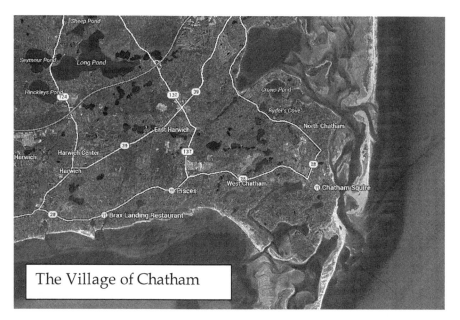

The Village of Chatham

Keeping with the theme of 'S' named streets Scatteree Road (apparently named by the native Monomoit tribe) fit the bill. I put Andy back in Chatham this time in the early 1980s.

During the time that I laid out this novel in my mind the case of the cleared government contractor Edward Snowden broke. It was a major international news story. At this point (June 2014) the Snowden case remains unresolved. Snowden claims he is a hero, the government sees him as a traitor. He is holed up in Russia and the government is on his trail. These events caused me to change the way in which I imagined the fictional Andy Reid would react to an increasingly Byzantine world of secrets and secrecy. Maybe it is because of my own experience as well.

My first brush with security and security clearances came in 1967 when I first was hired to work as a junior analyst at the Defense Intelligence Agency. Getting my first Secret Clearance was a mysterious event. I got calls and letters from relatives, coworkers and friends that they had been visited by badge carrying men asking questions about my character. Each of them assured me that they were honest, and that in spite of that honesty, I had nothing to fear.

I was given a final look over when I got to my first duty station. A security official, just slightly older than me, approached me and asked me penetrating questions, mostly about my behavior in college and my first year of graduate school. His questions focused on my binge drinking, partying and other ribald (for the mid-1960s) behavior. The gentleman was clearly not buying my assertion (which was true) that I never used any recreational drugs. He apparently had seen many applicants who proudly asserted that they had been 'casual' users. Being an experimenter was OK, anything self-reported more serious than that was a red flag. Another issue where being a liar gets you cleared, being honest might not.

Perturbed I asked the interviewer if he had used drugs in college. He refused to answer. The interview ended abruptly, I was given the Secret level clearance and started work. It was a strange place, Arlington Hall Station, located at the corner of Glebe Road and Route 50, Arlington Boulevard in Arlington, Virginia. Built as a girls' school and commandeered by the army in World War Two, it was the home of the Army Security Agency, one of the predecessors to the National Security Agency. It was also the home of one of the great unheralded successes in intelligence, the *Venona* Program.[3] That program, declassified in the mid-1990s, began at Arlington Hall on 1 February 1943 and lasted until 1980.

---

[3] See Nigel West, **Venona: The Greatest Secret of the Cold War,** Harper Collins, London, 1999, among others including the official NSA site for Venona, http://www.nsa.gov/public_info/declass/venona/

Now cleared I admit that I felt a kind of pride about being able to see the secrets of the world laid out before me. I felt honored that the government trusted me. Soon it became clear that many items crossing my desk were not really sensitive. As a young twenty something I had the knowledge of the ages at my fingertips. I was merely making an observation based on my vast knowledge of the world, or geopolitics and the like.

I never challenged any classification level, though various then current executive orders require a person with a clearance to do so. It became clear that the quickest way to end my nascent intelligence career was to make waves. A senior enlisted fellow in the National Military Command Center (the NMCC or the War Room) told me that 'cooperate and graduate' was his mantra and it might as well be mine.

In those days the counterintelligence people (nameless and faceless and almost universally despised) made nightly checks to ensure that all desks and containers were locked, and that all classified materials were safely tucked into safes that lined every office. They looked at GSA issued calendars to ensure that I and others had not somehow added our safe lock's combination in an inconspicuous place as a memory aid. The faceless ones left their calling cards, not congratulating me or others on being a rule follower, but admonishing us never to do anything wrong, ever.

Later in my career there was another round of interviews prior to granting me a Top Secret security clearance. I felt even more proud. I waited eagerly for the time when I might actually see a document marked with that level of security classification. It was a long wait.

While waiting, I attended basic intelligence school in a World War II era barracks in a remote part of Southeast Washington. It was memorable for one thing: there was a vending machine that dispensed cans of beer for a quarter in the break area of the lounge. We learned the craft, almost all of the lectures were not classified. We heard from long in the tooth practitioners, men and women who had risked their lives for their country in times of war and peace. The discussions centered on things that mattered and why. Security classification and clearances were pushed into the background.

Jobs came and went, the Army came and went. I got additional accesses, one of which most likely kept me out of combat in Vietnam. My clearances, like my badges, were on a string around my neck for all to see. I felt comfortable inside the world of secrets, perhaps not realizing there was life beyond the door that separated me from that outside world.

While working at the Pentagon in a secured area (still called a Sensitive Compartmented Information Facility or SCIF) I asked if I could bring in a small Sony portable radio, one with AM and FM. This request set off a firestorm of problems, including several sharply worded memos to me to the effect that I was getting a dispensation, but not to expect to see the radio for a while, if ever.

At one point after handing over the radio I asked for a receipt and was rebuffed. I was also told that the things that were going to happen to ensure that the radio was not a secret listening or transmitting device might actually destroy the radio. I imagined some death ray being focused on the little thing.

About six months later the radio arrived with a large tag indicating that it was never to leave the confines of the room in which it was stored. I listened to it faithfully, trying to drown out the steady hum of the Pentagon's HVAC system, known for spewing dirt than cool air. I left the building in 1987. I also left the radio. I assume since my office was one of those destroyed when hijacked American Airlines flight 77 crashed into the building on September 11 2001.

In the 1980s I had the chance to work with a dedicated bunch of people

trying to solve the cold war while not 'giving away the farm,' as we called it. Every step was one that we had never taken before and fraught with danger and even criminal sanctions. Writing an unclassified accounting of the enemy, which I did in **Soviet Military Power**[4], took every ounce of my nerve. I was called unpatriotic, a worthless piece of (fill in the blank), and other less flattering names. Agency heads told intermediaries that I was being watched; I am sure my home phone was tapped. There were a lot of nights without sleep, or catching a few winks on top of my very uncomfortable desk in the Pentagon.

We hoped that we might get a little play in the press, but more importantly, we might get a lot of column inches where it mattered, in NATO countries of Europe. Not only was that to happen but we generated a full-fledged international stir, bringing both supporters and detractors to the table.

Since the Soviet Military Power book was a huge success I was partially vindicated. Amazingly the world was turned upside down: the new idea was to make everything available to everyone, just as we had done. I was to become the Director of Public Affairs at the DIA, the first ever. That thrust me in the strangely bizarre world of media relations for the first time. Not a good place to be for someone who has spent decades locked away with information that was never to be released.

---

[4] **Soviet Military Power**, United States Department of Defense, Government Printing Office, 1981. One of the detractors reprinted the non-copyrighted book with annotations and corrections. See Tom Gervasi, **Soviet Military Power: The Pentagon's Propaganda Document, Annotated and Corrected,** New York: Random House, 1987.

In the mid-1980s my graduate studies started in earnest at Georgetown University courtesy of a generous grant from the Director of Central Intelligence's Exceptional Analyst Program.

Returning a year and half later with a PhD in government, I took a new job three thousand miles to the west, working at a newly created research center, called PERSEREC, the Defense Personnel Security and Education Center, I still needed and kept a clearance.

Our job was to look at bad people doing bad things and then recommend ways to prevent this kinds of actions in the future. I got involved with the Moynihan Commission[5] (the Senator was determined to unravel the twisted ball of string that held clearances and classification together.) along the way. I began to see the mentality of the spy in a completely different light. I never tried it but understood why some might. I talked with cabinet level officials about our research, getting mixed reviews and reactions. As in any challenge the challenged are wary.

My post-government life took me many places, but my clearance was in a hold status for a few years. I met former adversaries, including a retired KGB general.[6] I thought I would feel differently, either more or less alive, but it was all the same. Time spent teaching, listening and doing things I had never done before made me less concerned with the trappings of security and more concerned with the meaning of the thing. In 2010 my clearance was inactivated, but not before I had to endure a polygraph examination, one that was previously scheduled. For the first

---

[5] The report was issued in 1997 by the Government Printing Office and can be found here: http://www.gpo.gov/fdsys/pkg/GPO-CDOC-105sdoc2/content-detail.html

[6] Oleg Kalugin was a general officer in the KGB. He is now an American citizen and hopefully he would call me his friend.

time in over 40 years I was free (though the form[7] containing the non-disclosure agreement I signed would suggest otherwise for the next 50 years or so).

So, as you read this novel, look at what happens through the eyes of the participants. In some cases they are what I say to myself. In any case use this as a prism to understand what the characters are struggling with and how they view the world. In all cases, their thoughts and actions are products of my imagination, nothing more and nothing less.

I've included three short pieces as appendices about things mentioned in this novel. Hope they stimulate further discussion about secrets and secrecy. The first details the German's success in aerial reconnaissance during the Second World War. The second gives dimensionality to the Horten Bomber referenced in the prologue. The third is a short piece on the Nazi news operation.

Enjoy the journey, I did.

---

[7] Standard Form (SF) 312, **Classified Information Nondisclosure Agreement**, revised 2013, Office of the Director of National Intelligence, Washington DC

German Aerial Reconnaissance in World War II

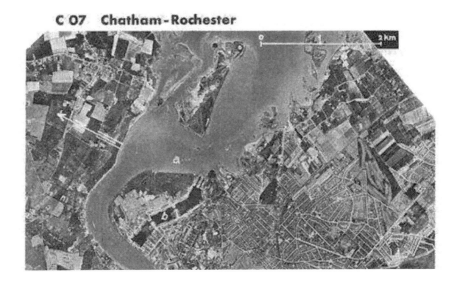

Recovered German 1940's aerial photograph of the harbor at Chatham, Kent, England. This photo was used by the Luftwaffe for targeting purposes.

At the end of the Second World War British and American troops discovered extensive German aerial reconnaissance imagery. Much of it was hidden by the German government and military across multiple locations in occupied Europe. Over one million photographic images cataloged have been cataloged since the discovery.

Project TURBAN, the codename for the handling of all the material found remained an intelligence priority for both countries to exploit. Much of the material came from Hitler's mountain retreat at Berchtesgaden in Bavaria, Germany. It was codenamed DICK TRACY for obvious reasons by an intelligence officer. An American team secured this only within a matter of hours of Russian forces arriving.

Other' collections include material found in: Vienna (codenamed ORWELL), Oslo (codenamed MONTHLY) and Berlin (codenamed TENANT).

In mid-June 1945, the material was packaged in crates and flown to Britain. Upon its arrival at RAF Medmenham, a Royal Air Force station based at Danesfield House in Buckinghamshire, England. There a British-American exploitation project began.

As the project developed all the imagery was tagged as 'GX'. The trove contained in GX was such a large quantity of imagery that preliminary sorting work went on until 1949. The intelligence discovery provided aerial imagery of Eastern Europe and the Soviet Union on a scale unachievable at the time and remained a key intelligence resource for more than two decades.

By 1960, much of the British and American target data consisted of predicted radar imagery of targets derived from the GX images. Although the British and Americans made a number of clandestine flights over the Soviet Union in the 1950s, the coverage obtained was small and GX was replaced with the arrival of satellite reconnaissance imagery in the 1960s.

No German imagery of the United States has been found. At least not yet.

German Stealth Bomber Technology in WWII

The Horten H.IX, RLM designation Ho 229 (often called Gotha Go 229 due to the identity of the chosen manufacturer of the aircraft) was a late-World War II prototype fighter/bomber designed by Reimar and Walter Horten and built by Gothaer Waggonfabrik. According to post war records the plane itself never flew, but a prototype was completed after the war and flown by the allies.

The plane was the first pure flying wing powered by a jet engine. It was designed to be more difficult to detect with radar - the first aircraft to incorporate what is now known as stealth technology. Postwar tests showed that the plane's shape and paint would have reduced its radar visibility by 20 percent.

It was a personal favorite of German Luftwaffe Reichsmarshall Hermann Göring. It was the only aircraft to come close to meeting his "1000, 1000, 1000" performance requirements. Its speed was estimated at 1,024 km/h (636 mph) and its ceiling 15,000 meters (49,213 ft.).

The remaining Horten prototype is now located at the Smithsonian's Garber Restoration Facility near Washington DC. Northrop Grumman built a scale model of the aircraft to test its radar absorbing qualities.

Concentration Camps, Paperclip, and Advanced Weapons

Jedem das Seine, uttered by the fictional Werner Rasmussen in the prologue of this novel, is a German proverb meaning "to each his own" or more appropriately, in this context, "to each what he deserves." It is a translation of the Latin phrase *suum cuique.* For more than two centuries, *suum cuique* ("to each his own") had been the official motto of the Prussian Order of the Black Eagle and today is the official motto of the German military police, Feldjäger.

During World War II, the phrase was used by the Nazis as slogan displayed at the main gate of Buchenwald concentration camp, built in 1937 near Weimar in Germany. Between April 1938 and April 1945, some 238,380 people of various nationalities including 350 Western Allied prisoners of war were incarcerated in Buchenwald. One estimate places the number of deaths at 56,000.

This camp and many others supplied workers, most of whom would be dead before war's end, to develop and then assemble the Nazi's war machines. One sidelight is the program finally known as Operation Paperclip[8] which brought Nazi scientists to the United States to begin the American space and rocket program, to improve the chemical and biological weapons program, and assist in the development of advanced weaponry.

---

[8] Much of the fine detail about Operation Paperclip has been lost or is still classified and not available for release. A recent book details the plans for and the lives of the men given special treatment by the Allies after the war. See for example, Annie Jacobsen, **Operation Paperclip**, New York, Little Brown and Company, 2014.

Germany's NAZI Daily Newspaper

The *Völkischer Beobachter* or "People's Observer" was a daily newspaper published by the Nazi Party in Germany from the 1920s until the fall of the Third Reich in 1945. The paper was originally founded in 1887 as a four-page Munich weekly, the *Münchner Beobachter*. It had become a daily anti-Semitic gossip sheet with a circulation of about 7,000 when it was bought by Adolph Hitler in 1923 to serve as the propaganda organ of his Nazi Party. In 1941 its circulation had passed 1.1 million.

There is not mention of the advanced weaponry, of the Horten brothers, or imagery of the United States in the newspaper's archives.

Made in the USA
Charleston, SC
09 July 2014